SAILOR'S WARNING

NOELLE GREENE

Text copyright © 2015 Anne Noelle Greene
All Rights Reserved

ISBN 978-0692442098

Cover designed by Scarlett Rugers Design
www.scarlettrugers.com

1

Rob McLain sprinted through his office door at precisely 9:05 a.m. His assistant looked up from her monitor. And froze at the sight of Luke, strapped across Rob's chest.

A delighted smile spread across the baby's face and he held his arms out to Mimi. She shook her head ruefully and waited while Rob let the diaper bag, portable playpen, and his briefcase thump on the floor. Then he hefted Luke out of the baby sling and onto Mimi's lap.

She nodded at the straps dangling from his waist. "Don't forget to unbuckle that thing."

"If Bill's already in the meeting, I may need this sling for my ass," he said. "I have a huge favor to ask. Letty called in sick and—"

"You're desperate," Mimi finished. "Go ahead. They're already in the conference room."

Rob pulled his son's sticky hands away from her keyboard. "You'll be okay here?"

"I raised three boys. I can handle one. Wait. You've got something yucky there." She put Luke on the floor and brushed dried rice cereal from Rob's forehead.

He closed his eyes to ward off the debris. In that one blink, when they were distracted, Luke bolted.

"Oh no," Rob said, leaping after him. His son had already disappeared around the corner. Damn it. How did a toddler run that fast? Hopefully someone would intercept him before he got too far. Everyone knew Luke; he tended to make an impression.

He heard her rich rolling laugh before he saw her. No one around here had a laugh like that, low and sexy. Sure enough, he found his son down the next hallway, tangled up with a pretty stranger.

It was official now. This had become the morning from hell.

"Whoa," she said, still laughing as she glanced up at Rob. She had crouched down to hold Luke by the waist and didn't seem to mind his flailing arms and legs. Luke had already managed to smear the lapel of her otherwise pristine jacket. Where had all this wet cereal come from? Did Luke keep a back-up blob in his pocket for snacking?

"I'm really sorry about this," Rob said. "Thank you for catching him. I'm late for a meeting but—I will definitely pay the dry cleaning bill. I'll find you later."

She cocked her head, bemused. She hadn't seen the stain yet.

Thankfully, she didn't get bent out of shape. She continued to smile as he apologized again. Then he realized her grin was for *him*—and the ridiculous contraption still flapping around his neck.

In the rush to get back to his office, Rob wondered briefly who she might be. Probably a temp. She couldn't possibly be from another department. Spontaneous laughter was too rare a commodity around here. Anyway, he would have noticed someone like her.

He handed Luke over to his assistant. "What about the webcast?" he asked as he tugged the baby carrier over his head.

"Up and running," Mimi said. "You better get in there."

Rob raced to the meeting. Since he had missed the big conference in New York last week, he'd moved heaven and earth to get industry legend Joseph Barranca and his research director in here. They'd agreed to accommodate him and give a presentation about their game-changing product. And now Rob was a full ten minutes late for the meeting he'd requested.

Just in time, he remembered the glass wall that offered a perfect view of this hallway. Starting right...here. He braked, took a deep breath and walked in to claim his place at the table.

The woman with the laser pointer ignored him. *Oh boy.* She wasn't smiling at him now and she definitely was not a temp. This would be the prodigy scientist he'd heard so much about. She looked too young to be in charge of research for a blockbuster cosmeceutical. Serious and straight-backed, she reminded him of that annoying girl in every high school honors class—the one in the front row with her hand permanently raised. Her long straight hair added to that impression.

He watched her run through the slides and his first impression shifted into something else entirely. The moment she began explaining her research, she became striking and lit by an inner glow. *There she was.* That vibrant woman he'd met in the hallway was back. Her eyes glittered and her faintly olive skin flushed. Her mouth was a bit wide, out of proportion to her narrow face. But he couldn't take his eyes away from that mouth. Lush, full and the color of a ripe berry. With the lights dimmed, he couldn't see her as well as he would have liked.

He leaned back and concentrated on the slides. The darkened room didn't help his concentration. How many hours sleep had he gotten in the last two days? Not enough. Never enough.

Meri Darrow brushed at the stain on her suit without much luck before she stood up to start the meeting. As she spoke, she gauged her audience—the last stop on the dog and pony show tour, as her boss called it—of biotech investors and fund managers.

Underwhelmed, they stared back at her. Their boredom didn't affect her one bit. Her research had been under wraps for three years. She'd given this presentation twenty times and her enthusiasm hadn't flagged once. If anything, she was more excited. She'd been told to curb her attitude, to play it cool and dignified. It wasn't easy. The research results were astonishing and she finally had permission to talk about them.

Her boss leaned forward. "You forgot to introduce yourself."

"Sorry. Got carried away." She tucked back a loose strand of hair and, started over. "I'm Dr. Meredith Darrow, research director—"

A latecomer walked in, in no particular hurry. She paused, frustrated by the interruption but since she was right in the middle of a slide, didn't actually look at him. Once he sat down, in a prominent spot left open for him, she recognized the guy she'd met in the hall. The one whose kid she'd collided with. He had the lanky frame of a runner and thick, longish brown hair. He was in his thirties, she guessed, and exceptionally, almost unfairly good-looking. He would be well aware of that fact. She didn't trust men that handsome.

Out in the hall, he had seemed nice. Down to earth. In here, with his colleagues, his manner and body language were completely different. He carried himself with a cool self-assurance that went beyond confidence. She couldn't have put her finger on how she got that impression, but somehow or other, he conveyed an annoying brashness. Maybe it was the way he looked at other people, including her. Like he was a 1980's master of the universe or something. Ambitious, one step ahead and ready to use every advantage at his disposal, including his luck in the genetic lottery.

Hard to tell if the people in this room were impressed by her presentation, but at least they were awake. Except for her arrogant friend. His stare had drilled holes in her forehead when he first sat down. Now his eyelids flickered and his head nodded. Slowly but surely, he dropped into a catnap. No one elbowed him. Maybe they didn't see him. She was tempted to call him out, give him a rude awakening. Just to see what he'd do.

A minute later, his head jerked. Then he looked at her almost proudly—superiority personified—as if he had been studying the inside of his eyelids as a personal favor to her. He pushed his cuff back to check his watch. For the next fifteen minutes, he alternated between staring at her intently and nodding off.

She moved through her slides and tried to ignore him. Which wasn't easy because when his eyes *were* open, he looked at her strangely, as if she was an exotic bird or something. The door opened as she wrapped up. A flustered woman with a lopsided chignon beckoned to him.

After he left the room, Meri started to take questions. There weren't many, which didn't surprise her. No one here understood biotechnology or life sciences beyond the numbers on their spreadsheets. Sometimes these finance types assumed she worked in marketing. They simply didn't expect a woman scientist. Last week a stodgy man in suspenders had asked—as if it were a matter of life and death—what she thought of "Clarence's strategic thrust and penetration." She'd choked on her coffee and it wasn't until she'd mopped her chin that she realized he'd been referring to Clarence Cosmeceuticals' new marketing strategy.

Fortunately, today she could direct any provocative questions about the competition to her boss, Dr. Barranca. So far, Joe Barranca had been mostly silent, composed and sophisticated in his crazy-expensive Italian suit. He preferred to let her do most of the talking—a trait that had surprised her at first but now she was used to. Joe had a laid-back style, preferring to stay above the fray, aloof and removed from details. She liked that about him—his willingness to delegate and let subordinates share the limelight. Then again, he'd been a prominent figure for so long, maybe the novelty had worn off. Since his reputation preceded him, his dignified, ageless appearance created a more powerful impression than mere words.

A young woman asked a question about potential side effects. Meri had just started to answer when movement on the other side of the glass wall caught her eye. The little boy she'd met earlier streaked down the hall. His chubby legs pumped as he sped by wearing only a t-shirt and an air of triumph.

His sleepy dad was wide awake now and in hot pursuit with a diaper. Shirttails and tie flew as he gave chase. The baby's glee and the dad's desperation were irresistible. A laugh exploded from her throat, deep, involuntary, and way too loud for the hushed conference room.

The guy turned his head as if he'd heard her. Their eyes met for a split second before he disappeared around the corner and galloped after the baby. Delighted by the flash of real life in the dull office, Meri waited a few beats, hoping they'd loop back around. No such luck. She turned back to her audience, still chuckling.

No one else was smiling. Only then did she realize her audience had missed the show. They watched her, slightly puzzled, with the same bored expectancy as before. Except for her boss, whose eyes narrowed. Now he was looking at the stain on her suit. His perpetual tan deepened—not a good sign. She gulped and rushed into speech without considering her words.

"So—side effects. We've seen some minor skin rashes, but very few. We believe our product is perfectly safe. However, we also know we're crossing a frontier. Frontiers are not risk-free. Remember, this cream contains particles so tiny it would take 100,000 of them to span the width of a human hair."

The young woman who'd asked the question leaned forward, her dark eyes glowing with intelligence and interest. "Can you explain how particle size might pose a risk to humans?"

Pleased that someone here took an interest in the science, Meri replied, "Some scientists have speculated that nanoparticles might pass through skin into the body's lymph system. It's a fascinating idea because—"

Joe Barranca cleared his throat and made a tiny motion with his head at the camera and microphone. *Crap.* She'd forgotten they were streaming live. Heat swam up her neck. "Anyway, that's pure speculation," she finished and sat down with a thump. Joe had coached her about staying on message. She'd given an honest answer. But she'd blundered. This webcast would be archived. Her remarks would stick around the Internet like gum on a shoe, impossible to shake off.

Cold sweat trickled inside her silk blouse. She'd speculated. About creeping nanoparticles of all things. As her mentor had repeatedly, patiently pointed out, she was now in a management role. She wasn't supposed to be honest, or rather, candid in her opinions. No one had ever told her to lie, but Joe had warned her about this very thing. *Don't talk too much. Don't volunteer unnecessary information or go off on speculative tangents. Never try to answer scientific "what-ifs". Whatever you do, don't let them pull you off-topic.*

She jiggled her foot nervously, wondering if she'd ever get used to a corporate mindset. There were days when she doubted she'd ever be polished and poised enough for this role. This was one of those days.

Joe concluded his remarks. She relaxed slightly. Everyone here knew his impressive track record with launching blockbuster pharmaceuticals. That's what the investors would remember. Not her.

Rob fastened the diaper, holding his son in place easily. Luke had run out of steam after his victory lap. Rob unzipped the cooler he'd packed at home and collapsed in his desk chair. Luke reached for his bottle eagerly. It wasn't yet 11:00 a.m. and Rob was wrung out. Now, if no one bothered him, he'd get this kid down for a nap and get some work done.

A familiar triple knock rattled the door.

Rob sat up straighter. "Come in."

When Bill entered, Luke stopped slurping and tracked Bill's entrance. Even Luke sensed the tension. Bill folded his arms and stared out at Newport Harbor. For a few moments, the only sound was the baby's resumed gulping.

"His nanny called in sick," Rob said. "The only way I could make it here today was to bring him along."

"I gathered that," Bill said. "You got lucky. Barranca's research director is the only one who saw you chasing your kid around the office."

"Did she?" The research director had been a surprise. Rob regretted missing so much of her segment. She had done a good job explaining why that new product was innovative. As crazy as the morning had been, when he'd heard that sexy, throaty laugh again, even through the glass, he hadn't been able to resist a last glance at that crushed rose mouth.

Bill swung around and faced Rob. "You look like hell. You've got a stain on your shoulder and don't tell me—I don't even want to know what that is. I can't believe you dozed off in that meeting. Barranca Labs looks to be the biggest initial public offering biotech has ever seen. You know this." He paused and cleared his throat. "I know you've been through a lot this last year…"

"Seventeen months," Rob said. His boss wouldn't understand the toll sleep deprivation could take. Luke hadn't slept through the night in weeks, not since he'd started teething. He doubted Bill had ever scrambled to find childcare. Bill's wife had always been there to pick up the slack.

"Look," Bill said. "Your performance—your fund's performance—reflects on me since I hired you. And I'm telling you right now—you need to step it up and travel more. You have to be realistic, Rob. Clients are watching. Get your priorities straight and your home life in order or you risk losing your portfolio."

Rob understood, all too well. This is how things worked in a pressure-cooker business. The market didn't care if you were having a bad day. Or, in his case, a bad year. Ironically, he'd never had much sympathy for associates who made excuses and complained of personal problems. But that was before. Before he'd been whacked with one of fate's two-by-fours. He might have appreciated the irony if this had happened to anyone else.

On the Friday after the investor tour, Meri swung out of her office and headed to her weekly status meeting. Joe Barranca insisted on face-to-face communication, an old-fashioned habit everyone complained about. For all matters other than the most mundane, and sometimes even those, the company actively discouraged electronic chats and correspondence, which meant, unfortunately, lots of boring meetings. It was the only aspect of her job she disliked. Today would be an exception. They had a lot to discuss. Strange data had popped up last night—too preliminary to overreact to or freak out about, but significant enough to take seriously.

She walked across the lobby to the executive wing and smiled at the security guard. "Hey Lou." Lou ducked his head without his usual teasing about her "sippy cup"—the stainless steel coffee mug she carried everywhere.

Meri hesitated at the threshold of her boss's office. Neither Joe nor his assistant were present at the polished steel table. Christine Rivera from Human Resources and Bryan Haskell from Information Technology waited there. Why would *they* be invited to a status meeting about the latest clinical trial results?

"Where's Joe?"

Haskell waved her in. "Close it." Haskell had overdone the cologne again. She could almost see the scent wafting towards her. He reminded her of the cartoon skunk, Pepe le Pew.

She sat, irritably wondering where Joe had gone. She didn't have time for administrative meetings that had nothing to do with research. Christine opened a file folder with silent precision, extracted one crisp sheet of paper and placed it in front of Meri. She glanced at it. Her mouth dropped open. "Is this a joke?"

Christine slid another piece of paper over.

"What the hell?" Meri said.

"We'll need you to sign this—acknowledging you had an exit interview—and I'll need your badge and company credit card."

Meri couldn't breathe. "This says I violated confidentiality. That's not true. Does Joe know about this? Where is he, anyway?"

Bryan Haskell angled his laptop and pointed to a list. "You left a virtual trail of breadcrumbs, Dr. Darrow. It's all here. Not one, but *five* e-mails leaking proprietary information to a competitor. Your friend Bob Peterson alerted his management at Viejo Pharmaceuticals after he got the e-mails—made sure he covered his ass. He says you two are acquainted but disavows any involvement with your scheme."

"Of course I know Bob, but I didn't send those e-mails. Someone must have hacked into my account. Joe will believe me."

"Why did you do it?" Haskell said.

"Exactly. Why would I do such a stupid, lame-ass thing like divulge manufacturing secrets?"

Haskell sighed. "I can only say…I'm shocked. We all are."

Angry tears threatened, but she refused to let them see. "I'm shocked too—that you people would believe this bullshit. How can you doubt my integrity? I've lived and breathed this job for three years. Six, sometimes seven days a week. Once again, I'd like to know—where is Joe Barranca? Does he know about this?"

"He's well aware," Haskell said. "He couldn't be here because of a family emergency. His father is gravely ill." He gave a sideways nod to the human resources manager, who opened the door and motioned to someone. Meri was lifted out of her seat by two burly security guards.

"Hold it!" she said, hooking her shoe on the chair leg. "What about the clinical trial results? You don't have anyone else on staff to deal with this next phase. You already laid off everyone who might have been qualified."

"Try for a little dignity," Haskell said.

They let her go to retrieve her purse and coffee mug from her desk and within three minutes, escorted her out, one on either side. What did they think she'd do, steal staplers on her way out the door?

A group of co-workers gaped from the front conference room window. They wouldn't have missed this show for anything. She wondered with sick resignation if any of them would believe in her integrity. She looked back at the gleaming building. At this distance, the tinted windows obscured her view. She thought she saw someone wave goodbye, although that might have been wishful thinking.

Her hands shook so much she couldn't retrieve her car keys. The security guys waited awkwardly. And all the while, people on their way to lunch gawked at her. She wanted to explain, but what would she say? She'd attended their weddings, bought them baby presents, and gone to Friday happy hour with them. Now she was on one side of a chasm and they were on the other.

Still in shock, she took one last look at the company she'd built her life around. The guards stood at the curb until she drove away.

Seven Weeks Later

Meri poured sunscreen into her palm before slathering Bella's shoulders. She moved on to Kelsey next, who waited patiently, her small face scrunched up against the onslaught of lotion. The smell of sunscreen and the heat rising from the redwood deck conjured up summer. Only the sun's low angle hinted at December.

"Aunt Meri, can we go now?" Bella shuffled her pink sparkly sandals impatiently.

"One more second, honey, while I finish putting sunscreen on your sister."

"One-Mississippi," Bella chanted. "Okay, it's been a second."

Meri rubbed lotion over her own forearms and feet, the only skin she intended to bare today. The kids tumbled down the steps and she followed at a slower pace. Santa Catalina Island shimmered in front of her like a mirage or a fake backdrop. She huffed and puffed all the way from the house to the shoreline. At least she felt better today than these past weeks, when her lungs caught fire whenever she walked more than ten feet.

She looked for a good spot to spread the bamboo mat.

"Eww!" Kelsey yelled. She had found a dead fish. Bella hurried over to help her sister shriek. By the time Meri found a clean spot upwind, they'd finished poking the fish with a stick and were heading for the water. "Come on, Aunt Meri. You have to put your feet in!"

Meri whooped when she ran into the icy water, then hiked up her gauze skirt and hopped the knee-high waves. After a measly ten jumps she was winded. But, she reminded herself, even in peak condition, she'd been no match for a five- and seven-year-old. She collapsed on a chunk of driftwood to catch her breath.

Three boys with skimboards ambled down the beach. Perhaps fifteen or sixteen, they wore board shorts tied ultra-low on their bony hips. The boys picked a spot nearby and took turns, waiting for the perfect moment to launch a diagonal run. In one fluid motion, each boy flung his board and ran onto it, skimming a thin layer of surf into a low wave. If the ride went well, he pivoted over the curl before landing in shallow water, triumphant. Waves and gravity always won, but whatever the ride, each boarder emerged grinning, whipping hair out of his eyes.

She envied the boys' attitudes. For them, failure was fun. Flamboyant wipeouts were applauded, cause for helpless laughter. They had the heartbreaking advantage of youth—believing themselves immune to serious injury or flat-out defeat.

Her nieces came over to snuggle next to her on the driftwood. Kelsey's hair was falling out of its yarn band. Meri fixed it and checked Bella's. Both girls had inherited the slippery white-blond Darrow hair. She would cheerfully kill for hair like that. In fact, any hair at all would do.

Another tow-head, a toddler, dashed over, drawn by the skimboarders. The child was transfixed, waiting for the moment when the boarder would either fly over the wave or pitch head first into the water. Either way, the little boy clapped when they landed. She smiled at him and at his father, who hung on to the back of the boy's swim diaper. The seat of the dad's shorts was soaked through. Like her, he hadn't bothered with a swim suit today. Only grown-ups were silly enough to think they wouldn't get soaking wet at the beach.

Something about the man's cinnamon brown hair—the way it curled against his neck—caught her attention. And his little boy looked familiar too. He sat down out of wave range and settled the boy in his lap. She recognized them then. This was the same guy who'd chased his son down the hall at that meeting a couple of months ago—right before her life imploded. Later she had learned he was considered a hot shot. What was his name? McLain. Robert McLain.

She risked a glance. His jaw sported a day's worth of stubble. In those soggy shorts and an old Cal t-shirt, he certainly didn't look like a biotech portfolio manager. He was nothing like the arrogant man she recalled. Of course, she wasn't the same either. She doubted he'd recognize her at all.

The skimboarders moved down the beach to find a steeper slope. The girls started to dig a hole. Before long the little boy was digging also, aided by Kelsey and Bella, who happily bossed him around. Robert McLain paced the shoreline, up and back twenty feet or so, keeping an eye on his son. He moved with nervous energy. Like he was walking off a problem.

No sign of mom, a diaper bag or towel. They must live nearby. Whatever. He was simply a dad on the beach. She didn't have to worry about influential investors anymore. Her silver lining.

Rob couldn't believe Luke had stayed in one place for more than ten seconds. It was good to be outside, enjoying the spectacular weather. What with all the scattered toys and mountains of laundry, the house seemed smaller every day. He watched his son attempt to dig a hole, imitating the two little girls who played nearby. Luke tried to fling sand over his shoulder—as the girls were doing—but the sand mostly landed on his head. Rob would be washing sand out of that scalp for days. Fair enough. A screaming shampoo later would be a fair exchange for a few minutes of peace now.

The girls' mother looked over at Rob and grinned in fellowship. He lifted his chin, acknowledging her. That woman wore quite a lot of clothes, considering the warm afternoon. Several layers of tops and a long skirt. Could be religious reasons. But her hair was hidden by a bandana and a baseball cap, rather than a traditional scarf. So that theory didn't fit.

"Aunt Meri, I'm hungry," the smallest girl called out.

"Rinse the sand off your hands and I'll get the snacks," she called back.

So she was their aunt, not their mother. That explained the difference. The girls were blondes, while the woman had darker coloring. Difficult to know for sure, since she was all covered up. The woman trudged over to their bamboo mat. Her skinny arms and legs poked through her clothes. As she neared him, he heard her inhale raggedly. An aura of illness hung over her. He hated looking at sick people. Hated knowing he was supposed to feel empathy. Instead he felt repulsion. Which meant he must be one callous son-of-a-bitch.

Luke made a beeline for the cookies she unpacked. She turned to Rob. "Is it okay if he has some?"

"Sure. Thanks." She turned to open the package. She reminded him of someone, but he couldn't remember who. He looked up in time to see Luke shove something in his mouth. "Ah—Luke! Don't eat the sand." He uncurled his son's chubby fists to check the contents.

"He'll be okay. My nieces used to do the same thing."

He held out his hand. "I'm Rob McLain. And this is Luke."

"Meri," she said, shaking it, not meeting his eyes. He couldn't see hers since the baseball cap shaded the top of her face.

"On the other hand," she said, more thoughtfully, "I wouldn't let him eat the stuff down by the water. I just read a study about bacteria on the beach. Wet sand is an incubator for microbes." She wrinkled her nose. "Gross, right?"

Alarmed, Rob reached for Luke to check his mouth.

"But this sand is hot and dry," she added quickly. "Bleached out by the sun. Don't worry."

He released his son's jaw, feeling a bit foolish. The girls clamored for their snacks and he watched the woman dole out food and juice boxes. Rob took a handful, too. They sat in silence, munching contentedly. The woman looked younger than he'd originally thought.

The wind kicked up then and sent low spirals of sand scudding across the beach. A gust caught the brim of the woman's cap. Alerted by her gasp, he ran after it. When he turned back, the children were giggling and the woman was plainly mortified. Her bandana had slipped, nearly covering one eye. She struggled to restore it and then yanked it off, revealing dark clumps of hair that stuck out in patchy tufts around her head. She was half-bald. *Oh, man.* Was she a cancer patient?

Pity came first, then a powerful reluctance to even look at her. At all. He kept his eyes trained on her bare feet as he handed her the cap. She thanked him. He resisted the urge to make an excuse and scoop up Luke. He'd be out of there in a heartbeat if he thought his son wouldn't protest loud and long.

The youngest girl piped up. "You looked just like a pirate, Aunt Meri! A funny-looking pirate!"

Rob held his breath, waiting for her to freak out. But the woman simply settled the cap back on her head and made a face at the little girl. "Thanks a lot, pumpkin."

"Let's play pirates!" the smaller girl said. "Luke can be our prisoner."

"You can be the captain," the older girl said, pointing at Rob. "Captain Wet Bottom." Startled into laughter, Rob forgot his discomfort.

"Go ahead," the aunt said, handing her bandana to the oldest girl. "You might as well use this for your costume since it won't stay on. I can't help but notice, girls, you're funny looking, too. Have you seen what you look like from the back? You have droopy drawers." Her voice lowered in mock accusation. "You have so much sand in your suits, you look like the *diaper* pirates of the Caribbean."

The girls twisted, horrified to see their aunt was right. Even Luke checked himself, imitating the girls. He trotted after them when they raced to rinse off.

Rob caught his son under the arms before a wave slapped him over. He had to hand it to that young woman. She was a good sport. He admired the courage it must have taken to come out here, looking the way she did. Lack of vanity was unusual in a young woman. In any woman. He couldn't imagine Julie handling a similar situation with such…pluck. She would have been too horrified to show herself in public, much less play with someone else's kids on a windy beach. When he glanced back, she was packing up. "Girls, come on up and get dried off now," she called.

One of the kids spotted a man coming down the beach. "Daddy!" When the girls turned, Luke turned also, following them like a baby duck. The girls rushed to him. "We're playing diaper pirates of the Caribbean!"

Their father held them at arms' length. "Hey, hey. Watch it. You two are a mess." He had the look of a lifelong surfer, with shoulder length hair and lines etched around his eyes.

The woman said, "Rob, this is my brother Jordan. Jordan, this is Rob McLain and his son, Luke."

Jordan nodded absently and turned to size up the surf. "Sloppy today. Doesn't seem that long ago," he said to the woman. "You and me, paddling out for the dawn patrol."

"It seems like a century ago to me," she replied.

"Can you take them next Sunday?"

"You have them two weekends in a row?"

"One day a week now. Nina says they need more quality time. Really, it's more like she needs more time to go to the gym and do her boyfriend. And it's been a real pain. I can't do *anything* with them around," he said carelessly.

The little girls were occupied with their sandals. Maybe they hadn't heard their father's remark. Their aunt certainly had. She assessed the kids' reaction before she stooped to collect their odds and ends.

"I'll be happy to have them with me next Sunday," she said in a low voice. "Or anytime. Just call." With a quick smile for Rob, she herded the girls up the beach, carrying most of their stuff. Her brother followed, empty-handed.

"Bye Captain Wet Bottom," the girls called. "Bye Lukie."

He picked Luke up to keep him from following his new friends. Then he swung the toddler in the air to distract him.

They had stopped to rinse their feet off, just a few doors down from his house. The woman's deep laugh floated on the breeze, followed by high-pitched shrieks from the kids. She was teasing her nieces with the hose. He liked her laugh, kind of throaty and sexy. Too bad her voice didn't match her appearance. Even from here, her silhouette was painfully thin. A pang in his mid-section caught him off-guard. He hoped she recovered. And he hoped he'd never lay eyes on her again.

2

Two weeks later Meri woke to the sound of gulls calling back and forth. For the first time in a long while, she had slept through the night. Best of all, unlike most days, her chest didn't feel like a Hummer had parked on it. She rolled out of bed, started the coffee, and unlocked the back door.

Most mornings, the Pacific Coast shivered under a bleak Army blanket of fog. This morning, much to her pleasure, sunshine greeted her. A warm breeze whispered through her cotton lawn nightgown and skimmed her bare arms. The coffeemaker finished spitting coffee back in the kitchen, but she stayed on the threshold, captivated by the watercolor sky.

A retired couple she now recognized as beach-walking regulars held hands as they crossed the sand to the coastal path. They took their time navigating the uneven surface and never let go of one another's hand. What would it be like—to be married that long? She couldn't imagine. When the path was clear, Meri went to lean on the railing. She inhaled warm salt air and with it, a trace of heady freedom and anticipation. The smell brought back memories of running into the surf with her old longboard, now relegated to the garage rafters.

Her neighbor, Rob McLain, approached with his son strapped in a jogging stroller. Where had he come from? Conscious of her skimpy nightgown, Meri dashed inside.

His footsteps pounded past. She closed the door and glanced around the dim house. The heavy pseudo-Spanish mission furniture had been ugly when new. Still, the place was an improvement over the apartment she'd moved out of last month. She'd chosen the apartment solely for its proximity to work. Plus it came furnished with fashionable neutral furniture. That beige furniture went with everything, but it had satisfied nothing in her soul. Which hardly mattered since she had spent most of her time working. That's the way she had designed her life. And until October, her life had gone according to plan. Since then, not at all.

She needed to get organized. Life required clothing. And catching up with laundry. Since the old machine inside chewed up her underwear, she washed all her delicates outside in a galvanized metal tub. A weakness for expensive lingerie was one thing—about the only thing— she had inherited from her mother. She hung the treasured bras and panties over a line she'd rigged on the deck.

At noon she made a sandwich and took it outside. Black dots rose and fell on the swells farther south, near the Wedge. Surfers chasing the ultimate wave. The advisory on TV had predicted monster waves this weekend, remnants of a Pacific storm thousands of miles offshore. A storm they would never even see. Only the waves would make it this far.

She shaded her eyes against the mid-day glare to watch the surfers for a while and then settled back in an Adirondack chair with a book. She was too out of shape to surf anywhere, much less that dangerous break. Before long, she gave in to fatigue and let her eyes close.

A child's scream woke her. She looked up and down the beach, but she couldn't see anyone. A ridge of sand blocked her view of the water's edge. She climbed on the deck bench and spotted them immediately. Rob McLain sprinted up from the shoreline with his howling son wrapped in a shirt. Ugly red scrapes marked the boy's face and arms. Rob's face was stark white. She ran down and met them halfway.

"I was right next to him the whole time and then a wave came out of nowhere," Rob said over his son's howls.

"The salt water on those scrapes is hurting him," she said. "I've got an idea. Follow me."

"I can take him home," Rob said. "We're just three doors down."

"This will be faster," she said and led the way up to the tub of rinse water she'd used earlier. "Pop him right in."

Rob lowered him into the washtub. The toddler's cries stopped abruptly as soon as he was immersed in water that must have felt tropical compared to the ocean. In those first few seconds of relief, the little boy looked up at her. His slow, sweet smile dawned when he met her eyes. And she understood. He was too young to say the words, but he didn't need them. He had thanked her perfectly.

She'd never known children so young could communicate so eloquently. In that instant, her heart was given over. She gently rinsed sand and salt from his scrapes while he splashed happily, his injuries forgotten.

"That's much better, isn't it?" she asked, scooping water over his shoulders. She beamed at his father. He grinned back, content to let her help, relaxed now that his son had stopped crying. Where exactly was this child's mother? Not in the picture? Possibly Rob had full custody. Which, of course, was none of her business.

Rob's chest was at eye level, only a foot away across the tub. She snuck quick peeks, trying not to be too obvious. A downy trail of hair tapered from his chest, trailed over lean abs and disappeared below the waist of his jeans. For one wild moment, she was tempted to stroke his skin to see if he was as warm and sleek as he appeared.

Rob shifted off his knees to sit more comfortably. He'd seen her out here this morning, her slim body outlined through her nightgown. And for a few seconds, he hadn't recognized the deliciously underdressed beauty. He hadn't even made the connection to the sickly woman he'd met a couple of weeks back. That woman had been drowning in clothes. This one was dressed normally, in board shorts and a tank top. Although she was still too thin, she appeared much healthier.

"We met on the beach, right?" he asked. "I'm Rob. Sorry, I've forgotten your name."

She hesitated and said, "Meri. And this is... Luke?"

"Thanks for coming to the rescue," he said. "You were a god-send. Except now I have to steel myself for the moment I pull him out of his spa tub and he starts to scream all over again."

"Let him stay for a bit. I'll get a dry towel and a cookie. That will keep him happy when the time comes."

"You seem experienced. Do you have kids?"

"I spend a lot of time with my nieces. Well, you met them."

When she went inside, he looked around. No sign of a male in residence. Sexy underwear hanging in the corner. He pictured her in that lacy bra. She wasn't well endowed but had nice curves. Just right. Those long tan legs would look good against a white lace thong.

Erotic images clouded his brain and desire surged, something he hadn't felt in a long, long time. It felt fantastic, until he realized she still wore that damn scarf on her head. What was wrong with him—to be attracted to a sick woman? She could be at death's door, for all he knew. The thought cooled him off fast. At least he could still get aroused. His libido had been muffled by fatigue for a long time. Until now. He'd been too busy to care. This encounter brought it home. He really needed to get a life outside of work and fatherhood. A normal life with a normal, healthy woman.

Meri set the box of cookies down and held the towel wide while Rob lifted the slippery baby out of the tub and wrapped him up. It was an awkward ballet and in the process, she brushed Rob's stomach with her knuckles. He reacted as if she'd burned him.

She stepped away, embarrassed, yet wanting to put him at ease. Poor guy was probably worried she had gotten the wrong idea. Briefly but unmistakably, his eyes had gone to her head, betraying alarm. She had forgotten. The bandana she wore didn't entirely hide her patchy scalp. She shook out the sandy towel and folded it carefully. *Don't worry. I get it.*

He sat down on a chaise with Luke bundled on his lap. "Only two cookies. I limit his sweets."

"Would you like a drink? I've got orange juice, water…"

"No, nothing. I should get him home," he said. An odd look flitted across his face.

If she didn't know better, she would have said he was afraid. Since that idea made no sense, she promptly dismissed the notion. "Do you want another towel?"

"No, he's fine," he said.

She hadn't offered the towel for Luke. The man was oblivious to the amount of skin he bared.

She dug into the box of animal crackers. Luke swiped the first cookie out of her hand. She laughed and sat on the lounge chair opposite Rob.

"Are you renting this place?" he asked.

"Sort of. It's my father's. He offered me the temporary use of the house for a few months." She'd almost added, *until I get back on my feet.* "I'll probably move out before the rental season kicks into gear. It's usually empty at this time of year anyway, so I lucked out."

"I don't recall seeing you around."

"I haven't spent any time here in years."

Luke squirmed. Rob let him go, only to scoop him up again when Luke tried to climb back into the washtub. She indulged herself with a long look while Rob was distracted by his son. There was something incredibly attractive in the casually tender way he handled his little boy. She wondered what it would be like to curl into this man's wide, warm chest. To turn her face into his skin.

He let Luke explore another corner of the deck and then sat down, apparently unaware of the effect he was having on her. She retied her bandana and hoped her face wasn't too flushed.

Rob asked, "Have we met? Before last week?"

"Actually," she said, "We *have*. I gave a presentation to the people in your office a few months ago."

His eyes narrowed.

"I was working for Barranca Labs at the time, as research director—"

He interrupted her. "Dr. Meredith Darrow."

"I only use the doctor title professionally."

"I thought you seemed familiar," he said, "but I didn't recognize you. You're very—different than you were then."

She took a short, painful breath and tried not to care. Luke came over to her chair and patted her knee, as if he sensed her distress. When she smiled in reassurance, he wandered off again.

"Wait a second," Rob said. "On the beach last week, you said your name was *Mary*."

"It is. Short for Meredith. But I spell it M-e-r-i."

"Shouldn't it be M-e-r-e?"

"No, my Dad always said that spelling was too close to 'merde'." When Rob didn't crack a smile, she added, "French for—well, never mind. I didn't intend to mislead you that day on the beach. I just wasn't ready to explain then and there."

"I heard you left the company under a cloud. There were rumors you shared inside information with a boyfriend or something."

"Not even close," she said. "I would never do something so unethical, not to mention stupid. Someone set me up."

"It's been a couple of months. If you're innocent, why haven't you fought back?"

"I've been fairly sick for the last—well, ever since—and then just had a string of bad luck. Someone broke into my apartment last month. I didn't feel comfortable there anymore so I talked my father into letting me stay down here." She jumped up to make sure his son didn't fall down the stairs. "Anyway, everything is better now and I feel stronger all the time. The beach is nature's cure-all, don't you think?"

Rob kept his eyes trained on the surfers. "So what actually happened? What's the real story?"

"I wish I knew," she said, not understanding the look of confusion that crossed his face. "I've tried to talk to my boss, but he won't return my calls. Honestly, I still don't understand."

"Actually, I meant…never mind. So this all went down pretty soon after the meeting at my office."

"Yeah, I sort of messed up that day, but—"

He interrupted. "That's bullshit, you did an excellent job."

"Thank you," she said, brightening.

"Anything else happen around that time? Anything unusual?"

"There *was* something," she said slowly, "but I didn't want to believe there was a connection. The day before, some preliminary data came in, indicating problems with the new drug. Probably not serious but troubling results, nevertheless."

"And?"

"I don't want to elaborate."

"But you do suspect someone set you up?"

"It's the only explanation. Unfortunately, Joe has people around him that are—I don't know—unscrupulous."

"But Joe is not?"

"No," she said firmly. "Not Joe. He's a scientific genius." She turned her head to cough.

"Maybe so but he's also got a genius for greasing the wheels of government bureaucracy. And for landing on his feet."

"What does that mean?" she said.

"How did you manage to get this far and still be so naive? Didn't you investigate or ask around before you went to work for him?" The look on her face must have given her away because he didn't give her a chance to answer. "Joseph Barranca made his first million when you were in elementary school."

"So?" she said.

"I'm just saying—he's been around a lot longer than you or me. And he's achieved great things, but you'll want to keep your eyes wide open and tread carefully from now on."

"What are you trying to say?"

"Nothing except what anyone paying attention already knows. Barranca has never failed in an industry with a notorious failure rate. He's always managed to get the most influential government scientists on his payroll as consultants. I won't say much more, but if I were you, I'd get a good lawyer. And soon."

She opened her mouth to defend her mentor and then closed it, remembering a few instances when Joe had disappointed her. But she'd never seen him do anything unethical or illegal. "As it happens, I've got an appointment on Tuesday."

"So what's up with your—with your health?" He said it like he didn't actually want to know, like she'd forced the question. And now he stared out at the ocean again, rather than facing her. "Are you undergoing chemotherapy? Is that why you lost your hair?"

"Oh God no, it's not cancer. Thankfully. No one's been able to fully explain the hair loss. It started falling out right before I was—before I left the company. And then I got sick. Stress, I suppose. Maybe vitamin deficiency. My hair's been growing back since I started new vitamins. I felt pretty lousy for a while there, but I'm improving by leaps and bounds. I've gotten over the worst of it, whatever it was. The illness stumped numerous doctors. They couldn't tell me what was wrong and none of their diagnoses were correct."

"How do you know they weren't correct?" Rob asked.

"I can tell. I observed my symptoms and researched the possible diagnoses."

"Uh-huh," he said skeptically.

"You know how when you're doing a jigsaw puzzle, sometimes a piece appears to fit? And you can make it fit if you force it. But when you don't hear that satisfying click, it's not the right piece."

Luke toddled over to Meri, wearing her underwear like a sun hat. He'd cleverly slung a bra over each shoulder pistolero style. The molded cups dangled on either side of him.

"Where does he learn this stuff?" Rob muttered. "Sorry." Luke proceeded to drag her clean bras up and down the sandy deck. Rob chased him to retrieve the lingerie. When Luke loudly protested, Rob glanced around with a harassed expression, spotted the animal crackers and handed him the box. Luke dropped the bras and plunged both fists into the cookies.

Meri's bout of laughter cost her. Her chest tightened and in seconds, she could hardly breathe through her constricted airway. She excused herself and hurried into the house. The coughing fit started before she made it to the bathroom. She got through it, used her inhaler and went back outside. "Sorry, my asthma flared up," she said. "But that laugh was *so* worth it."

Rob stood by the beach stairs, apparently anxious to get going. She'd never seen him sit for more than a few minutes. He was restless, with the lean physique of a long distance runner. And, she noted, he still didn't want to look at her.

Luke stood in the far corner of her deck, cramming cookies into his mouth and keeping a weather eye out for his dad. When he saw her approach, he said, "Mine," through a large mouthful.

"That's the first time I've heard him talk," she said.

"He's got a few words," Rob said. "Most are variations on 'no.' I should get him home for his nap."

"Take this dry towel. The wind is picking up."

Rob sat to pry the box away from Luke and wrap him in the towel. "There's rumblings of a big announcement coming from Barranca Labs. I would guess they'll be filing to go public soon."

"Probably," she said. "You would know more than me. Quite a few of my colleagues—well, ex-colleagues—are looking forward to that."

"But not you."

"No, not me." She stooped to tidy up around the washtub, keeping her back to him.

"That must have been a bitter blow."

"What?"

"Losing your stock options. If—as you say—it was a wrongful termination, you're missing out on a pretty sweet deal. You were in management. Your compensation package must have included a significant amount of stock. If it were me, I'd be angry. And yet, you don't seem angry at all."

"Sure, the money would have been nice. The thing is, missing out on a chunk of change isn't nearly as important as losing my job—my whole career, really. I don't care about those stock options."

"If you say so," he said, chuckling.

"I do say so." She issued a challenging look, daring him to meet her eyes. To her astonishment, this time he did and their silent exchange felt more comfortable than confrontational. He showed no sign of discomfort with her calm scrutiny.

An unusual guy, then. She took her time, evaluating what she knew about him, weighing the facts as she understood them, drawing her own conclusions. In her experience, many, if not most, men didn't like a woman challenging them, even when the challenge wasn't personal. But Rob McLain didn't mind. He wasn't irritated and uncomfortable with her observations, unlike her last boyfriend. In fact, he looked more amused than anything. Stewart had been a sensitive man. Rob McLain did not strike her as the least bit sensitive.

She shook her head, sharing his amusement. "I can see you don't get it. Geeks like me—money isn't what gets us out of bed in the morning. Exploring, inventing, and creating? That's what matters—that's what we do. But you—you're an investor. People like you—you're motivated by one thing and one thing only. And by the way, this isn't a personal thing—I truly mean no offense. After all, I grew up here in Newport Beach. I've been studying the humans in this habitat for almost thirty years. I ought to know."

A fog bank had moved in just offshore, cooling the air. She shivered, while Rob appeared at ease, still warm and comfortable without a shirt. His chest was toned and strong. Just the way she liked—fit without being muscle-bound. She forced herself to look away. This would not do. Rob might not be super-sensitive but he wasn't stupid.

He'd notice her drooling. Awkward would not begin to describe her mortification.

He leaned back and watched her face. "You grew up here, on the beach?"

"Not here but yes, on the beach. I spent summers at Crystal Cove with my grandparents, closer to Laguna. My parents' house—I mean the house they had while they were married—that was here in Newport. My dad's a developer. Commercial real estate, mostly. As was my grandfather."

Rob had acquired a satisfied grin, an "I've got your number now, sister" expression. "So your people are the old guard—the established, old money. Unlike me, the carpetbagger." A distinct southern accent had crept into his voice. Hence the carpetbagger reference.

"No, no you misunderstand," she said. "That's not who I am. Not anymore. You probably have more in common with my family than I do."

"You think so?" His smile became enigmatic. "You know quite a lot about me, then?"

She tapped her lip. "Let's see. Politically, you lean conservative. Moderately so. You're a Christian but you don't attend church anymore. You drive a luxury sedan, probably a lease so that you always have the latest model. When absolutely necessary, you wear very expensive suits and silk ties, otherwise you skip the tie and stick with tailored dress shirts—probably slim fit. No executive cut for you. You definitely work out regularly because it's just who you are and appearances matter in Southern California, they really do. You live at the beach because it seemed like a great idea before you had a child but you'll probably move up soon, either to Newport Coast or maybe even Laguna, if you can swing it—" She stopped to catch her breath. "Well, you get the idea. I'm not judging."

"Yes, you are," he said.

Luke climbed into Rob's lap, pursed his lips and stared at Meri like she was a mystery to be solved, his expression nearly identical to his father's.

"Well, was I wrong?" she asked.

"No," Rob said, without rancor. He projected nothing more than cheerful calm. He wasn't the alpha dog she'd assumed. Or maybe he was the Big Kahuna at work but, unlike many high-powered men and women, he had a sense of humor about himself. Either he had a tough hide or he didn't mind verbal sparring. Possibly both. "You nailed it. So you've decided, then? I'm not your people."

"Afraid not." She smiled tentatively. "You don't mind my honesty."

"Far from it. A lot of people dance around the truth. You don't. You're...different, aren't you?" He said it like that was a good thing, something to be proud of. Which would be a first. She'd been told she was different her whole life, and it had never been a compliment.

So are you. She couldn't say it aloud. The words, once spoken, might take on an awkward life of their own. Compliments could be tricky.

When he smiled a slow smile, right *at* her this time, Meri swallowed hard. She actually went weak in the knees and had to hold on to the deck railing. The weakness must stem from her mystery illness. It must. She wasn't the weak-kneed type and never had been.

When his glance flicked over her legs, the air between them became charged. His eyes went up to her head and before he masked it, she saw queasy chagrin there.

For all her talk about honesty, she couldn't be honest— not even with herself—about her swoony reaction to this man. Some things were best swept under the rug. And sometimes hypocrisy saved one a world of hurt.

Rob hoisted his son over his shoulder. "Well, thanks for everything. And good luck. But remember what I said about your former boss. You may have a blind spot there."

That night she looked up the latest news releases and announcements about Barranca Labs. There was no sign of any negative news, not the slightest hint of any delay in the product launch. Joe might not have a research director—they still hadn't hired her replacement—but he certainly kept the public relations people busy. All this time, she'd truly believed that if Barranca had been up to something nefarious, she would have known. But what if Rob was right? Her trust in her boss—and her illness— may have kept her from seeing the obvious.

The information she *hadn't* shared with Rob began to eat at her. Could this whole ugly business be about the last phase of the clinical trial? If so, the data monitoring committee would be meeting soon to review all the available data. If they knew what to look for, or even if they didn't, they would zero in on any results out of the ordinary. After all, there were too many safeguards in place and too many people involved for Barranca to rig the data. She just needed to alert the right people to make sure nothing fell through the cracks. She'd made her decision.

The next morning, she looked up Dr. Chamberlain's number. His phone rang through to his assistant.

"Professor Chamberlain won't return until after the holidays."

"It's urgent. I need to speak with him as soon as he returns," Meri said. "He knows me from Barranca Labs." The secretary, at least, wouldn't know she no longer worked there. "This is regarding a committee he chairs— data monitoring for a clinical trial. I'm not certain when they meet next."

"That committee meets quarterly. Hang on, I'll check his calendar." The secretary came back on. "He's got the meeting on his calendar for February 2nd."

At 10:00 on Christmas morning, Meri drove down to Jordan's condo in Mission Viejo. She had been dressed and ready since 8:00, but she'd waited, not wanting to intrude on her brother's first Christmas morning with his daughters in three years. He and his ex-wife had negotiated the arrangement for months, until their lawyers finally resolved the dispute. A dreary and not atypical solution in the Darrow family.

Christmas had been very different when her grandparents were alive. They always decorated the Carnation Cove house and dock with hundreds of multi-colored bulbs. No subtle white lights for them. Grandma used to joke about Santa Claus identifying their house from miles out at sea. She and Grandpa had loved bundling up the grandchildren to sit on the dock and look for the Christmas star on Christmas Eve.

Meri herself had gone down to the beach last night to continue the tradition—as a way of remembering them and their Technicolor approach to the holidays and life in general. She'd been lucky to know them. Especially given the fact that neither of her parents made any effort to create family traditions, then or now. This year, like most years, her parents spent the holiday with their current partners—Mom with her husband in Whistler, Dad with his wife in Aspen.

Meri, however, did have her nieces nearby and couldn't wait to see Kelsey and Bella's reaction to their gifts. Last week she'd picked up vintage hats, gloves, and jewelry for dress-up at the thrift store. Once she'd washed and repaired everything, she was pleased, even a little conceited about her ingenuity. No one else in their lives would have thought of these gifts, and she knew how they loved playing dress-up.

She juggled boxes to ring Jordan's doorbell and tried to remember if she'd brought her camera.

Jordan opened the door. "You just missed them."

"Oh." Her voice hitched on the word and she could only stare at him.

"Nina picked them up early," he said sourly.

She swallowed a lump. "I thought they were supposed to spend the day here."

"Change of plans. They had to get their party dresses on. Nina makes a big friggin' deal about dressing up for Christmas dinner with her parents."

"I'm sorry, Jordan. I know how much you were looking forward to this morning."

"They were ready to bail out of here, anyway."

She shifted the boxes in her arms. "Did you have a good time?"

"Aside from getting woken up at 6:00 a.m., sure."

"I'm glad you were together. That's what really matters. So—what should I do with the girls' gifts?"

Jordan shrugged. "Hold on to 'em. They've got too many presents as it is. And tonight they'll be getting a stack from her parents. Tell you what: I'll bring the kids over next weekend. Or—no. That won't work." A roar went up from the basketball game on his giant TV. He looked over his shoulder to check the score. "Uh, I'll call you later?"

"That's fine. See you." She walked back to her car and drove home slowly. No rush. No one waited for her. No one at all.

3

Carolyn Ling, her old school friend and now her lawyer, came over on New Year's Eve afternoon. They walked down to Newport Pier and back, soaking up the butterscotch light. The afternoon sun's low angle created an illusion of summer, even as the minutes ticked toward January. Winter in Southern California.

Her life and Carolyn's had diverged in recent years, and they hadn't seen much of one another until early December when Meri had asked for Carolyn's help negotiating with her former employer.

About half a mile into their walk, Carolyn pointed to a modest bungalow sandwiched between two massive contemporaries. "How much would that house go for?"

Meri lifted her shoulders. "No idea. I haven't followed prices here."

"Well, you wouldn't have to, would you? You already own a beach house."

"It's my dad's house, not mine. Trust me, the only reason I'm here is because it's the low season and he didn't have renters. He wants me out by Easter."

"You're getting oceanfront property for free," Carolyn said. "I'd say this is a pretty sweet deal for as long as it lasts. I wouldn't complain if I were you."

Meri studied her curiously. She hadn't been complaining and Carolyn knew it. Her friend's vivid features, usually so pretty, were twisted in sour resentment.

When Carolyn tossed her dark hair, the spiky fashionable layers fell into place and she became once again her exquisite friend, the girl all the boys noticed in school, somehow never minding that she was smarter than every one of them. "Yes, it's quite a world you have here," Carolyn added.

Meri would have delved deeper but right then, a rogue wave rushed in. Carolyn took the brunt of it, shrieking with shock when the icy water smashed into her.

Laughing, Meri pulled her to higher ground. "Never turn your back on the sea."

Carolyn groaned. "Ugh. My capris are wet all the way to my ass."

"Let's go back so you can change."

Meri tossed steaks and vegetable kabobs on the grill right after sunset. Carolyn sat in a deck chair drinking wine.

"How are your parents? Do you get to see them often?" Meri said.

"Every Sunday for dim sum," Carolyn said.

"They must be so proud of you—a successful attorney."

"No, actually. They're more embarrassed than proud that I haven't settled down with a nice Chinese boy. Hey, do you know this kid?"

Meri looked over the grill hood. Luke was tearing up from the water, headed straight for them. A plump woman she didn't recognize trailed him by a good thirty feet. The toddler waved and babbled at Meri, telling her something incomprehensible. She turned off the grill and intercepted him at the foot of the stairs. "Hey there. Where do you think you're going?" She settled him on her hip and only just managed to save her dangling earring from his reach.

The plump woman caught up and held her side, speaking between gasps. "This boy is quick. One minute we're looking at a crab… next thing I know… he's taken off. He's faster than my dog… and my dog's a Jack Daniels terrier. Jack Daniels are *not* slow dogs."

Meri smiled uncertainly. Surely she meant Jack *Russell?*

Carolyn leaned over the railing. "Maybe he smelled the steaks."

"My dog can smell a mile away—oh you mean Luke," the woman said in an unmistakable southern drawl. "Could be. Thanks for catchin' him, darlin'." She had a friendly round face, topped by a beehive of pinkish blond hair. "I'm Betty Jo McLain, this little one's grandma."

Luke wiggled out of Meri's arms and promptly scrambled up the deck stairs. "I bet he's looking for the laundry tub," Meri said. "He played in it recently. So you're visiting for the holidays?"

"Just got here from Tennessee last week, but it looks like I'm going to extend my visit," Betty Jo said. "My son needs my help with this little speed demon." She watched Meri deftly scoop up Luke before he reached the grill. "You know my Robert?"

"We've met a few times," Meri said, before introducing herself and Carolyn.

"Here comes his daddy now," Betty Jo said. "And hooboy, by the look of him, he's got a bone to pick."

Rob was dressed to go out, in black trousers and a silky cream shirt. He addressed his mother in a tight voice. "Where have you been?"

"Your son went exploring. Why didn't you tell me he moves like greased lightning?"

"It's past his dinnertime," he said.

Meri picked her way down the wooden steps to hand Luke over to his father. Luke promptly climbed his father's chest to get a bead on a flock of gulls.

"Son, it's not the end of the world if we deviate from your *schedule*," Betty Jo said. "New Year's Eve parties don't start till later on anyway."

"His feet are like ice cubes," Rob said. "And I don't want him running onto strangers' property."

"No harm done," Meri said. Rob hadn't even said hello, however the once-over he gave her was plenty thorough, eyes lingering on her bare arms and legs.

"They aren't strangers," Betty Jo said. "Meri and Carolyn, right?" When Rob didn't respond, his mother frowned at him in a way only a mother could. "Well, your son made a beeline for these pretty gals like they were Miss America and Elmo rolled into one."

"Hard to say if he was heading for us or those steaks," Carolyn said.

"They do smell good," Betty Jo said. "Glad to know someone around here eats something other than kale."

"You're getting healthier," Rob said to Meri. "More fit." He hadn't stopped staring, hadn't acknowledged Carolyn.

"Working on it," Meri said. Why he thought it appropriate to comment on her bod, she didn't know. Surely this wasn't sexual interest.

"I've seen you riding your bike in the morning," he said, his stance and tone almost aggressive.

"And I see you running," she replied, matching his tone on principle more than anything else, because she really did not understand what was happening here.

He continued to stare, issuing a wordless challenge. "Maybe I'll see you out there."

Meri backed up, forgetting the stairs, and scraped her heel. "Ouch." She sat on the step and maneuvered her foot, attempting to see the cut.

Rob put Luke down and crouched beside her. When he took hold of her foot, she flinched in surprise. Unfazed, Rob inspected the scrape. She hadn't realized she was cold until he turned her foot in his big warm hands. His fingers were strong and capable. Delicious heat spread from his hands to her foot and travelled up her leg. She looked down at his thick hair. She wanted to put her hands in it.

His shampoo smelled nice, kind of like sandalwood, very herbal. Oh, she liked this, she liked how he touched her. So much. Her eyes closed and a sigh rippled through her entire body. She hadn't felt this good in what felt like a very long time.

"You better go wash this scrape," he said. "You've got sand in it."

Above them, Carolyn rested her chin on the deck rail and mimed mock adoration behind Rob's back.

Rob, meanwhile, sat back on his heels, seemingly baffled as to how he'd ended up holding her foot. He dropped it like a hot potato and stood up. He didn't look at her again, but he did smile at Carolyn once he had Luke in his arms. "We better go. Happy New Year, ladies."

Luke bobbed away, beaming at them over his father's shoulder and waving. She waved back, noting the grubby handprints all over Rob's back. He'd have to change again before going out to his New Year's Eve party. She allowed herself to wonder briefly who he'd go to the party with. In all likelihood, some babe-a-licious blonde.

Betty Jo shivered and pulled her floral cardigan together. "I don't how y'all are wearing shorts. I'm freezing. Nice meeting you gals." She hurried off.

Carolyn poked Meri in the ribs. "Well, shut my mouth. Robert McLain—was that his name? He's a cutie. And he wasn't wearing a ring. He's not married?"

"I've never seen a wife. But I don't know."

"How can you not know that?"

Meri cradled her raw heel. "I actually met him through work, some months back." She explained how they'd met at his office. "He's not interested in me, Carolyn. And even if he were, he'd need to steer clear. He's at the center of the biotech investor universe—it's a little awkward under the circumstances."

"Oh, he's interested all right," Carolyn said.

"Sweet of you to say so."

"No one's ever accused me of that," Carolyn said irritably. She looked around the beach and then at the setting sun, an orb of liquid gold melting into the ocean. "And a very lovely and privileged world it is. So—have you talked to this Rob guy about what happened? How much does he know?"

"He knows I lost my job. He may even believe my side of the story."

"What story is that?"

Taken aback, Meri said, "Well, that I'm innocent. As you know."

"He could be using you. You've got family connections and even if you don't socialize with your father's friends, you'll always be a member of the Newport Beach elite. Old money."

Meri chortled. "Money so old it's evaporated. No, I don't think that's his style."

"I suppose he'd have to disclose anything he learns to investment clients. Wouldn't he?"

"I don't have a clue," Meri said. "What do I know about high finance?"

"Exactly," Carolyn said. "Why wouldn't he use you? You were privy to juicy inside information."

Meri eyed her friend. "I trust him."

"You trust everyone," Carolyn said and then shrugged. "Don't want to see you get hurt, that's all. What, specifically, did you tell him?"

"Nothing too specific about the negative results I came across before I left. But he agrees something fishy is happening. He thinks I've got a blind spot when it comes to Barranca. And I'm starting to think he's right. It's taken me long enough. That mystery illness must have fogged my brain."

"Speaking of which, what makes you so sure your illness wasn't caused by those crazy nanoparticles in that product you've been working on?" Carolyn asked. "You might have been exposed to something in the lab."

"I've thought about that a lot. I don't see how. I didn't work directly with the product. At all. If anyone was exposed, it would have been one of my lab techs and they're all fine. I've been in touch with my lab supervisor and she says I'm the only person who's been ill. So it can't be related to work."

"Tell me more about those side effects."

"Mine?"

"No, the ones you said that patients in the clinical trial were starting to have."

Meri hesitated. Carolyn would be bound by attorney-client privilege. So it should be fine to tell her. "Some of the trial participants—both men and women—had just reported side effects we'd never seen, not in any of the earlier phases of testing the drug. The patients had developed painful lumps. The men, in particular, reported lumps in their groin area."

Carolyn grimaced. "Eww. So. How big a deal is that?"

"Hard to say. I never had a chance to find out. It's possible it was some fluke thing, unrelated to the anti-aging cream."

"Good lord, were they putting the stuff *down there?*"

"Seems unlikely," Meri said. "I need to get assurances that the study was run properly and the data is all there. Because what if it's something to do with the lymph system? Something that takes a while for—"

"What do you care?" Carolyn said. "It's not your problem anymore. All you have to do is let me handle the settlement—and I'll make it happen eventually—and then put this experience behind you. And next time, be smarter. Didn't you ever wonder why an industry titan like Barranca would hire you?"

Meri felt the color leave her face.

"Oh, you know what I mean," Carolyn said. "You're brilliant, of course you are. Haven't you always been? But you are very young to head a research department and you had no corporate experience before you went there."

"I won't argue that point. Because you're right. I guess I was flattered and believed they wanted my expertise. Be that as it may, I can only move forward and try to do the right thing. I have to find out if those side effects are a real thing, a mistake, or what. And if so, what the company is planning to do about it. And maybe in this whole process, I'll find out who set me up. I suspect something else is going on here, something bigger than me getting forced out of the company."

"What do you mean?" Carolyn asked.

"Right before Christmas I got a call from a reporter with the *Orange County Business Weekly*. He said he was working on a story about the company. He knew I'd been fired and wanted the scoop. He was digging around for some tidbit or other; I'm not sure what."

"What was this reporter's name? And what did you say?"

"Nothing. His name was Seth something. I didn't talk to him. I have no intention of making a public stink. Negative publicity—especially if it's just speculation—will only hurt a great many people. Not just investors but all the employees. Good people who've been working their tails off for years to get the company off the ground."

"Your loyalty is misplaced," Carolyn said.

"Those people were my friends."

"Have any of these 'friends' called to check on you since you left—any of them?"

"One did," Meri said. "The woman I just mentioned. And she did so at some risk to herself because I'm sure she isn't supposed to communicate with me. Anyway, that isn't the point. Jeanie and many others have been killing themselves 60-70 hours a week to make this company succeed. This coming year is supposed to be the one when all that hardship will pay off. I've seen their sacrifices. Jeanie's marriage broke up and her kids are struggling. She hardly sees them. That's no joke. It's the price she's paid, all this time waiting for her ship to come in."

"So don't get involved. Let me handle this from here on in. Let it go."

"I can't do that either. How could I sleep at night if I'm not sure the clinical trial participants are okay and getting the right follow-up? And what if that product really does have these side effects?"

"Look at you," Carolyn said. "The quiet mouse turns crusader. What are you proposing to do?"

"First I need to find out what really happened." She explained her plan to alert the data monitoring committee.

"That professor will think you're a disgruntled employee," Carolyn said. "And he's probably already aware of any issues. Why would he give you the time of day?"

"It's an independent committee and he's a biostatistician. If the numbers have been falsified, he'll want to know."

On the Monday after New Year's, Professor Chamberlain's assistant called at 9 a.m. To Meri's astonishment, the professor not only wanted to meet, he wanted to meet for lunch the following day at Sherman Library and Gardens.

The next morning Meri unearthed one of her business suits. The skirt had to be safety-pinned at the waist but with the suit jacket buttoned, the safety pin didn't show. After applying a careful layer of make-up, she congratulated herself on achieving a close facsimile of her old self. Except for the scarf. She pulled it off and assessed herself using two mirrors, an inspection she ordinarily avoided. Her scalp didn't look too bad. No awful bald patches anymore. Just her own light brown hair that looked almost—not quite—normal. Too short to qualify as a pixie cut, the meagre length branded her a sick woman. But so did the scarf, especially in business attire.

With distaste, she unwrapped a wig that one of the nurses at the doctor's office had given her. Meri had initially refused the offer. She hated the idea and she hated the wig. The nurse had insisted Meri take the wig—a freebie someone had donated—and as the nurse said, one never knew. At that point, a few weeks into her illness, Meri had been certain that she'd never resort to wearing a wig. Her hair had been falling out, sure, but she'd had no idea how extensive the hair loss would become. Plus she'd felt so ill that she couldn't imagine caring enough about her appearance to bother.

She sighed and anchored the page boy style on her head. The hair was too dark, nowhere near her own color. But the professor wouldn't know that. They'd never met in person. Anyway, better to look silly than sickly. The wig would have to do.

She almost missed the sign on Coast Highway for the public garden. Twenty-first century Corona del Mar had sprung up all around it, creating an incongruous oasis. She'd been here as a kid, but not since. The grounds were eerily unchanged. Entering the hushed and mossy brick courtyard was like walking through a time warp into her grandmother's day. Humidity and the sickly sweet odor of exotic plants wafted from an old glass conservatory.

A ruddy fortyish-man waited at a window table in the café. Dressed in a pastel polo shirt and plaid pants, he resembled a golfer more than a professor.

"Dennis Chamberlain?" she said.

"Dr. Darrow," he said, rising to shake her hand. Once they were both seated, he regarded her coolly. "You must be aware, Dr. Darrow, this is not standard procedure, not by any stretch. I agreed to meet as a professional courtesy. My role as committee head for monitoring the drug trial data means I have to operate within guidelines, but you're no longer coordinating the clinical trial. Don't expect more than a limited conversation. With that said, what is this urgent matter you mentioned to my assistant?"

"I know you'll be reviewing adverse event data," Meri said. "Perhaps you already have since the committee will convene in a few weeks."

"As it happens," he said, "I have reviewed the data. A first pass, anyway."

"So you know why I'm concerned."

The waitress took their drink orders. Meri studied the professor and saw no spark of awareness or prior knowledge. He checked his watch repeatedly, apparently not concerned about anything more serious than making his scheduled tee time.

"I won't be ordering lunch," he said. "I suggest you cut to the chase."

"Unexpected side effects were reported near the end of the last trial, several months ago. Troubling and serious results. And yet, from what I gather, Barranca Labs hasn't delayed the product launch."

Chamberlain steepled his fingers but said nothing.

"If you're not aware of these side effects," Meri said, "then there's a problem. A serious one."

"Are you saying the study didn't follow good clinical practice?"

"Under my watch it did, but after that, I can't be sure. I don't know if this happened through negligence or—or, what—but I believe there's missing data."

"What makes you think so?"

"Because I saw negative results disappear overnight. The problems *were* reported, by the patients I mean. The night before—before they terminated me—I reviewed results that had just been uploaded to the database."

"Uploaded by whom?" Chamberlain said.

"The contractor—well, likely a night shift clerk because they're back east—had just uploaded numbers from the current trial. It was early—raw data. Ordinarily I wouldn't have noticed so quickly. But I happened to see these results right away, just by chance."

Meri paused while the waitress brought their drinks. Chamberlain looked at his phone and then out the window. Meri followed his glance out to the courtyard and the conservatory. "What is it?"

"I just saw an acquaintance," he said. "Will you excuse me a moment?"

She looked at him. "Oh. Okay." She watched from the window as he disappeared into the adjacent steamy conservatory. What a strange man. He came out after five minutes or so and then returned to the table. "An old friend I hadn't seen in a long time," he said. "Go on."

Meri observed no sign of tension in the professor's flushed face. "Anyway," she said, "on my last night at the lab, when I ran across the data online—I was actually looking for something else. I just happened to see that a new file had been loaded. And there it was—a sudden influx of patients reporting painful lumps, often in the groin area. I mean, this was the proverbial bolt out of the blue, more significant than anything we'd seen in previous trials."

Chamberlain quizzed her about the side effects for no more than a minute before asking, "And when did you say this occurred?"

"October. Nineteenth or twentieth."

"Almost three months ago. And I understand you became very ill around then. You could be misremembering." He said it neutrally, without accusation or alarm. Either he knew nothing about this or he was an exceptional liar.

"No," she said. "I have a specific recollection of jotting ▸wn some of the codes we use for the side effects because

I thought someone had goofed. I figured it probably was a mistake in the data entry. But then, the next morning, that file had disappeared. It was just gone. I sent off an e-mail to the contractor, but I never got a chance to get to the bottom of it."

"You're saying you saw something that no one else saw or has seen since. Highly unlikely."

Meri straightened her spine. "Why would I make that up?"

He shrugged. "Spite."

"Really?" she said, staggered. "Would you say that to a man who just told you about a suspicious development in a drug trial?"

"Sorry," he said. "Disgruntled wom—employees do all sorts of things. I doubt you're any more immune to bitterness than other people. Think very carefully before you make accusations. You wouldn't want to de-rail your career."

They both knew her career had already careened off the tracks and skidded into a ditch. She took a deep breath and spoke softly, deliberately, because if she didn't, she'd raise her voice, which would only confirm his offensive theory. "I'm not accusing anyone. I am waving a red flag. You monitor patient health and safety data. What if someone deleted that file containing negative results?"

"My fail-safe methodology will catch any sort of cheating or deception."

"Okay, good," Meri said. "I'm simply asking you to review the patient data with a fine-toothed comb before your committee gives the go-ahead."

Chamberlain crossed his arms, clearly impressed with himself. "That goes without saying. Maybe you've not heard of my innovation some years back. Now it's used throughout the industry. With my patented method, I can determine, with absolute certainty, if any files have been removed or corrupted in the course of a clinical trial. If a single line of code has been altered, I'll find out. It's what I do. If something has been removed, I will ferret it out. And by the way, you haven't considered the obvious fact that others will have records of these issues. The nurses who handle the day-to-day interactions or the patients themselves. Not to mention that the Federal Drug Administration encourages patients to report adverse side effects directly."

"They could report, but they might not. Some people, especially *men*," she said, almost relishing the dig, "won't report health problems, especially if these problems are embarrassing. Certainly it warrants investigation to make certain there aren't others suffering in silence. Patients trust the process and the institutions. Which leads us back to your committee." She met his eyes. "Can these patients trust us to do the right thing?"

"There is no 'us', Dr. Darrow."

"Oh yes," she said. "There is. Now you've been alerted. And I'm not going anywhere."

"Well, I will most certainly be checking all data from all sources." He pushed his chair back, preparing to leave. "Let me know if you have anything else more tangible to offer the committee."

"There is one tangible thing," she said. "That I only just recalled. My lab notebook. I know I wrote a few key facts down: dates, dosage, specific side effects. Some of the patients have code numbers—I jotted those down. I like to write things down in my notebook right before leaving the office. Something about the old school method helps me process information. It's not actual proof of course, but it's at least *something* tangible to back up my story."

"Not that it will prove much, but where is this lab notebook? Did you leave it in your office at Barranca Labs?"

"Maybe," she said. "Unless…unless I brought the notebook home with me that night." She paused to think.

"Sometimes I stick it in my bag if I want to finish notes at home. I don't know. I'll look for it."

"Don't worry about it," he said. "As I said, if a file was expunged, I'll know."

Meri looked at her phone. He'd given her twenty minutes.

Joseph Barranca adjusted his sunglasses and kept an eye on activity across the street. He watched Chamberlain hurry to his car and winced at the man's plaid pants. Why anyone would choose to dress like a buffoon was one of life's unsolved mysteries. Was the man auditioning for the circus? Mind-boggling, really. Chamberlain might well be the worst-dressed gay man in Orange County.

Joe touched a button to raise the tinted window of the Mercedes. He didn't need Chamberlain waving and making kissy faces across Coast Highway. That five minutes of flirting and flattering earlier had been a risky enough gambit. Joe didn't delude himself, however. The risk of meeting in public, in such close proximity to the oh-so-earnest Dr. Darrow had been half the fun.

He reached for his phone to give Bryan Haskell an update and to arrange a meeting at the office later. Once that was done, he called his partner of ten years. As ever, skillful redirection worked best. Happily, Derek picked up right away.

"Dear one," Joe said, "You won't believe this. I have to meet some investors for cocktails and dinner tonight...It just came up...No, no spouses this time, I'm afraid...You're the best. How was your visit with Dad?"

He bided his time while Derek vented his concern about the heavy doses of opiates the hospice team had prescribed for Joe's father "I'm sure you're right," Joe said. "You're my rock. You know that, don't you? I'll see you tonight. But don't wait up."

Pragmatism was Joe's religion. Giving oneself up, even devoting oneself to that idea had a timeless elegance. Pragmatism had served him well. Exceedingly, breathtakingly well. Allowing him to support Derek in the manner to which he'd become accustomed. For the rest of their lives.

Truth was, their relationship had always hinged on the fact that Joe was a fabulous provider. Derek expected no less than opulence. Being poor simply wasn't an option for the two of them. Particularly not Derek, who would be the first to laugh as he enumerated all the luxuries he expected Joe to provide: fashion week in Milan with Joe's credit card in hand, the second home in Cabo, the gourmet kitchen when Derek felt like cooking, and the giant spa kept at a toasty temperature year-round, though they rarely skinny-dipped anymore. Derek had grown self-conscious about his hips. Which was ridiculous and he'd told him so many times.

As he took another call, Joe idly watched a slim dark-haired woman exit the public gardens. Her long stride caught his attention, even as he chatted with yet another attorney. He'd had so many of these conversations; the exchange only required a tenth of his attention and even less of his intellect.

The dark-haired woman unlocked Meredith Darrow's sedan. After the first twitch of confusion, Joe found himself smiling. A wig. She had surprised him, unlike most of the people he dealt with. Even a tiny surprise brightened his day. That's all it was, because she wasn't playing secret agent or anything, which would have entertained him even more. No, the wig revealed vanity over the rather startling hair loss she'd endured.

At least Meri wasn't stupid. Hopelessly idealistic, yes. Hamstrung by daddy issues, yes. But always sharp. He'd hired Meri for her unusual combination of skills and presence—both things the company needed for this last, critical phase before gaining drug approval. Until she'd lost that lovely head of hair, she'd possessed the perfect mix of looks, intelligence, and dorky naiveté that investors loved. They just ate that shit up.

In fact, he'd enjoyed mentoring her, until the day she'd found results no one was supposed to see. Uncanny, really, how she'd found them. Virtually seconds before Haskell hacked into the database.

Meri was the fly in the ointment, he thought, enjoying the pun. The contractor running the clinical trial, blissfully ignorant, had accepted his hefty bonus without a blink, no questions asked. Even Bryan Haskell had no clue of the data's significance. And since Joe had taken his usual measures, none of the medical staff knew any extraordinary patterns or data had emerged from this phase of the clinical trial.

He'd learned early on, once you understood how to control people, they really preferred being told what to believe. Especially once they thought themselves integral to a groundbreaking venture. Part of a winning team. Everyone loved a success and Joseph Barranca delivered success. Time after time.

Now he had a new situation. He'd thought they had eliminated Meri from the equation. Even weak and ugly as a newborn kitten, she had become a stubborn thorn in his side. She wouldn't have asked for this meeting with Chamberlain if she didn't suspect something. Which meant the next move was his. He knew how to handle inconsequential players in a game. It wasn't difficult to marginalize even the brightest and the best. And Meri Darrow was neither.

A few seconds of silence alerted him. The attorney on the other end of the conversation expected a response.

"We have no reason to think he's dangerous," he said, "but we'll continue to investigate. Our corporate counsel advised we proceed carefully. Hence the delay, but now we can clear the air and compensate her for this ordeal. You'll be hearing from us about a generous severance package. Trust me, she'll be pleased with the settlement."

He infused his voice with amused indulgence. "I'd rather talk about *your* next step. I've dealt with many attorneys over the years and you—you're exceptional. You know that, don't you? I'd hire you in a heartbeat. Does your firm appreciate what they have in you? Talent like yours ought to be nurtured. Maybe we should talk about your future in corporate law, once this current issue is resolved."

He checked his teeth in the mirror while she responded predictably. When she stopped chattering, he took his cue.

"In the meantime, I know you'll help your client make smart choices. This settlement will require absolute discretion. I don't have to tell you one careless word from her could destroy all the negotiating and hard work you've done on her behalf."

He tilted his head to inspect his nose hairs while she answered.

"Why not tomorrow?" he said. "I look forward to it."

Joe slipped his phone inside his jacket pocket. He'd learned at a young age—the easiest way to manipulate was to massage the ego. No one was immune to flattery. And in some cases, massaging other things worked nicely too. Witness that mini-tryst in the conservatory. All he'd had to do was offer the eminent professor a compliment and a quick tickle—a sneak preview of the ecstasy he could expect later.

Naturally things might get sticky if Derek ever got wind of the affair. As devoted a partner as one could ask for, Derek's jealous nature created some fireworks on occasion. But Joe liked that. Derek's sassy volatility kept their relationship exciting.

Things were going well. Yes, he'd had to adjust course several times, but nothing he wasn't prepared for. Even this slight complication with the intrepid Dr. Darrow had created a mildly amusing detour on the inevitable road to success. She was simply a loose end, thanks to Haskell's inept and ill-timed maneuvers last October. He wasn't worried, not in the least. He had a plan, a back-up plan, and various alternatives in the unlikely event she continued to make waves. No one—not even a girl genius—ever became too difficult or unpredictable for him. He always found a way. Nothing could distract him from taking the company public and then launching this blockbuster drug. His lifelong goal of creating the ultimate anti-aging product informed every decision he made, every step along the way. The culmination of his whole career. His beginning, his middle, and his end.

4

Just after sunset, someone pounded urgently on the front door. Meri froze until she registered the southern accent. "It's Betty Jo McLain." Rob's mother stood on the doorstep with a tear-drenched Luke. "I'm so sorry to bother you honey, but I don't know anyone else. This child went and put something up his nose."

Meri stifled a laugh. "What?"

"The nanny went home and everything was fine and dandy. He was playing on the floor. And the next thing I know, he's screaming and holding his nose." Luke held his arms out and Betty Jo, on the verge of tears herself, passed him over.

"What do you think it was?" Meri asked.

"I don't know. I just don't know. He's been crying up a storm. He only just stopped when he saw you. I don't know what to do! Rob's at a dinner meeting with some VIP or other. I left a message for him, but he won't get it till later. He said his phone would be off until at least 9:00."

Meri sat Luke down and crouched at his eye level. His nose ran profusely. "Luke, did you put something in there?" She tapped her own nose.

Comprehension shone in his blue eyes. He nodded, tearing up again.

She hunkered down below him and tilted his head. She couldn't see a thing. "What was it Lukie, can you tell us?"

"Rock," he said in a nasal tone.

"Ohh. Those stupid rocks," Betty Jo moaned. "I should have *known* better. But Tina Marie insisted on sending those polished rocks. I don't expect her girls ever put a rock up any orifice."

Luke started to cry again. His grandmother's panic increased with his volume. Or maybe his volume increased with her panic. Meri got a flashlight. She still couldn't see anything in there. Even harder to see when he was bellowing.

Betty Jo wrung her hands. "Rob is going to have kittens."

Meri took a deep breath. "So you left a message for him? Okay, this is what we'll do. I'll go back home with you now. We'll call the pediatrician and take it from there."

The pediatrician and Rob arrived at the emergency room within minutes of each other. Rob rushed in the door, white and drawn. Meri guided him to his son before slipping out to the waiting room. Five minutes later, a nurse escorted his exhausted grandmother out to sit with her.

Betty Jo took up her monologue where she had left off earlier. "I tried to tell Rob what happened, but I don't think he was listening. Tina Marie—Rob's sister—sent a souvenir bag of pretty rocks. I *told* Tina Luke was too young. But she wanted to send something special and she remembered how Rob loved his rock collection when he was a kid. Believe it or not, I'm well-acquainted with helping people in pain, but my grandbaby shoving a rock up his nose really threw me for a loop."

Rob came out soon after, only slightly less pale than he'd been. "Dr. Fox got the pebble out. He's going to be fine. But he's got a low fever and they want to keep him for observation."

"The poor baby," Betty Jo said. "Can I go see him?"

"Go ahead, Mom. I'll join you in a minute."

Meri shifted her bag to her shoulder and stood up. "How long will they keep him?"

Rob rubbed the back of his neck. "A few more hours. I hate to ask for another favor…"

"It's fine. What do you need?"

"Mom should go home—she'll need her blood pressure medicine and she's been through the wringer tonight. I'd feel better if she wasn't sitting here for hours, waiting on us. Could you drive her back?"

"Of course. I have Luke's car seat though, so I should pull that out for you."

"It's an extra one. I'll get it tomorrow."

He looked lost, she thought. His blue eyes had darkened and taken on an eerie vacancy that disturbed her. He wasn't fully present. She didn't know where the cheerful arrogant Rob had gone, but he wasn't here.

"What about you?" she said. "Are you going to be okay?"

"Yeah, sure," he said slowly. He still had very little color in his face. Even his lips were pale. "Thank you for helping us. My mother's first message was so garbled I didn't know *what* was going on. I just heard 'emergency room.' The second message wasn't much better. I thought…I thought something really bad happened."

"Would it be okay—?" She hesitated. "Would you mind if I came back here, after I drop your mom off at home?"

His eyes re-focused and he came back to the moment, back to her. "You would do that?"

She'd gotten used to the way he carried himself, a contradictory mix of relaxed humor and pent-up energy. But this nervy tension and his anxious stare—as if he thought she might disappear—it wasn't consistent with her image of him. He wasn't the same man she'd met on the beach. She hated seeing him like this.

"I want to wait with you," she said. "I've gotten attached to your boy."

"I noticed," he said. "He's lucky that way."

She dug out her car keys and edged toward the door. "I'll be back as soon as I can. I'll go pull the car up now so your mom doesn't have to walk too far in this mist."

"The fog has gotten dense," Rob said, glancing over her head. "Be careful."

She returned in less than an hour, after dropping Betty Jo at home. On the drive back, Meri wrestled with her reaction to Rob's anguish. Her discomfort shamed her. She wasn't skilled at handling people or family problems—her default was to withdraw from family dramas and hide with a book—but he deserved better and so did his family.

Rob lifted his head when she came in, almost pitifully glad to see her. His reaction wasn't for her; she knew that. This was gratitude for any emotional support, even if it came from a relative stranger. Luke slept peacefully. The only signs of his ordeal were the hospital bracelet he wore and the teddy bear he clutched.

"Where did the teddy come from?" she asked.

"It's a duplicate of his bear at home. I keep an extra one in my trunk. For emergencies."

"This would qualify." She moved the extra chair to sit beside him. Better if she wasn't facing Rob. Not that he particularly cared one way or another, but she'd be more comfortable.

"He's fine," Rob said.

"You don't sound convinced." She glanced at him. Poor guy looked so tired and anxious. If this is what parenthood did to you, she didn't want to join the club. In any case, with the notable exception of the last few months, her career took all her time and attention. She expected it always would.

"I know he's going to be alright," Rob said. "He woke up a while ago. Once I got him calmed down again, I asked him why he put the rock up his nose. I mean, I know he's not even two, but I gave him more credit."

She had to laugh at that. "You did?"

"He *is* very bright."

"Well, of course he is," she said, touching his hand without stopping to think. "That's why he's such a handful." Rob seized her fingers and didn't let go. An automatic response. He wasn't thinking either. Once again, she wondered about Luke's mother. No one had mentioned calling her.

"I'd been careful to keep those rocks out of his reach since Christmas," Rob said. "When Mom let him play with them today, he must have rightly figured I'd take them away once I got home. So I asked him, 'Why did you put a rock up your nose?'"

"Well what did he say?"

"He pointed down and said, 'no pocket'."

Meri grinned. "Impressive logic."

"I thought so," Rob said. His color had returned. He looked like himself again. "Thank you for coming back."

"May I ask—where is Luke's mom now?"

Rob stiffened and released her fingers. His face took on a gray hue again.

"Sorry. If it's a sensitive subject…"

"No, no. It's a reasonable question. My fault, not yours. Most people I talk to on a daily basis already know. Julie died the night he was born."

It was her turn to stiffen. "I'm so sorry. I had no idea." The possibility hadn't even occurred to her. She'd simply assumed he was divorced, like most people around here.

"You had no way of knowing," he said. "For some reason, I didn't think—I'm so used to people already knowing what happened to Julie that I didn't think to explain."

So what *had* happened? Who died in childbirth anymore? Especially here and now, to a couple with money and access to the best medical care. Too mortified to ask, she said nothing. Rob was lost in thought again. No wonder he'd been upset. He'd had to watch his young wife die suddenly on the one day that should have been his happiest.

When Luke stirred, Rob stood and felt his son's forehead.

"Is he okay?"

"If he still has a fever, it's a low one."

"Do you want me to get a nurse?"

"No, we're in no rush. I'm not looking forward to taking him out of this warm bed. You know, you can go home anytime. You don't have to stay."

"No, I'll wait. I have nowhere I need to be."

Rob had grown so quiet. On impulse, she reached for his hand. He gripped her hand like it was a lifeline and held it close to his chest. He said nothing more and she couldn't ask. So they held hands and sat in the hard plastic chairs, watching the small figure in the bed until it was time to go home.

The rusty sunset had faded from the horizon on the following evening when Meri's doorbell rang again. She checked the peephole. Rob stood on the front steps holding a shocking purple florist's hydrangea.

"You didn't have to do that," she said.

"Yes, I did." He handed it over.

"Would you like to come in? I was just about to celebrate."

He walked straight to the picture window that overlooked the beach. "Your view's better than mine. What are we celebrating?"

The angles of his face intrigued her. There was a crease in one cheek, probably from the wide grin he flashed from time to time. His hair brushed his collar, almost, but not quite as messy as that first time she'd seen him. When she'd thought he was an arrogant know-it-all. Now she saw a man who knew what he wanted, who was forthright and direct.

He filled the room in a way she couldn't quite figure out. In crisp trousers and a blue oxford shirt—more conservative than the tangerine one he'd worn that first time she'd seen him—he gave off an air of authority. She'd seen him last night in work clothes, but everything had been different. Last night he'd been vulnerable. He'd been a neighbor who needed her help, a worried young father. This man—this tall, too-fine man—was Robert McLain, smart, capable, and sure of himself. Supremely confident about who he was and his place in the world. Every hair in place and looking like a model in a menswear catalog. Except more masculine and definitely more powerful.

Everything that she was not, at least not at the moment, in her rumpled skinny corduroys and V-neck sweater, unemployed and uncertain of her future.

He looked at her expectantly. She had forgotten what he'd asked her. "What are you celebrating?" he repeated.

"I finished writing a paper I started years ago. I always intended to publish, but never got around to it. Would you like some wine?"

"Sounds good."

She went to get a second glass, taking the opportunity to give herself a mental slap upside the head.

"What's the paper about?" he called out.

"It compares topical skin cancer treatments," she said, coming back in. He stood by the fireplace, studying the old photo of her grandparents in their heyday, clowning around with their friends. The picture drew people like a magnet and Rob was no exception. They were all beautiful young athletes and their timeless vitality practically jumped out of the picture frame.

"Who are these people?" he said. "That guy in front looks like Tarzan."

"Good eye. It is. Johnny Weissmuller before his Tarzan days. He was an Olympic swimmer, like my grandmother." She tapped a pretty young woman in a long tank suit. "Cissy Lopez. The blond god behind Grandma is her future husband, Louis Darrow."

"Your grandmother was an Olympic swimmer? No kidding. When was this?"

"Late 1920's. Before they married."

"Wait. These are your grandparents, not your great-grandparents?"

"My dad is considerably older than my mom. My brother Jordan—remember you met him on the beach—and I are from the second marriage. Dad's on wife number four now. And counting."

"Are those surfboards? They're huge."

"Yeah, the boards were like ten feet long and super heavy—close to 100 pounds. This Hawaiian man here is Duke Kahanamoku. Pretty famous in surfing circles. He did some acting, too."

"Your grandma was a babe." He took the glass from her and sat down.

"She was something. That group surfed at Corona del Mar on weekends. The break was completely different back then, before the Newport jetty. Anyway, the boys taught Grandma Cissy to surf. But the boards were really too heavy for her. She mostly tandem surfed with my grandfather. I saw them do it once when I was little. Showing off for the grandkids."

She sat across from him and cradled her glass.

"So you were saying you wrote a paper about skin cancer treatments?" Rob asked. "Not cosmeceuticals?"

She heard the faint scorn in his tone. "My doctorate is in skin cancer biology. It's still my real interest."

"Skin cancer. Serious stuff. So why go work for Barranca on his expensive anti-aging creams?"

"Rob, are you implying I'm a sell-out?"

He shrugged. Humor and intelligence lit those blue eyes. She liked that he didn't backpedal or apologize. A spade was a spade. A cosmetic product—however groundbreaking—didn't command the same respect. Why would it? Anything less than honesty would only have annoyed her. Interesting that he guessed that.

"Joe knew about my work researching nanoparticles. And he made me an offer I couldn't refuse. I needed the money after graduate school. Student loans and so forth, so I took the job and never looked back."

"And now you're getting back to the serious stuff? Like what?"

She set her glass down and leaned forward. "I'm interested in the use of vitamins topically. There's possibilities. Can you believe—the paper only needed minor tweaking to make it current? It's just been accepted for publication in one of the dermatology journals."

"Congratulations," he said.

"Thanks. How's your boy today? Is he keeping his nose clean?"

"Ha. He's forgotten all about it. It's my mother who's not taking it well. She's wrung her hands and apologized at least a dozen times. Says she'd forgotten about toddlers. My brother and sister's kids are older. And she keeps reminding me none of them ever stuck a rock up their nose."

"And where do they all live?"

"Everyone's still in Tennessee. After my Dad died, I bought my Mom a new house and my sister moved into my parents' old place. My brother is nearby."

"You're the only one who moved away?"

He settled back in the chair. The reading lamp shone on the thick waves of his hair and she noticed for the first time that the brown was mixed with auburn, thick and glossy. "My mother never lets me forget it," he said.

"How long will she be visiting?"

"At least six weeks, but I'm hoping she'll stay longer. Luke's nanny can't stay nights and weekends and I'm in a bind with all the business trips I've put off. My boss has cut me slack for almost two years now, but the truth is, the job requires travel. People will be sympathetic to my uh, situation, for only so long. And now I've pretty much used up my sympathy quota."

She liked this. He was relaxed and relaxing. Interesting to talk to. Most men she dated were introverts and not the most observant creatures. Stewart, the man she'd been seeing last year, before everything happened, hadn't even noticed as she got steadily sicker. The last time she'd seen Stewart, around Halloween, she'd had to explain that she wasn't well enough to go out to dinner. He'd taken it as a personal rejection and simply stopped calling after that. Which was okay with her. Good riddance.

She could have sat there all night listening to Rob, except for the fact that her airways were slowly constricting. A coughing spell was coming and she didn't want to have it in front of him. "Excuse me," she said and left the room quickly.

He heard her coughing. It sounded painful. He looked around her house. Other than the photograph, there were few personal items, and the furniture was curiously stodgy and dated. Nothing new or particularly nice. Then again, this was a rental property, not her home at all. What had she said about that? He could recall only that the place belonged to her father.

When she returned, her mouth was a straight, almost grim line. She didn't look nearly as fit as she pretended to be. He saw the boring salad on her table.

"Would you like to come back and have dinner with us? My mom's making fried chicken. It was her idea." He noted Meri's cool reaction. In his world, the way he was raised, it was polite to emphasize the hostess wanted your company.

"Thank you but not tonight. Maybe another time?"

"I better go," he said. "What I really want to do is get a run in before dinner. It's the only time I'm alone, except for driving to and from work. I need that time for my sanity."

"I know what you mean. Not that I have your responsibilities." She glanced at her watch. "Listen, I want to ask you something. We could kill two birds—get a quick walk in now—to the jetty and back?"

"You're sure you're well enough?" She ignored him and headed for the back door. He saw she wasn't pleased. "Hold on now, where's your jacket?"

"Oh, it doesn't matter."

"Yes it does. You've been ill."

She looked as if she wanted to argue, but went to pull a hoodie from the closet instead. He waited at the back door, letting her go first. But she paused as well, as if she expected him to go first. They looked at each other, mutually confused.

Finally, she stepped out onto the deck. "Aren't you going to lock it?" he said.

"We're only going to the jetty and back. Ten minutes, tops."

He followed her down the back stairs. The night was clear, with no fog, just an icy wind whipping across the beach. She was already well ahead, striding over the sand. He didn't know what to make of her. Why not wait for him before striding into the darkness? "Wait up."

She paused, a slim figure outlined against the ocean's dark mass. Though not short, she looked fragile enough to be carried away with the next gust. He caught up, took her arm and she jumped. She must not be used to a man taking her arm. Or letting her go first through the door. What sort of jerks did she hang out with?

They walked south toward the harbor entrance. She paced beside him with her head bent, hidden from view except for the short strands of hair that escaped from her scarf. He hauled her up short. "This won't do. You need to keep your head warm." He reached for her hood.

"I can do it," she said, batting at his hands.

He tugged it over her ears and forgot to let go. He didn't want to be attracted. He could see the illness in the hollows of her face and the circles under her eyes. Not like October, when she'd been healthy and vibrant. At least her mouth hadn't changed—a lovely crushed rose. And his curiosity bloomed anew. Her lips looked so sweet and soft. What would she taste like? He gripped her hood, tempted past self-control.

He couldn't wait and he sensed the same impatience in her. He bent to taste her. His reward was delicate lemongrass. Nice. And she was kissing him back. He went in again and she met him eagerly. Her lips warmed and clung to his. He slid his hands inside her hood and along her delicate jaw line. She made a low noise in her throat, a murmur of pleasure. He answered her with a wordless sound of his own. With each kiss, they went deeper, hotter, and longer.

His hands wandered and hunted for treasure of the best kind. He crept under her sweater and along the baby soft skin of her stomach. He slipped a few inches below her waistband. Even softer skin there. He wanted more but that could wait.

He needed to learn her breasts. Each perfect mound, surprisingly full. They grew heavier in his hands. The sensitive pads of his fingers rubbed the peaks through the silky bra. They hardened for him. She told him what she wanted with wordless language, exquisite little noises, telling him how much she liked his kisses, his touch.

He wanted more of her. More warmth, more sweetness. He cradled her closer and rocked her against his thighs. His hands fit around her hips easily, cupping her close against his cock so she fit him just right.

Then his thumbs met prominent sharp hip bones. Bones so sharp they poked through her corduroys, startling him. As if someone had dumped a cold bucket of ice down his pants.

When Rob jumped, Meri thought something must have happened behind her. She even looked around. But, no. He stepped back a pace, his hands held out stiffly, as if his hands had acted of their own volition. He appeared embarrassed and sorry. Was he sorry he kissed her, sorry they'd had their hands all over each other? Or was he just physically repulsed? He'd been very hard and hot. There was no mistaking that. No doubt in her mind, he had wanted her. And then, not at all. She knew revulsion when she saw it. And felt it.

"It's all right," she said faintly. "No worries."

"Look, I want to—"

"Forget it." She resumed walking and hoped to God he wouldn't try to explain. He carefully kept his distance. The wind tore through the gap between them. She was colder than she would have been if he'd never sheltered her at all. And then the obvious occurred to her. The man probably hadn't had many sexual encounters since his wife had died. What with the job and a baby, he wouldn't have had much free time. She hadn't heard any reference to a girlfriend. So any woman who touched Rob intimately would have gotten a rise out of him. Initially.

They were halfway to the jetty when Rob broke the silence. "What did you want to talk to me about?"

"If you can't do it, I will totally understand, okay? Because I—"

Rob interrupted. "Just tell me."

"I've been following Barranca Labs' announcements. I've seen nothing about the current drug trial and its status.

I was wondering if you can keep me posted as to any news. I mean, that's something you'd need to know. And they'd need to fill you in, right?"

"Typically, yes. What are you saying?"

"I'm not comfortable getting into details."

"Maybe I can make this easier," he said. "Does Barranca cut corners or bend the rules in clinical trials?"

She took a long time answering. "Not that I know of."

"So you have doubts."

"Yes."

"Such as?"

"I can't say. But I am…concerned."

"You're not the only one."

She glanced over, unsure what he meant. "I expected to hear more by now. I know that Joe Barranca has been under a great deal of strain, at home and at work."

"Sounds like you're making excuses for him."

"No, not at all. His father is very ill, probably dying. I'm wondering if that's a factor."

He waved dismissively. "Never mind. I'll see what I can learn. I'll keep you informed, within limits. It's likely my company will buy shares in that IPO. Anyone with a financial stake needs to watch out for ethics violations."

"I'll appreciate whatever you can do. I wouldn't want to get you in hot water."

"After your help last night, it's the least I can do. Ready to go back?"

They turned into the wind. She huddled deeper into the jacket and clutched the hood to keep it on. After a few minutes of trudging at a pace that apparently didn't meet his approval, he put his hand on the small of her back to propel her up the beach.

"Have you gotten a final diagnosis yet?" he asked.

"No." She tried to shake him off, but he ignored her effort and kept his hand, solid and warm just above her rear end. Warmth spread from his hand and into her muscles, up through her spine. Her back felt strong and supple and a sense of well-being rose to the back of her neck. It wasn't fair—how good he made her feel—considering how one-sided this attraction was. "I worked crazy hours for months on end last year. The doctor said stress and exhaustion must have created a perfect storm when a virus hit."

"Why did you say your hair fell out?"

"Like I said, stress." With that, the pressure from his hand increased again, pushing her forward. "Man, you're in a hurry. Are you always like this?"

"Always," he said.

The energetic pace he set brought them parallel to her house within five minutes. He took her arm, towed her across the sand, marched her in the back door, and steered her to the couch. She plopped down with relief.

"Do you need something?" he said.

"No thank you. Not a thing."

"I'll get you a glass of water," he said and went to the kitchen.

More exhausted than she ought to be after a short walk, Meri closed her eyes and wondered why he'd bothered to ask if he was just going to do what he wanted to do in the first place.

Meri sat up and fuzzily checked the time. She'd been asleep half an hour. An old blanket had slipped to the floor. Rob must have covered her up before leaving. She picked up the business card he'd left on the coffee table and read his scribbled note saying he'd be in touch.

She'd heard women talk about the southern gentleman thing. A magnetic charm. She'd scoffed at the idea. Now she understood. She, plain old Meri Darrow, was not immune, not by a long shot. Whether it was his slight accent or courtly manner, something had lit the fuse of sensual awareness between them. For him, that fuse had lit briefly, then fizzled.

Point taken. She'd been so caught up, she'd forgotten all about his earlier reactions to her. This wouldn't go anywhere. For several reasons. Not least of which—she and Rob weren't people who would ordinarily even socialize, much less hook up. And things were complicated enough right now.

She pushed herself off the couch. He'd help her learn what she needed to know. Wanting him was irrelevant.

Over the next two weeks, Meri rode her bike every day and applied for jobs she had no prayer of getting. She had posted her resume on various sites, written and called every industry contact she had. People who actually answered their phones sounded surprised and ill at ease. No one called her back. Then, one morning, someone finally did. Moses Chen, an old friend from graduate school, reported he was now working in San Francisco. Kind and friendly as ever, he agreed to meet her for coffee in a few weeks when he planned to be in the area. She took heart from this small but significant step in the right direction.

Her doctor pronounced her almost recovered, except for the asthma flare-ups that were becoming less frequent. Her hair continued to grow in and she wore a baseball cap only when she went outside, more to protect her scalp from the sun than anything.

Rob had started travelling a lot so she rarely saw him, but she often met Betty Jo and Luke on the beach. They soon formed the comfortable habit of stopping to chat. Rob's mother loved to tell stories about the folks back home. Before long, Meri knew enough dirt to blackmail half of Rob's family. Some of his mother's stories, however, resembled tall tales.

One morning, Betty Jo told Meri about the family's heritage. "One-sixteenth native American," Betty Jo said proudly. "We traced the line back to a young Cherokee who just said 'No sirree' to the Trail of Tears. He wasn't going to put up with that nonsense and walk all the way to Oklahoma. So he didn't. On the other side of the family tree, we have the faith healers. My side, of course. My daddy, my granddaddy, and his daddy before him had a long and proud tradition. People today would likely have a different name for it. But we called it faith healing."

Meri looked up from the sand castle she and Luke were building. "You mean like a ministry or something?"

"Oh my, yes. My family has always preached and practiced whenever and wherever the good Lord required. Tents, churches, campgrounds, you name it. That's how I spent my childhood, travelling all over the South. I suspect even before my ancestors embraced the gospel, they were healing. Folk healing has been a Carter family tradition all the way back to who knows when. The gift is passed down from generation to generation."

"Hmm," Meri said, unwilling to engage such a nice lady in debate over what she herself believed to be pure hogwash. She didn't disrespect Betty Jo's spiritual beliefs; in fact, she envied her faith. But honestly, the idea that one person could possibly heal another couldn't be taken seriously. None of that stuff ever withstood rigorous examination. It was folklore.

Later that same day, Meri heard again from Seth Bernstein, the journalist for the *Orange County Business Weekly*.

"You're persistent," she said.

"My sources tell me you have the inside scoop about what's happening down at Barranca Labs. I'd like to hear your side of the story."

"Who are your sources?" Meri said.

"Sorry, can't divulge that."

"I'm sorry too, because I can't talk to you."

"Why not?"

"I—well—I just can't."

"So you're still in talks with the company."

"I really won't comment."

"Tell you what," he said. "I'll send you my contact info and you can let me know when you change your mind. I have a feeling you'll have lots to say before this is all over."

"I'll keep you in mind," she said and disconnected.

Barranca's attorneys had dropped strong hints that more information would soon be forthcoming. An investigation into what had happened with those incriminating e-mails was underway—a very good sign, according to Carolyn. For weeks now, her friend had counseled patience, emphasizing the need to keep a low profile during negotiations, a drawn out process she assured Meri was par for the course. But Meri felt increasingly restless and impatient. Her savings was dwindling, so she'd have to find gainful employment soon. She couldn't move forward until the wrongful termination was resolved. But if the settlement didn't include clearing her name, she didn't have much of a future anyway.

5

Rob managed to catch a flight that landed at John Wayne airport two hours earlier than planned. He'd been away three days and missed Luke more than he would have thought possible. They'd never been apart this long. On his first trip earlier in the month, he had enjoyed his freedom. By the second trip, that freedom felt more like loss. On this trip, his third, he resented the lonely dinners and sterile hotel rooms. He even resented waking to an alarm instead of the sound of his son talking to himself in his crib. Every day Luke learned new words, formed whole sentences, and got into more trouble. His grandmother wasn't used to boys and thought he was too wild. Luke needed someone who understood him to tuck him in at night.

As soon as Rob paid the driver off, he rushed into the house only to find it empty and quiet. His mother had mentioned that Letty, their nanny, had been sick. A note on the counter in Betty Jo's writing explained that she'd taken Luke to the park. Rob looked closer. She'd addressed the note to Meri? Interesting.

Rob loosened his tie and dumped his luggage by the stairs. Now what? He could go for a run, return phone calls, even work from home uninterrupted, a rare opportunity. But none of those things appealed. He just wanted to see his family.

He walked over to look out at the beach. And jumped. A woman slept in the reclining chair next to him, facing the window. Half-covered by a blanket, with her arms wrapped around her middle, her feet tucked beneath her, she slept curled up like a kitten.

He didn't recognize her at first. Not counting when they'd first met, he'd never seen her without that god-awful scarf or a hat. She had hair. Caramel-brown and too-short, the hair was, in fact, quite pretty, with gold-tipped tendrils framing her face. He didn't know why the sight surprised him. He hadn't considered how she'd look. His fantasies so far, and there had been plenty, centered on her long legs and expressive mouth.

He moved closer. Watching her now, rosy with sleep and lips turned down in a cute pout, he wondered at his lack of imagination. She'd be downright beautiful once she regained her health. When they'd shared that kiss on the beach a few weeks back, he'd managed, briefly, to forget the aura of illness that lingered around her.

He wasn't proud of his reaction then. The rejection had come from his gut—a wrenching dread he had surprisingly little control over. Since then, he'd done his best to repress the attraction. And here she was again, and the mixed feelings had come roaring back. All this time he'd tried not to think too deeply about this pull he felt. The last thing he needed in his life was a woman with chronic health problems. If that made him shallow, so be it. He had Luke to think of. They'd been through too much already.

However. If he were honest with himself, his caution wasn't for Luke's sake. The sorry truth was—even the slightest chance of losing another person he cared about was enough to send him howling into the night.

Meri gave a little sigh, turned her face into her hand and slept on.

To keep from touching her, as he wanted—suddenly, fiercely—to do, he sat and watched her sleep. He had been attracted to her from the get-go but tried to ignore the whole baffling situation. Now he understood why he'd been fantasizing. She was a lot more than a pretty mouth and long legs. It was her. He knew her better—or at least he was starting to know her. She was utterly unique—honest and braver in some ways than anyone he knew. Even as thin as she was—still too thin to be healthy—he recognized her innate strength. Her attitude toward the challenges she faced attracted him almost as much as the physical attributes. Almost.

He got up and edged a bit closer to see if she'd stir. She didn't. Like a voyeur, he stood above her, looking down at the rise and fall of her chest, at the golden skin exposed by the slipping blanket. Just because Meri was here and just because he wanted her, that didn't mean he should act on that desire. He ought to let her sleep. She was so mouthwatering, though.

He bent over her sleeping form. He was less than an inch away, hovering between her jaw and her ear, close enough to breathe in her scent. Close enough to see the smooth silky texture of her skin. He wanted to kiss her neck. To taste her. Her lips twitched and pouted that adorable pout. And that was it. Too much temptation for him to withstand. He'd been hard since the second he saw her cuddled up in his chair, like she'd been waiting for him.

He put one hand out to touch the swell of her breast—then stopped barely an inch away. Once done, there'd be no turning back. She'd be upset and uncomfortable. Understandably. He'd have to explain and apologize and everything would change. He didn't want her to wake up frightened and then go away. He wanted her to stay.

Rob stepped back. How would he explain his obvious arousal? Here she was, innocently sleeping, completely unaware of the slobbering beast poised above her. He wouldn't be able to explain his behavior because he didn't understand it either. He returned to the couch and put a pillow over his lap. And laughed at himself.

That's when she woke up. After a few sleepy blinks, she saw him sitting across from her and smiled the most beautiful smile. Welcoming him home.

"Hey there Sleeping Beauty," he said.

She blinked again and her smile died. Her face changed and became wary, hurt even. What had he said?

"Where is everyone?" she said, sitting up and clutching the blanket with both hands.

"Mom and Luke went to the park."

She looked embarrassed. "Sorry, I didn't mean to fall asleep here. I'll get going."

"Don't rush on my account," he said. "You look so comfortable." Although in fact, she did not. Not anymore.

She glanced around. "I just have to find my shoes. Your mom was showing me some foot reflexology pressure points. I guess I got a little too comfortable. Luke went down for his nap and I must have done the same. She said she'd wake me before you got home."

"I'm early," he said. "And you must have been sleeping so soundly she didn't want to wake you."

"That must be it," Meri said. "I don't even recall getting sleepy. I must have passed out." She shook out the blanket and folded it. "I feel so rested, like I got a full night's sleep."

"Good," Rob said. "You must have needed it."

"Apparently, I did," she said, smiling again, completely unaware of how turned on he was. Still. With one graceful movement, she rose and located her shoes. "I'll see you around."

"Wait," he said. "I'll walk you home." She didn't seem to want to look at him anymore so at least he wouldn't have to explain the erection. He'd be spared that embarrassment.

He took her arm as they descended the steps to the beach and once again, he noted her surprised flinch before she let him help her. Not that she needed the help—she was stronger now. Still, it was a good excuse to touch her. He kept her arm in his as they trudged over the uneven sand down to her house.

"I have news," he said. "One of my people has been tracking what's happening at your former company. Priya called me with an update this afternoon. Barranca Labs just got the green light to proceed with the new drug."

She stopped dead. "That can't be right. The data monitoring committee isn't meeting till February."

"According to Priya, the meeting got moved up. They convened earlier this week and approved the results. It's all systems go for submitting a new drug application to the government agency and then moving on to the next phase."

Meri sank onto the bottom step of her stairs, as if her knees had given out. "I let this happen. All this time, Carolyn has been negotiating on my behalf. And I thought things would work themselves out if we played by the rules."

"What do you mean? Your *friend* is negotiating? You said you had an attorney."

"She is an attorney."

"What sort of an attorney?"

"Intellectual property, something like that."

"Not employment law?"

"Not usually, but she's handling this as a favor."

Rob shook his head. "I wish I'd known."

"Why would you need to know?"

"Because I would have helped you find someone to represent you who actually does this sort of thing for a living."

Meri's eyes widened. "I realize you want to help, but you're out of line."

"Maybe you need someone who's out of line."

Her expressive face revealed both irritation and amusement. "Because I'm so helpless?"

"I didn't say that. I know when I'm right, though."

"Are you always so overbearing?"

"When I have to be. So, where do you stand? What has your friend done so far?"

"As a matter of fact, she said yesterday the company told her they had investigated and found out who set me up."

"And?"

"Guy named Bryan Haskell. I know him. Knew him. They've already fired him, but he used to be the information technology manager. They've apparently got proof that he was behind all this."

"Why would this Haskell guy want to get you fired?"

"They told Carolyn it had something to do with him working for a competitor and trying to sabotage the company's progress."

"Do you believe that?"

"Not really. There's a great deal I don't understand. Haskell's machinations don't quite add up and then there's the data that went missing right before they fired me. Of course there's more going on. And if so—if I'm correct in my suspicions—why wouldn't Barranca just disclose any potential problems in a forthright way? Why would he take such a risk?"

"Pose the same question from his viewpoint," Rob said. "Why would he take a risk and disclose anything that might delay or jeopardize taking the company public?"

"Ethics aside, he's too smart to make such a big mistake." She ran her hand through her short hair.

"Look," Rob said, sighing. "I know you've got some kind of hero worship thing for him."

"Not anymore. I need to take action. I'm not going to sit around and wait for someone else to make the next move. I've done too much of that already."

"I don't think you understand what you're up against. Powerful people have a lot at stake. Why did you wait so long to tell me all this?"

A few seconds ticked by while she gave him a deadpan look. "Like I said, I appreciate the help. But why would I involve you?"

"Don't do anything until we have a chance to talk some more. We need to plan your next move."

We? She nearly said the word aloud. His apparent worry had touched her at first, but now he'd gone too far. Telling her what to do and what not to do. Really?

"I'm serious," he said.

"I can see that."

"What exactly were these side effects, anyway?"

More than ready to be done with the inquisition, she gave him a broad stroke overview, more or less what she'd told Carolyn and Chamberlain. When Rob appeared ready to argue further, she said, "You know what, I'll let you get back to your family and we'll catch up another time."

"Hold it. Do you expect these problems to solve themselves?"

"Of course not. What do you suggest? A smackdown?"

"I don't want you to get hurt." His words, slightly too loud and blunt, hung in the air and he immediately looked chagrined.

Though startled, Meri didn't jump to conclusions. He hadn't meant anything by it. Or perhaps he had, but he certainly had not intended his concern to come across so intense or personal. She could almost see his thoughts running like a ticker tape across his forehead. *Oops. Hope she doesn't read too much into that.*

She even felt sorry for him. "Thank you for your concern. I do appreciate it." She patted his shoulder. "Good night, then."

He said a somewhat dazed goodbye that struck her as comical.

Back inside on her own couch, she pulled her legs up and rested her chin on her knees. She really did appreciate having him worry about her. She wasn't used to that and it was a nice change. But honestly? Her problems were her own to handle. Growing up with self-involved parents, she'd learned how to cope and make decisions on her own, and for the most part, managed pretty well. Until recently.

Her decision made, she left a message for Seth Bernstein, the reporter who'd called earlier in the week. "I've changed my mind. I'd like to talk. How is Friday afternoon?"

A water pipe burst at Carolyn's apartment so she stayed over a few nights while repairs were made. On Thursday night, Carolyn brought in Thai food and they discussed the latest developments.

"We're getting very close to a tidy settlement," Carolyn said. "Just be patient."

"That's what you've been saying for weeks now," Meri said. "I don't know how much longer I can wait. And not just for myself. What about those people who might have gotten swept under the rug? Is there anyone looking out for them?"

"You don't know for sure if that drug has side effects, isn't that correct?"

"You're talking like a lawyer," Meri said.

"Give it some time and let people do their jobs."

"I've done that. And I am thankful for your help in getting a settlement and some formal means of clearing my name. But now that we're finally getting there, it's past time to alert someone else who can investigate. That pompous professor was useless. I need someone willing to flip over rocks to see what crawls out." She explained her plan to meet the business journalist the following day.

"You're really going to talk to that journalist?" Carolyn said, her voice rising. "You're willing to jeopardize all the work I've done on your behalf, and willfully risk this lucrative settlement they're about to offer you?"

"Some things are more important than money."

Carolyn stood up quickly. "Says the girl who grew up rolling in it."

"I'm sorry you feel that way," Meri said. "And it's not true about my family's wealth, you know. My parents and now my brother always blew through more money than they made. They're consistent that way. All three of them are truer to that habit than anything or anyone."

"You seem to have forgotten—if you screw this up with Barranca, you're screwing me over too—I won't get paid."

"Not necessarily." Meri watched while Carolyn angrily stacked dishes. "Look, let's take this one step at a time. We can talk more over the next few days."

"Fine," Carolyn said. "Wait a second. Didn't you say you were meeting with your grad school friend tomorrow? You've got both of those meetings tomorrow?"

"Yes it's perfect, actually. I only have to put on make-up once. Two birds with one stone. After I talk to that reporter I'll meet Moses before he catches his flight back to San Francisco. He may not be interested in hiring me. But I'm excited to hear about his research."

"I see," Carolyn said. She looked marginally less angry. "Hey, I'm out of here in ten minutes. I'm meeting someone for a drink in Laguna Beach. What about you? Are you going out tonight?"

"No, I'm turning in early. You have your key?"

Once Carolyn left, Meri locked up behind her, showered, put on her favorite purple pajamas with the Lucy-and-Ethel pattern and climbed into bed.

She lay there for a while, thinking about this rift with Carolyn. They had spent more time together over the last couple of months than they had since high school. Always prone to envy, Carolyn had become more bitter over the years. Meri had never quite understood why. The two of them were very different people; but surely a friendship of such long standing would outweigh any disagreement over money.

A long time later, the phone rang. It kept ringing. And ringing. Meri curled into the fetal position. *Obnoxious*, she thought vaguely. Why didn't people turn off their phones? She wanted a glass of water but she was still too tired and couldn't be bothered. Sleep took priority. Another wave of exhaustion rushed in and she went under again.

The ringing started up again. She raised her head and finally understood the noise came from her own phone. She felt around on the nightstand, nabbed it and lay back, exhaling on "Hello?"

"It's Seth Bernstein. I've been trying to get you all morning."

"All morning?" She couldn't quite compute his meaning. Her head was a cantaloupe thumped one time too many. "I'm sorry—*who* is this?"

He repeated himself and said, "I'm outside your door right now. Didn't you hear the doorbell at all?"

"No," she croaked. "Listen, it's too early."

"It's noon," he said. "You're the one who moved our meeting up by an hour, remember?"

"I did?" She squinted, noting the full sunlight behind the blinds. The room spun. She closed her eyes to stop the slow rotation. "Refresh my memory. Why are you here?"

"You agreed to an interview. I won't keep you long."

She clutched the phone to her ear and willed the spinning to stop. "What day is today?"

"Friday," he said. "I can wait."

"Give me a few minutes." She heaved herself to her feet. A high-frequency noise buzzed in her ears. She parked herself on the edge of the bed. Her head felt awful. And her jaw was sore.

The doorbell rang. She stood up, steadied herself, and shuffled to the front door. A sandy-haired young man waited on the porch, digital recorder in hand. His jaw dropped and so did his gaze.

Meri automatically reached to tug at her pajama bottoms and got a fistful of air. She glanced down at bare legs. When had she taken off her pajama bottoms? Good thing the top hung past her thighs. Otherwise, she was bare-assed.

"Ah, thanks for seeing me," the young man said. "I promise this won't take long."

She gazed at Seth Bernstein blearily. "I can't talk to you now."

"Come on," he protested. "After all this?"

Her field of vision narrowed. The high-pitched noise resumed and a metal curtain clanged shut behind her eyes. Convinced her head was going to explode, she held on to the doorknob for dear life. "I'm going to have to reschedule." She started to close the door.

Someone shouted, "Hold it!"

A blue light flashed and spots danced in her eyes. Bernstein turned around and yelled, "Hey, this is my interview—who sent you?"

Something large and dark took off down the alley. Meri blinked. "Did someone just take a picture? Where'd he come from?"

Bernstein said, "A black Range Rover. Standard for paparazzi. Why would you rate paparazzi?"

The pain in her head jackhammered relentlessly. "I don't." She couldn't think. The pain crowded out any embarrassment over her appearance and messing up the interview.

As soon as she got rid of the journalist, she stumbled back to bed. Later, when she finally managed to get up, she called her doctor's office and asked them to fit her in. Then, after bobbing and weaving under the shower for a period of time that might have been five minutes or twenty, she dressed slowly. Still disoriented, she looked around the house. Her missing pajama bottoms sat in the laundry basket. She must have taken them off in the middle of the night.

Then she noticed Carolyn's bed hadn't been slept in. She called Carolyn, who said, "I didn't sleep in my bed because I got lucky. I didn't go back to your place last night."

"I see. Well, something really odd happened to me today."

"Can you hold that thought?" Carolyn said. "My client is walking in the door—I'll call you later."

Next, Meri called Moses Chen. He didn't pick up so she left him a message cancelling due to her illness. As he was only in town for the day, she'd effectively lost the only networking opportunity she'd had in three months. She hoped he wouldn't hold it against her.

Since driving was out of the question, Meri summoned a car service to get to the doctor's office.

The doctor was stumped. "Your chest is gravelly," he said, leafing through his notes. "Better than the last time I saw you, though. Vertigo, you say?"

Meri ran her fingertips along her jaw line. "And kind of sore here."

Dr. Hanks poked a tongue depressor in her mouth. "The inside of your cheek is red. Did you eat an ice pop before coming in here?"

"I haven't eaten anything today."

"Hmm. I'm going to order some tests and see what we can find out. Wait here for my nurse and she'll get what we need. We might not get results till Monday; I'll call you then."

Depressed she'd had such a distressing relapse, Meri got another ride home and watched TV until bedtime. When Carolyn finally called back, she was sympathetic but in a rush. Her apartment was habitable again and she didn't need a place to stay anymore.

Meri woke early on Saturday. She sat up, tested her equilibrium, and checked for aches and pains. To her amazement, she felt perfectly fine. The headache and lethargy were gone, as if nothing had happened. Yesterday had been surreal. But the humiliation she felt now—she'd greeted that journalist dressed only in her pajama top—all too real.

Mid-morning she went out to check her mail and heard a kid crying in the distance. She recognized Luke's scratchy wail, coming closer, continuing unabated until he and his father arrived in the alleyway, where acoustics compounded the noise. A rigid-jawed Rob walked with his son slung over his shoulder. Luke bounced along, spitting outrage. Half was gibberish and half sounded remarkably like insults directed at his father's back.

"Didn't want to leave the playground," Rob said. He juggled the squirming toddler with one arm and a load of toys and clothes in the other.

Luke delivered a solid kick to his father's ribs. When Rob grabbed Luke's legs to prevent the kicking, everything he carried landed in the gutter.

"I'll get it," Meri said. She retrieved the stuff and jogged to catch up.

"I have to hose him down before we go in," Rob said and stalked to the back of his house. Luke's legs and feet were filthy, coated with dirt and sand. Meri bent down to twist the faucet on and felt a whoosh of air as Luke tore past, making a break for it.

Rob caught him ten seconds later. He held him aloft and got right in his face. "Why can't you behave?" he yelled. "You just drag me down, you little brat—" He broke off mid-sentence and turned parchment white.

Father and son stared at each other, with Luke shocked into temporary silence. Rob continued to hold his son with stiff arms, out of kicking range. Then Luke resumed crying and Rob hauled him up their back steps.

Meri followed. "Is your mom here?"

Rob shook his head, his lips a tight line. "Hair appointment."

"Let me take over. You go for a run or something."

"I'll be fine."

Ignoring that, she held her arms out. When Luke lunged for her, Rob handed him over wordlessly, turned around and left. She took Luke upstairs, rinsed him off in the tub and then, after finding a clean diaper and t-shirt, put him in his crib for a nap.

She walked downstairs, taking the opportunity to check out the house.

Rob's wife had had good taste. Though this house was smaller and older than her father's, it was far more welcoming. Natural rattan and sea grass furniture was arranged on sisal rugs. The walls were pale blue, the color of dawn over the ocean. If you overlooked the building blocks, various ride-on toys, and bright orange plastic slide, this living room could have been featured in a magazine.

Meri couldn't decorate her way out of a paper bag. In each of her apartments, the walls had been plain beige. She didn't even like beige, but the idea of choosing a paint color made her freeze up. Her mother had always told her to leave the interior decorating to professionals. As a result, she didn't trust her own instincts, at least not with domestic decisions.

A framed wedding picture hung above the fireplace. They smiled at the camera, a confident, attractive couple launching a lifetime together. Julie, Rob's wife, was blond and pretty, the quintessential California girl. Meri had no idea what sort of person she had been. Betty Jo had not revealed much about her daughter-in-law and Rob said next to nothing. Meri looked closer at the younger Rob. He was better looking now, she thought. His face had more character.

A short time later, she stepped back outside into a distinct chill. The clear walls around Rob's deck deflected most of the wind, but not all of it. The ocean had turned dark and choppy under an overcast sky. She surveyed the beach. His figure was indistinct, but somehow she recognized the sprinting figure. Something about the way he moved. Single-minded and driven. Other people jogged. Not him. He either sprinted or he walked with the loose grace of an athlete, as he did now. He circled the neighbors' volleyball net a few times, cooling down or, more likely, putting off coming home.

Finally, he came up the stairs. She pushed a chair out, which he took without meeting her eyes. He lifted the edge of his t-shirt to blot the sweat from his face. She tried not to stare. His stomach was tanned, even now, in the middle of winter.

"Is he asleep?"

She nodded.

"How'd you do it?"

"Rubbed his back. He couldn't keep his eyes open. Although I think he was trying to tell me his side. I understood about one word out of five. Are you doing better?"

"Yeah." He sat for a few minutes, staring at the horizon.

"Tell me about it."

"Are you sure you really want to know?"

Fair question, she thought. "I can see you're having a bad day."

"I'm going inside for a drink," he said. "Did you want something?"

She declined, uncertain whether to go home or stay here and drag it out of him. He came back with an organic lemonade and his unhappy face decided it for her. She stayed.

He sat in a different chair, farther away. "What I said to Luke—that's what my father used to say to me." He stretched his legs and contemplated his feet. "It's horrible to hear your father's voice come out of your mouth. Incidentally, please don't repeat this. My mom has a revisionist view of family history. She pretends not to remember anything bad about my dad, even more so since he died."

"I won't mention it."

"I loved him, but he wasn't a man who had much going for him. And he wasn't good to my mom or us kids. He got riled up at the drop of a hat so we all walked on eggshells around him. We were the reason he never succeeded, or so he said. He'd change jobs or start a new business every year—one year it was ostriches, another year it was ferrets."

Sidetracked by that, she asked, "What did you raise ferrets for?"

"Pets, mostly."

"Sorry. Go on."

"None of that ever worked out. He was always angry." Rob's face reflected a mix of bafflement and annoyance. "You don't want to hear this."

"I asked," she said. "And I don't mind."

"I can't remember having a real conversation with the man. I told myself I'd never be that kind of father. Then today I heard my father's words come out of my mouth." He rubbed the back of his neck. "Part of the problem was—I got a call earlier. From my boss. He was at the 19th hole at Pelican Hill with a client. Wanted me to join them. Right then."

Her confusion must have shown. Rob laughed shortly. "How can you grow up in Newport Beach and still not know what the 19th hole is? The bar, Meri. The bar. Bill wanted me to drop everything and come have a drink with a client. And I had to tell him I couldn't do it. My mom had just left, and I didn't think I should bring Luke along to a bar. Maybe I should have. Then again, Bill barely tolerates his own kids. Anyway, it definitely wasn't what he wanted to hear. I've been trying to get my career back on track. Sometimes I wonder if it'll ever happen."

"You could still go down there," Meri said. "I'll stay with Luke."

"No. Too late now. They'll be gone." His eyes refocused on her. "Funny, I hoped we'd run into you. I didn't picture it quite like this. Why did you rush inside the other night?"

She tipped her head. "When?"

"After I walked you home, the day I found you sleeping here."

"I thought we were all done and we got to my door."

"I offered to help," he said, "and you blew me off."

"You were just being polite."

"You were wrong."

She squirmed under his glare. "I'm used to handling my own problems."

"Nice sentiment but not necessarily the smartest approach," Rob said. "I've been e-mailing a friend at the Institutes of Health. He got back to me yesterday with some ideas—other ways to challenge what's happening at your old company."

Meri made an impatient noise. "I've been attempting to contact people at various government agencies. No one returned *my* calls or e-mails."

"I'll just give you his info right now." He went inside to retrieve his phone. "I don't think I have your number yet," he said on his way out.

She wasn't surprised. Why would he? She gave him the number and Rob got busy forwarding his friend's contact info. "Once you alert them about what you suspect," he said, "let the authorities handle Barranca."

"Here's the thing," she said. "I'm not convinced the authorities will act quickly or effectively. I'm always hearing how they're understaffed and underfunded and how they can't do this or that anymore. 'Sorry, we don't have funding for that.' After what I've seen the last couple of months, I don't know if I trust anyone to do the right thing."

"This habit of yours—handling problems on your own—it'll come back to bite you in the ass."

Meri stood up. "There's your mom pulling into the alley."

"Anyway," he added hastily. "Thanks for your help today. Luke is a holy terror sometimes."

"I think he's supposed to be at his age."

"He's so much easier to manage when he's around other kids. He's too busy watching them to cause trouble."

"My nieces are visiting me tomorrow," Meri called over her shoulder. "We're going down to Crystal Cove to whale-watch and look at tide pools. You're welcome to join us."

That night, Rob's mother came downstairs after reading Luke a story. "He's ready for you to say good night. You know, I think it's great y'all are going whale-watching with Meri."

"Aren't you coming?" Rob said.

Betty Jo rolled her eyes. "My hair finally looks nice and you want me to go out in the wind and mess it up? It cost me an arm and a leg. The prices here are mind-boggling."

"Go shopping then, instead. My treat. You deserve it after all the time you've put in with your grandson this week."

"Maybe I will. You and Meri can get to know one another a little better. She's a lovely girl."

Rob nodded. So he'd been right. No accident Meri had been sleeping in his chair like Goldilocks that day he'd come home early. He suspected Meri had no clue she was a pawn in his mom's plans. For once, he didn't mind Betty Jo's interference or her wacky ideas about folk healing. He couldn't argue with her results.

"She loves Luke," Betty Jo said.

"She likes his company more than mine," Rob said, well aware he sounded peevish.

Betty Jo laughed. "Work with what you got, son."

"Meaning?"

"It means, so what? There's your leverage. I'm surprised I have to tell you that, Mr. Investor."

6

The scent of sunscreen filled the car. Rob watched Meri buckle her nieces in on either side of Luke's car seat. Yesterday's cold front had moved on and temperatures had warmed up again. Meri settled beside him in the front seat, looking good in her board shorts. He could see the outline of a bikini top under her t-shirt. He wished she didn't feel the need to wear that baseball cap, but at least it didn't hide her pretty hair entirely.

Intercepting his glance, she shot him a look he couldn't decipher. Meri was different from other women. Her response just now wasn't flirtatious. He didn't understand what that was. He'd always been able to read Julie. She hadn't been one to think very deeply about, well, anything. He hadn't minded. Because that was Julie. Uncomplicated.

The ten-minute ride was loud and cheerful. Rob glanced in the rear view mirror at his son. Luke quietly listened to Bella and Kelsey's chatter. Meri admonished the girls to keep their feet off Rob's leather seats. "We're going to have to put lots of towels down later," she said to Rob. "Otherwise we'll mess up this nice car."

"Don't worry about it," Rob said. "I don't care." And to his surprise, he actually didn't. He pulled into the state beach parking lot.

While he unstrapped Luke and gathered towels, Bella pointed to a yellow food stand nearby. "What's that place?"

"That's the Shake Shack," Meri said. "Your daddy and I used to go there when we were kids. For root beer floats."

"Can we go? Can we go?"

Meri exchanged glances with Rob. "If you girls are very, very good today—you have to leave when I say it's time, with no arguing"—the girls nodded vigorously—"then we'll take you on the way home."

Rob kept a firm grip on Luke's hand and paused at the top of a rocky cliff, staggered by the view. Three miles of rare, undeveloped coastline spread below them. "Do you know," he said, "I've never been here before."

"It's so different from our beach," Meri said. "Right? Not nearly as groomed and boring."

Golden cliffs loomed over wide beaches. Teal blue water washed into a series of coves. Above the coves, natural watercourses had shaped canyons alive with sage and wildflowers now, in late winter. The view north presented an unfortunate contrast. Smog flowed out to sea from the Port of Long Beach and Los Angeles Basin. A khaki layer streamed toward Santa Catalina. Beyond the island, the smog dissipated and the sky, mercifully, cleared to a pale blue wash. Out there, the seascape was untouched.

They made their way down the rough path. The kids found a spot close to the tide pools and spent an enjoyable hour poking around. Meri pointed out sea urchins and crabs hiding in plain sight. The kids marveled at rocks plastered with thousands of mussels.

Eventually, she joined Rob on the blanket to watch the children dart back and forth. Much like that December afternoon when they'd first met on their beach. Yet so different. Then, she had simply been a lady he pitied. He hadn't seen past the surface. Now he saw a vibrantly attractive woman. Riveting even. The slim arms she'd covered before were bare and toned from her bike rides. Her face had rounded enough to balance her aquiline features. Her board shorts revealed beautiful long legs. Not as interesting as a bikini, but he would take what he could get.

"So you're feeling much better these days," he said, not really asking. "All recovered."

She gave him an uncertain look. "Pretty much. Except I had an odd relapse the other day. The strangest thing happened—"

Rob cut her off. "Overall though, you're way better, right? Bottom line—you're not sick anymore."

"I guess so. Although—"

"Well, you're healthy now," he said. "And that's all that matters."

She turned away to line up the kids' flip-flops and brush sand from the blanket. He wasn't so insensitive that he missed her frustration. The truth was, he didn't want to hear any details that weren't one-hundred-percent positive.

He couldn't explain. Not without coming off as a self-centered jerk. Or without telling her how he'd failed his wife. The truth was, he needed Meri to be well. Anything that didn't reinforce that belief, that need, could not be tolerated. He just couldn't handle any other possibility. He didn't want to hear it.

After a few minutes of silence, and searching for a distraction, he asked her about the ramshackle cottages scattered along the hillside. "Why are there broken-down shanties on a state beach?"

"Back in the day, this was a movie set," she said. "Those palm trees over there were probably planted for a 1920's picture. Then it became a summer resort for regular folks who stayed in tent cabins. Eventually Crystal Cove evolved into a real community. The state owns it now, but the idea is to keep the cottages rustic. You can camp out in them. If you can get a reservation."

"Those places look like they ought to be condemned," he said.

"Crystal Cove was never fancy. People often built with salvaged wood. Some friends of my grandmother used teak that washed up from a shipwrecked yacht. Only problem was, there were big gaps in the floorboards. I fell through once. They liked to joke that they were waiting for another shipwreck so they could fix it."

"I didn't know this area was prone to shipwrecks."

"In fact, there were a few that my grandparents witnessed over the years, in various spots. In the 1920's my grandfather went out with Duke Kahanamoku to rescue some fishermen whose boat capsized near Corona del Mar. A huge southern swell hit them. It became well known because the rescuers used their surfboards. Grandpa wouldn't talk about it. They couldn't save everyone."

"How do you know all this?"

"I stayed here with my grandparents for a few weeks every summer. And heard many stories around bonfires."

"I thought you said they lived in Corona del Mar."

"They spent weeks at a time here in the summer, and they liked having us kids with them. My parents never understood why anyone would want to 'slum it', as they put it. Maybe it's nostalgia but I always felt—" She slanted a grin at him. "Don't laugh. This place was magical for me."

Rob snorted. "I'll tell you right now—nothing magical about living in a shack. Or looking through holes in floorboards."

"I didn't mean to imply poverty was magical."

"Seeing as how you have so much experience." He saw her discomfort and added, more gently, "Summer is magic for most kids. Go on."

"I suppose you're right. It's hard to explain why it seemed magical. People behaved differently here. They were interested in other people. As opposed to material things like houses, cars, and yachts. Let's just say, the vibe wasn't anything like Newport Beach. I'll always regret that I missed the last summer they spent down here."

"Why'd you miss that summer?" he asked.

"I was eleven and I'd been begging for science camp at Lake Arrowhead."

"Why would you need to beg? Your family had money." He himself had never been to camp. Growing up, none of the kids he knew went to camp. Camp was for rich kids or kids in the movies.

"I was a geek," she explained ruefully. "As you might guess. My dad thought science camp would make me geekier. That summer, my parents relented. I remember driving into the mountain camp and seeing all these girls running around. I was so excited to be with girls like me. I didn't catch on until the lady at the sign-in desk asked if I'd forgotten my pom-poms. I looked around for my Dad. You know, to tell him we'd come to the wrong camp. By then, the only sign of him was a cloud of gravel dust."

"He tricked you into cheerleading camp?"

"Can you imagine? Those poor counselors. They had no idea what to do with me."

Rob stared, bemused by her laugh. Not a word of self-pity. Her sympathy was with the counselors.

A yell from one of the girls caught their attention. Kelsey pointed several hundred yards offshore. Rob caught a fleeting glimpse of a spray of water. He turned to Meri. "Was that—?"

"Maybe," she said, jumping up to shade her eyes. "I don't think I've ever seen a whale this close to shore. I told the kids we'd whale-watch today just to get them interested in going someplace new. You often can't see much unless you're out on one of those whale-watching excursions." Another explosion of air and mist shot up. The whale breeched, its dark body slipping out of the water. "There it goes." The whale disappeared before the words were out of her mouth. Meri picked up Luke to show him. "I think it's a blue whale. It could be 80 feet long. This is too good to miss. Did you see how fast he was moving? Let's go."

She didn't wait for Rob or even ask whether he wanted to come. She grabbed the children and ran down the beach, as excited as they were. Rob watched them for a minute and then kicked back on the blanket, enjoying his chance to relax.

From the corner of his eye, he noticed a figure on the cliff. A man in business attire stood with elbows locked and binoculars trained, not at the water, but down at the beach.

The whale breeched again 100 yards south. Meri stayed even with the whale. Regardless of what she'd said about a relapse, anyone who could run like that and carry Luke at the same time had to be strong.

Rob glanced back at the man. From this angle, it was hard to know for sure. The man appeared more interested in tracking beachgoers than the whale. For the next few minutes, Rob alternated between watching the man on the cliff and watching Meri and the children. The more he observed, the more convinced he became. The guy's binoculars moved with them when Meri turned the kids back at the end of the cove.

Rob strained his eyes and saw water spouts four or five more times before the whale swam out of sight. The water spouts were dramatic enough that other people on the cliff called to each other and pointed. But the man's binoculars followed Meri and the kids.

As the group straggled back, he heard Meri say, "I don't know why he was alone."

"Did he get lost from his mommy and daddy?" Kelsey asked.

"I don't know, honey. Maybe this *was* a daddy whale. A lot of mommy whales are already in Mexico."

"The daddy whale is coming home late from work," Bella said.

When the kids were distracted again, Rob pointed the man out to Meri. "Any idea why someone would be watching you and the girls?"

Meri looked up. The man on the cliff lowered his binoculars. "He's whale watching."

"I don't think so," Rob said. "I've been watching him. Anyway, who wears a tie to the beach?"

"Someone who just went to church?" A troubled expression came over her face. "Was he taking pictures?"

"Not that I could see."

"My brother and his ex-wife have an ugly history," she said in Rob's ear. "Hiring detectives to spy on each other. Maybe they're at it again. I don't know why either would care about what we're up to here. We're a pretty wholesome bunch."

Her breath tickled his ear when she leaned in. He needed to think of more reasons for her to whisper in his ear. "You're great with those girls," he said, settling for the truth. "They're lucky to have you."

She rewarded him with a wide smile but said nothing.

Later on, while they drank root beer floats up on the cliff, the kids faced the ocean, dangling their legs from the picnic bench. Rob and Meri sat on the other side of the table, supporting Luke between them. He watched her interact with the children, smiling and laughing far more than she had with him.

"You obviously like kids," he said. "Why don't you have children of your own?"

"Me? I don't want to be a single parent. It's way too hard."

"Who says you'd be single?"

"I'm not getting married," she said, flatly certain. "And if I did…" She slushed her straw up and down. "Please. Everyone becomes a single parent. No one intends to, but everyone ends up that way, eventually. And it's just too hard." Then she covered her mouth, stricken. "I'm sorry. I didn't mean to be insensitive…your situation as a single parent is obviously different. You didn't choose—"

"It's all right," he said, waving away her concern. "So you really believe this?"

"I don't want it to be true," she said wistfully. "I wish I *didn't* know better." She whispered so the kids couldn't hear. "Just like I wish the Easter Bunny and Santa Claus were real. Part of me would love to put logic aside. Ignore the evidence."

"What evidence?"

She set her drink down. "You don't really want to know my views on this."

"Yes, I do. Why don't you believe people can stay married?"

"All right then," she said, with an 'I warned you' look. "Here's what I've observed. People in love see what they want to see. Lovers create an illusion—a version of the other person to fall in love with. The illusion has nothing to do with reality. Couples who beat the odds and stay married are couples who wear rose-colored glasses. They choose what they want to believe about their partner, seeing who they want to see, as opposed to who that person actually is. And if *both* partners manage to pull off that miracle in mutual delusion, then yay, they stay together and live happily ever after," she finished with a big flourish of her arms.

Bella, Kelsey and Luke giggled. Despite the warmth of the sun, Rob felt a chill, seeing something very different than theatrics. He saw cynicism that ran deep. He didn't know how to respond. So he said nothing and she clammed up after that.

They soon corralled the kids into the hot car and drove home with the windows rolled down to capture the breeze blowing off the Pacific.

Meri hosed the sand off the girls outside and then delivered them directly back to their dad's house. By the time she arrived home again, it was late afternoon.

She noticed the smell the moment she walked in. A sporty masculine scent. A scent that had not been present when she left.

The house looked the same, dull and quiet as ever. Light from the setting sun stippled the walls. The windows and the back door were all closed and locked. Perhaps the smell came from one of Carolyn's fashion magazines—one of those perfume sample inserts. She looked around and then remembered recycling those magazines. Maybe she herself had brought some scent into the house. A candle or shower gel? But she knew she hadn't.

She walked through the gloomy rooms, finding nothing out of the ordinary. Except—a slight stirring in the atmosphere. And a lingering smell. The hairs on the back of her neck stood up. A man's scent. It reminded her of Eric, a young lab assistant who'd worked for her. Everyone had teased him about the strong aftershave he favored.

She took a quick inventory. All the electronics were still here, unsurprising since most of the media equipment and devices were quite dated, except for her own computer. With that thought, she darted to the kitchen. Her laptop sat on the table where it always did. Her breakfast dishes were in the sink. The kitchen clock clicked to the next minute.

She examined the sliding door that led to the back deck. The wooden dowel she kept on the runners as a jamming device hadn't been dislodged. She flicked the lock. It seemed a little loose, but otherwise fine.

Back in the bedroom, her pulse sped up. The smell was stronger in here, though the room appeared normal. She'd made the bed earlier with her sloppy, but good-enough method, sheets and comforter hastily pulled up. The bathroom medicine cabinet hung slightly ajar, which happened all the time because the little magnet in the rusty frame sat off center. Unless she took the time to firmly click the door into place, it stayed open. The medicine cabinet's contents—aspirin, cold medicine, and two extra inhalers for her asthma—were undisturbed.

She returned to the bedroom and finally spotted a difference. She'd switched purses this morning, after grabbing a couple of essentials from the old one. That handbag sat where she'd left it, right on top of the dresser. Upright. She never left it like that. She always placed the bag on its side with the outside key pocket facing up. A small habit, but a consistent one. Which meant her instincts had been correct.

Someone had been here.

She went to the dresser, dreading what she'd find. Credit card fraud thrived in Orange County. The extra wallet where she kept her credit cards would be gone. And probably her checkbook too. She gingerly opened the purse, holding it away from her body as if a stink bomb might go off. Strangely, the wallet was still inside and intact, as was her checkbook. She went through both rapidly, checking the credit cards and extra cash. It was all there. A hairbrush, an inhaler, and a package of tissues—still there. She went through the house once again. Most of her stuff was in storage so it wasn't hard to come to the same conclusion. Nothing whatsoever had been stolen. So why had they bothered?

She walked to the living room and sat down with her purse in her lap. Did this have anything to do with the man Rob had seen on the cliff? She doubted any connection, just as she doubted the man had, in fact, been spying on them.

But this? What were the odds that twice in nearly three months she'd come home to find evidence of a mid-day break-in? First, her apartment in Irvine—when thieves stole a tablet computer and a six-pack of beer. And now here, the place she'd thought of as her safe haven.

Back in November, the cops told her mid-day burglaries weren't uncommon. And that kids often stole alcohol and small electronics. And yet this time, she'd lost nothing. So—what now? If she called this in, what would she say? "Please come investigate—my house smells like a man." That statement would do wonders for her credibility.

The wind kicked up on Monday. Sand blew in Meri's face and stung her skin when she tried to ride her bike. She finally gave up and retreated inside to read. A quick call to the doctor's office to get her lab results yielded exactly nothing. The nurse read the results over the phone.

"Nothing popped out of normal range?" Meri said.

"Nothing," the nurse said. "It's a standard toxicology screen plus blood tests and nothing unusual showed up. The doctor wants to see you for a follow-up in a few weeks."

Whatever had ailed her on Friday, it wasn't anything to worry about, apparently. She'd felt perfectly fine since.

Rob knocked on her door around 5:00 p.m. He wore a leather bomber jacket and a hostile expression. The wind from the alleyway whistled around him.

"Come on in," she said. "This is a wind tunnel."

He shook his head. "I can't stay." He held up a copy of the *Orange County Business Weekly*. "Did you see this article?"

Dread bubbled up. She'd done her best to pretend nothing would come of that non-interview. She hadn't even checked online.

He unfolded the paper and read aloud: "'In a brief interview at her residence, former research director Meredith Darrow appeared confused and incoherent. She was unable to comment on rumors of misconduct or corporate espionage.'"

She wilted against the doorframe. "Is there a picture?"

"No. Did you expect one? Why didn't you tell me about this? We were together half the weekend."

"I tried to tell you yesterday and you cut me off."

"You could have tried harder. Why does he say you were confused?"

"I *was* confused. When he came by on Friday, I wasn't well."

"Sure, but incoherent?" Rob handed her the paper. "You can keep this. I don't want it."

"Now wait a second—"

"This was an opportunity to set the record straight," he said. "Instead you gave Seth Bernstein a terrible impression. And why the hell does he say you were half-dressed?"

"I answered the door in my pajamas." No way would she volunteer that she'd answered the door without pajama bottoms.

A lock of hair blew into Rob's eye. He shook it away and watched her, as if he expected her to say something else. Whatever he wanted, she wished she could give it to him. His concern warmed her heart. Nice to have someone on her side. He believed in her. He must. Otherwise he wouldn't be here.

"Are you feeling all right now?" he said. "You didn't seem sick yesterday at the beach. You were running around with the kids."

"I'm fine. That incident Friday was a relapse but I've recovered. Look, why don't you come in?"

He looked toward his house. "I haven't been home yet. I came straight here. So...I should go." But he stayed on the front porch, staring at her. "I thought maybe—"

"What?"

He stuffed his hands in his jacket pockets. "Nothing. It boggles the mind. Your reputation is deeper in the dumpster than before." His tie blew across his shoulder.

"Thank you for letting me know. I think." She made an effort to chuckle.

He shrugged. "Hey, I tried."

"What do you mean, you 'tried'? Did you have something to do with that reporter calling me?"

"I might have given him a nudge in the right direction."

"A nudge? He's been calling since December, before Christmas."

Rob scowled and zipped the bomber jacket. "I don't know what else I can do for you." He started to walk away.

Something twisted in her chest. "I know. It's all right."

He retraced his steps and looked at her hard, with laser beam focus. "Why don't you call and check in with Betty Jo from time to time? Let her know you're okay. Otherwise, she'll worry about you."

"Of course," she said, smiling. "Absolutely." She waved and stepped behind the not-quite closed door. He walked down the alley, eager to get home. She watched him until he was out of sight, knowing he wouldn't look back. His mother would worry. Not him.

Pink jasmine curled around the porch post. Blooming early this year. Some people found the scent cloying. She loved it, even though, for her, the scent evoked a creeping sense of isolation.

She blew a raspberry noise to dispel self-pity. Smiling—even when you didn't feel like it, even when you wanted to cry—helped you become happier. She flashed a phony smile in the hall mirror. If the mask was good enough to fool Rob, she could fool others, too. With practice, she might fool herself.

The buzzing of her phone woke Meri the next morning at 7:00 am.

Rob's voice was urgent. "Are you online yet?"

"I'm still in bed."

"You better have a look at the BioReport blog."

His harsh tone woke her up fully. "Want to give me a hint?"

"Just look," he said and disconnected.

She made coffee while she waited for her laptop to boot up. Whatever waited wasn't good. Otherwise Rob would have told her. Good news got passed along immediately. Bad news languished like an unclaimed body at the morgue.

She sat down with a strong cup of coffee and took a deep breath before searching for the blog. Steve Ewell had modeled his web log after celebrity-slam sites, filled with entertaining gossip about the industry's more flamboyant characters. Everyone in the industry scorned his blog as an offensive example of pseudo-journalism. But everyone in the industry read it religiously.

The home page appeared. So far, so good. Nothing dramatic. She gulped coffee and burned her tongue. Clicked a link. Her brain registered the high-resolution photograph and she stopped breathing.

Her dazed face stared from the screen in crisp detail. Stark white face. Bride of Frankenstein hair. The purple Lucy and Ethel pajama top barely skimming the top of her thighs. The caption read: *Meredith Darrow, ready for her close-up?*

The next photo was a grainy shot taken at Crystal Cove on Sunday. She and Rob had their heads together. They looked like a couple. He held his arm protectively, just behind her shoulder. She'd been completely unaware of that. The blog identified Rob by name and title, with snarky references to pillow talk. The misleading impression that they were a couple was bad enough, but the insinuation that she shared confidential information with Rob was far worse.

She herself had often laughed at posts on this site. The comments, pictures, and witty observations could be entertaining. That's why everyone read them. Those poison darts were hilarious. Unless you were the bullseye.

Rob clicked to exit the site, got up, and started to pace. If only he could wipe the image from his brain. He hated the way she stared at the camera. So glassy-eyed and frightened. He'd had to get off the phone quickly to avoid yelling at her. How had she allowed this to happen? Now he knew why she'd asked him yesterday if there had been a picture in the paper. That business article had gone easy on her, compared to this blog post. None of it boded well for her attempts to clear her name. He didn't care about the other picture, the one of them on the beach. Other than regretting he had not run up and throttled that creep on the cliff when he'd had the chance.

Till now, he'd thought of Steve Ewell as a harmless gadfly. Rob had met him at a party once at the BioReport office down in Laguna Niguel. The guy had been smooth and pleasant enough. However, even then, Ewell's face had reminded Rob of his father's ferrets.

Mimi stuck her head in. "Hey, did you see that 'deer in the headlights' picture of—"

Rob sent his chair spinning into the bookshelf. "I saw it. And I may just go pound on Steve Ewell. Want to come along and shoot video? You can post it on YouTube."

Mimi recoiled.

"Well?"

Her alarmed expression jolted him back to rationality. "I'm sorry. You caught me at a bad moment." He paced some more. "What is the deal with this whole business model of…taking pleasure and glee from another person's misfortune?"

"It's human nature," Mimi said. She came in and sat down. "If you ask me, gossiping is programmed into our DNA. So—if you're planning to reform all of mankind—

good luck with that. Now what's the deal—is she a friend of yours?"

"Yeah. A neighbor." He suspected Mimi was managing him. And it was working. His fury settled into a low flame.

"Is this the same Meredith Darrow who visited that day last fall with Barranca? What's wrong with her?"

"She's been ill."

"How did those pictures wind up on the Internet?"

"Good question."

Mimi studied his face, nodded, and went back to her desk. The analytical voice in his head pointed out that if he didn't know Meri, he might have readily believed the worst about her. Someone had orchestrated the whole stinking situation. It was either Barranca or someone connected to him. Who else would have an interest in hurting her? Rob was tempted to drive down to Laguna Niguel and beat the answer out of Steve Ewell. The sorry truth was, he'd lost any objectivity when it came to Meri.

Bill walked in a minute later, steaming. "I hope that little piece of tail is worth it because this sort of attention is exactly what this company doesn't need right now. Nor do you. This could blow up in your face. And I'm not just talking about your fund. Do you know what this looks like? Clients will drop us like hot potatoes."

"As long as we're not in the quiet period—"

"But we are. Barranca Labs just made the announcement—they're filing to go public. Any firm connected to this upcoming IPO will be under a microscope for potential ethical violations. The Securities and Exchange Commission got so many complaints after those tech IPO scandals last year—hell, they're sharpening their knives. If they suspect you received insider information from your lady friend, those government lawyers will be only too happy to carve you up and serve your head on a platter."

7

Rob pulled into his garage, glancing toward Meri's front door, as he did every morning and every night. He hadn't laid eyes on her since that windy afternoon two weeks ago. She had called his office several times, after the photos appeared and the next day, when the photos disappeared. He'd had Mimi lie for him both times and say he was busy. Which was true. He had been travelling on and off ever since. He dropped his briefcase in the front hall.

Luke sat in his high chair and Betty Jo stood at the stove. Their nanny was getting ready to leave.

"Daddy. Pissgetti." Luke held up a fistful of noodles and sauce. He wore half of it on his face and neck. The other half had splattered on the floor and wall. Rob wondered wearily if he ought to take him outside to hose him down.

"There you are," his mother said. "Well, sit down and eat. Sorry about the mess. I never dreamed he'd get so—involved—with spaghetti. Your sister's girls never had a problem, once they learned to twirl their forks. They were eating like little ladies by the time they were two."

Rob patted the top of his son's head, the only clean spot he could find. "I don't see Luke twirling his spaghetti anytime soon."

"Guess not," she said.

He looked out the window. "Mom, have you seen Meri around?"

"That's the third time you've asked me that. I hardly ever see her."

Letty coughed.

He looked up at the nanny. "You okay, Letty?" When she nodded, he said, "Hey, thanks for everything."

Letty blew a kiss to Luke and grinned at Rob.

"She was all smiles," Rob said after the nanny had gone.

"Letty likes it when I cook," Betty Jo said. "Where were we?"

"I was wondering how Meri is doing. Do you think she's eating right?"

"No idea."

"She should have called you like I asked her to."

"She's not likely to call if she's feeling poorly," Betty Jo said. "Anyway, she wasn't put on this earth to follow your orders. I don't know where you got this bossy streak from. No one else in the family is as bossy as you."

He frowned at his plate and got up for a beer. "You think she's sick again?"

"Should I see if she wants to try out my folk healing?"

Rob groaned. "No. Please don't. She'll think we're even more country than we are. Country crackpots."

"Speak for yourself." Betty Jo wiped her hands on a towel. "Son, if you're going to worry, you might as well enjoy her company while you worry. Just call her up."

"It's not wise."

"For you or her?" his mother said.

He thought about that. About all the reasons he shouldn't pursue her. And all the reasons he wasn't right for her either. "Probably both."

Once he got Luke to bed, he strolled over, telling himself he'd just keep an eye out for her. He could do that, couldn't he? From a distance. Harmless enough. But her house was dark. Pitch-dark. Not even a light by the back door, which she usually kept on at night. He stood on the beach for a long time. He missed her, but he didn't know what to do about it. He hated this—behaving like an obsessed stalker. Disgusted with himself, he went home.

The following night, his mother still claimed ignorance of Meri's whereabouts. He walked down the beach and stood outside her house. Still dark. Had she gone out of town? Good idea. Let things cool down. Or maybe she was out with friends. It was a Friday night. The bars in Newport would be packed. He thought about how he might find out where she was without actually contacting her. Maybe locate her brother? The surfer dude. What was his name—Jordan—Joshua—Jacob?

Someone's ignition key beeped one street over. The alley was quiet except for a few garage lights. All shapes and shadows were static. All the garages were closed. The neighbors were in for the night.

A light bobbed behind a side window of Meri's house. Not a normal lamp. A pinpoint or beam of light. Was that a bedroom? It had to be. Her living room and kitchen were on the beach side. If she were home, would she be walking around with a flashlight or candle?

He walked closer. No. She wouldn't. No other houses had lost power. Dense fog shrouded the beach, insulating noise and blurring visibility. Maybe this fog created optical illusions. But he didn't think so. Though the curtains were closed, a circle beamed on the glass. A brief, unmistakable ring of light.

Meri opened the garage door with the remote and pulled in. She had just gotten out of the car when a tall figure moved swiftly in from the alley. The figure rushed toward her. She jumped back and gasped—nearly screamed—and then recognized Rob. "You almost gave me a heart attack."

He put one finger over her lips. "Hush. Come with me."

With one arm around her waist and the other on her upper arm, he guided her around the side of the house and out to the beach. "Keep quiet," he said and pointed at the back sliding door, visible through the deck railing. And there it was. A light beam bounced off the ceiling and walls. Inside her dark house.

"A flashlight?" she whispered.

"Looks like it." Rob moved her well away from the deck and kept a firm hold on her.

Her heart raced as her mind ticked through rational explanations. The only people with keys were her father and brother. Both would have switched on the lights and broadcast his presence loud and clear.

She was glad Rob was with her, warm and solid at her back. "What should we do?" she asked. "My phone's in my purse back in the car."

"Wait." His mouth tickled her ear. "Okay, he's moved into another room. Run straight to my house. The back door is open. My mom's there. Go inside and wait." He squeezed her shoulders. "Ready?"

"What about you?"

"I'll be right behind you. You first." He gave her a push. "Go!"

She scooted away but stopped on the far side of her neighbor's house. Rob had moved also, right after she did, but she couldn't see him now. He wasn't behind her at all. She strained to see through the fog. A muffled crash came next and a light flared inside the house. He'd lied. Rob had gone up to her deck to do something heroic. Or stupid. Or both.

She dashed back to find him, took the stairs two at a time and met Rob halfway. He cursed, pulled her back down the stairs, and hauled her well away.

He gripped her arm in a painful squeeze. "Why can't you follow directions?"

"I couldn't just leave you," she said. "Why didn't you follow *me*?"

He yanked his phone from a pocket. As he thumbed the screen, she said, "You have a phone?"

He ignored her and called 911, relaying the facts to the dispatcher.

She hugged herself to stop trembling. Rob pulled her against his body and said, "They're on the way." To the dispatcher, he said, "I think the intruder just left. Yeah, I'll stay on."

She had her face against his chest and smelled his sweat, mixed with cotton t-shirt and salt air. Thankfully, no metallic smell of blood. Just in case, she started to pat him up and down, checking for injuries.

Rob covered the phone. "I'm not hurt. You can stop fussing."

She wanted to either clock him or kiss him. Instead she wrapped her arms around him and held on tight. He kept her close and within two minutes, flashing police cruiser lights appeared in the alley. A car door slammed and radios squawked.

Inside the front hall a few minutes later, the senior cop, a bulky man with spiky gray hair, said, "How do you know it was one guy?"

"I saw only one light," Meri said. She turned to Rob. "Did he see you?"

Rob shook his head. "He couldn't have. He may have heard me try the back slider but it was locked. He got spooked and ran out the front."

"How did he get in?"

"No windows were forced," the officer said. "The front door wasn't forced. The lock is intact. You probably forgot to lock the door."

"No, I locked the door," Meri said, frowning.

"Ma'am, you ought to check again to see if anything is missing," Officer Martinez said.

"I have no valuables," Meri said. "That's what's so ironic. This guy picked the worst house in the neighborhood. Even my laptop is a couple years old, which makes it practically ancient."

"We're gonna' go ahead and dust for prints," the cop said. "Why don't you look around one more time?"

She hadn't let go of Rob this whole time. Though she knew the intruder was long gone, a nasty sense of violation remained. The thief had riffled through all her drawers. She shuddered at the thought of someone touching her panties. She would wash them before wearing a single thing.

"I'll go with you," Rob said. He hadn't once tried to disengage or pull away, a kindness she wouldn't forget.

They passed another cop in the kitchen attacking paperwork with bored efficiency. Meri stopped to tell him about the previous incident when nothing had been taken, as well as the burglary of her apartment in November. Rob's eyebrows went up while she spoke and he began to look extremely pissed-off. At her.

Once the cops were gone, Rob lost what little patience he had left. "Don't be ridiculous," he said. "You know you'll feel much safer with us. You can have my bed and I'll take the couch."

"What will your mother think?"

"She'll think you're sensible, under the circumstances. You'll be doing me a favor. I'll never hear the end of it if I leave you by yourself tonight." He saw her mouth tremble and put his hand on the back of her neck, gentling her.

"Okay," she said, surprising him with the sudden turnabout. She watched him with those green, green eyes, wide and vulnerable. "You don't think I'm safe here?"

"I don't know Meri," he said. Unable to resist, he kissed her forehead. "Come home with me and we'll talk about it tomorrow. Along with those break-ins you never told me about. I'm in this now, for better or for worse, so you may as well get used to sharing information and accepting help. What *is* it that these goons want from you?"

The blue-gray light of dawn streamed in the high clerestory windows. Meri looked up and around, orienting herself. His bedroom. She turned her face into the pillow and caught the faint scent of Rob's hair. If he were beside her in this bed, she'd burrow into his back and breathe in all of him. Wrap her legs around his long body and absorb his warmth. But he wasn't here. And rolling around with him in his wife's bed wasn't in the cards for her.

She yanked down the shirt Rob had loaned her and looked around. His room didn't look like him. Dainty white furniture. Flowered chintz fabrics. Obviously his wife's choices. She hopped out of bed and slipped on the dress she'd worn yesterday. It felt like three days since she'd put that on at her brother's house yesterday morning.

She made the bed and tiptoed downstairs to find her shoes. Rob still slept on the sofa. He must have had an uncomfortable night. His head was tilted awkwardly and his feet dangled over the couch armrest. She started over to wake him, to tell him he could move back to his bed, and then thought again. Why disturb him? Luke would be up soon enough. A toddler's household woke early. She cast one last glance at Rob's face before letting herself out quietly.

All too soon, she faced her house. Dead silence greeted her. She wanted to shower but she couldn't bring herself to go into the bedroom. Instead, she sat on the couch and watched TV with a pillow clutched to her stomach. She stared mindlessly at an infomercial for a cosmetic surgeon. The commercial looped over and over. She must have slept then because the next time she looked, they were selling fruit dehydrators. Wrinkles out, wrinkles in.

At 9:00 a.m. she sent Jordan a text. If he had company, a likely possibility on a Saturday morning, he wouldn't respond anytime soon. His active love life had been one of the motivating factors for her to come back here yesterday. Plus it was time to move on. She'd been helping him out with the girls on and off the past two weeks while his ex-wife was on vacation. When the kids were in school, she'd cleaned just about every surface in his condo to keep busy.

She had better luck with her father. Harrison Darrow answered his cell on the second ring. "Meri—perfect timing! Tamara and I just got on the lift. You wouldn't believe the powder here."

"You're skiing?" Of course he was skiing. Even at his age, closing in on eighty, her father prided himself on his fitness and vigor. He needed to keep up with his wife, a strategy that worked quite well for him.

"Why are you calling?" he said. "You've got less than two minutes till we get to the top of the mountain."

She told him about the break-in, as succinctly as she could.

He agreed to pay for an emergency locksmith. But he balked at installing an alarm system. "Let me think about that," he said. "This is the first burglary we've had in over 30 years. You go ahead and get those locks changed. I'll see you when I get back."

Rob and Luke showed up a few minutes later, bright-eyed and grinning. Rob in jeans and sweatshirt, his son much the same, along with a sticky bib. Luke locked his arms around her knees. She was effectively trapped in the doorway, unable to hide unexpected hot tears that welled up.

"You were out of the house early," Rob said. "We came to fetch you for buttermilk pancakes. Luke likes his maple syrup so he's probably stuck to you by now."

"He shouldn't be here," she said thickly. "There's broken glass." She tried to keep her face averted. She'd been holding herself together okay until just this minute. They'd become so dear to her in such a short period of time.

Rob assessed her with a level look before unlocking his son from her legs. "I'll be right back." Luke didn't understand why he had to leave and watched her mournfully as Rob carried him home to his grandmother.

Rob came back and immediately began issuing orders. "I'm taking you home, too. Get a change of clothes and your toothbrush. I'll sweep up later."

"I need to call a locksmith."

"Then go wait at my house while I handle it."

"I don't think so," she said, "but thank you."

He made an impatient noise low in his throat. "Have you eaten anything? You haven't showered or changed."

"I didn't want to go in there," she said, indicating the bedroom.

He went to the threshold and touched the door frame. "What's all this black stuff?" He answered his own question. "Fingerprint powder. They just leave it like that? So on top of getting burglarized, you have to clean up after the cops?"

She stood beside him, eyeing the mess. All the glass explained the crash she'd heard on the beach last night. Turned out the inept intruder had found valuables after all. The framed photos he'd smashed were the only prints she had of her grandparents. She slumped. The prospect of cleaning and washing everything overwhelmed her.

Without turning his head, Rob found her hand. "I'll make the first pass at cleaning while you shower. Do you have a robe?"

Too tired to object, she started for the closet. He restrained her by holding his arm like an iron bar against her stomach. She couldn't budge.

"Stay," he said. "There's glass on the floor." First, he carefully picked up her photos and stacked them on her dresser. Then he found the robe and hustled her into the bathroom.

He shut the door and left her to it. The shower, blessedly hot, washed away exhaustion and fear, except for a new one—she already depended on him too much. She desperately wanted to lean on him, let him take over. And that scared her more than any intruder.

Rob wiped away powder, swept up glass, and vacuumed the floor. Then he stripped her bed and loaded the sheets in the washing machine. The shower valve shut off and he heard her get out. He found fresh sheets and a blanket and made up the bed.

He was done with worrying. About his sinking career, about the future, about the double mortgage payments that would commence in March. And about Meri. Worrying about her safety and well-being had become an obsession. He didn't know why, but why hardly mattered. The situation had become untenable. If he could, he'd keep her close until her problems were resolved. And then they'd both move on. He knew nothing permanent could come of this. Anyway, she seemed more attached to his family than to him.

He looked closer at the bent-up photographs on her dresser. The largest, an 8 x 10, had the look of old Kodachrome film—drenched with vivid color. A crowd gathered around a flagpole, saluting a flag as it was hoisted. An older man and woman stood in the foreground. They grinned widely, as did the little girl between them. The little girl had eyes too big for her narrow face and an expression of part wonder and part glee.

"I'll need to re-frame that," Meri said in a subdued voice. Damp and rosy, she stood in the doorway wrapped in a terry cloth robe.

He pointed to the little girl in the photo. "That's you, isn't it?"

She leaned on the door jamb and then recoiled from a bit of fingerprint powder Rob had missed. "That's me. And those are my grandparents."

He looked closer. "Summertime at Crystal Cove?"

"Recognize that house? It's the one painted turquoise now."

"What's the occasion?"

"Raising the margarita flag. The party started every day at 4:30. Everyone dropped what they were doing—kids stopped swimming, moms quit cooking, artists covered canvases."

"Looks like everyone is having a blast."

"We were. That guy"—she pointed to an older man with a generous belly—"blew the bugle while another man raised the flag. And the grown-ups started pouring margaritas—fruit punch for us kids. After dinner, the adults would hang out and talk. The kids played games, built bonfires, and generally ran wild until we were called in for bedtime."

"Sounds idyllic," he said.

"I took it for granted. Looking back now, I see how special it was. Not just the margarita flag, but what it stood for." She flushed and looked at her bare feet.

"What did it stand for?"

"A community. People who knew how to have fun. And the fun was contagious. They knew the ritual was important, in its own goofy way."

"You could have that again," he said. "Not there and not with them. But somewhere."

"I doubt it," she said. "Seriously. It doesn't exist anymore. Think about it. Can you picture your neighbors in Newport doing anything so undignified? People hanging out. All ages, shapes and sizes in their swimsuits. And no one giving two hoots about the shape of their bellies or thighs?"

"No," he admitted. "I can't picture that."

"People aren't like that anymore," she said. "And to be fair, it's so expensive to stay anywhere near a beach, even for a holiday, this experience is out of reach for most families."

"Not completely," he said. "If you go down to the pier on Sundays, families are together, having fun. People still make an effort to gather and hang out."

"That's true." She turned the picture face down. "I have this tendency to idealize the past."

"Nothing wrong with fond memories," he said. "As long as you keep making more. You're talking like an old lady."

She bristled and sat down on the bed. "I am not."

"Like all your happy times are behind you. You need to have more fun." He sat beside her with enough bounce to pop her in the air.

Knocked off-balance, she fell over. He caught her in time and her robe opened, revealing olive-gold skin in that soft, smooth space between her breasts. She laughed and then abruptly stopped, her full lips forming a question she didn't need to ask. Her narrow face glowed in the amber morning light. The caramel-tipped hair, slightly longer now, was a tousled sexy mess. He pushed a tendril out of her eyes, loving the silky feel of her hair. She was far from the polished, put-together sort of woman he'd always thought his ideal. And far more beautiful. Just like this. And just his.

"Meri?" he said.

8

She nodded. So serious. So sweet and completely beguiling. He slid one hand inside her robe and found the warm weight of her breast. When she leaned into him, her nipples hardened against his open palm. Her head came up and she looked at his mouth.

Their lips clung and caught fire. He kissed her with slow sweet precision, again and again until she was flushed and ready, a gift waiting to be unwrapped. He slipped the robe off her shoulders and held her waist. She obviously hadn't had great or even half-decent lovers because she was caught off-guard by some of his moves, not anticipating that he'd want to sample her breasts and nip little love bites along her shoulders. And yet she kissed him back with an artless enthusiasm he found adorable. She moaned her pleasure at every surprise. He suspected the sound of her throaty voice alone could make him come. Unwilling to let that happen before he gave her complete pleasure, he sank to the floor and got a sumptuous view of creamy white breasts that tightened under his gaze.

"Perfect," he said and buried his face between her breasts. She held his head as he suckled. Her scent was all around him, herbal and green. The tender intoxication of spring. He loved the faintly sweet taste as he lavished each nipple with attention. Her hands threaded his hair. He felt her gasp when he tugged and then soothed with his tongue.

She tried to pull him up.

"Oh, no, this is still my turn," he said and tasted his way down to her lower belly. So smooth and slim, she jerked and responded to every touch of his mouth so he almost lost control before he'd even gotten out of his jeans. He couldn't allow that. He wanted to dive into that long lovely body and explore its mysteries. She murmured something and moved to open her legs to give him better access.

She cried out suddenly.

"What is it?"

She lifted her foot. Blood dripped from it. "I found more glass."

"Sorry, sugar. I thought I got it all." He went to get a towel from the bathroom. "I'll do it. Don't touch the glass."

By the time he got back, she'd already swung her foot over her knee and plucked out the shard.

He made her sit still while he dabbed, cleaned, and applied a bandage. "All done," he said, holding her foot in both his hands. "There's always one more piece of glass, somewhere. Why don't you let people help you?"

"I just did."

He sat back on his heels and held onto her knees. "What am I going to do with you?"

She issued a lopsided smile. "I wrecked the mood, huh."

"No," he said. "You couldn't do that."

She said, "Come back up here." Her hands felt small and light when she slid into his waistband and undid his jeans with greedy curiosity.

He went still, shaking with need. It had been so long. If she kept this up, he'd explode prematurely. "I should remind you. It's been a while so unless you want this to be over in five seconds, just take it easy. Plus, I might be a little rusty."

"Like the tin man?" She traced the outline of his still-confined penis, rubbing him lightly through the straining fabric. "But he needed oil." She grasped his cock assertively. Claiming him as hers. Such sweet intensity. "You won't."

He dragged her hands away. "Meri, you're killing me."

He held her head very still, not letting her move. She tasted like honey. With his fingers in her hair, he played her with his tongue, defying the urge to devour her. Kneeling once more, he ran his hands up her silky inner thighs. He put a single finger up to stroke her soft heat, the dainty folds unfurling for him.

He searched out her sensitive spots and she trembled under his hands and mouth. He kissed the inside of her knees, tickled her legs and slowly worked his way back up to her stomach. She tangled her fingers in his hair and tugged. He slid up to kiss her mouth before working his way back down again. She jumped when he found her clitoris, a tiny bud throbbing with need. He restrained and steadied her all at once.

"This is mine," he said. "Let me." He cupped her bottom with both hands and gently pulled the pink folds apart with his thumbs. When he found the center of her desire, he created shock waves with his tongue. She tried to escape the intensity and meet it at the same time. He yanked her closer, increasing the pressure as she danced on his tongue. His hunger fed and blended with hers. She held his head and her body rose on a wild slick wave, brutal and relentless as it peaked. She bucked with silent need but when the wave finally broke, her cry was harsh and hoarse.

He settled over her and buried his head between her neck and her shoulder. "Damn," he said. "I don't have a condom. I don't suppose—"

"I can't think," she said. "I must have one somewhere."

She rolled off the bed and limped into the bathroom. He watched her move, a nude study in gold skin and soft curves. She came back with a condom, ripped it open swiftly and helped him put it on. He wanted to learn her, trace every curve and plane. Too much to learn. Too many pretty little hollows and angles to explore.

Covering her body, he set his jaw and entered as slowly as he possibly could. So tight. One long thrust and then an easy pull back. When he sank into her again, she moaned, husky and low.

"So sweet," he muttered and plunged again. She gripped him with her inner muscles and he was caught, held in a blissful trap. Making her come had sharpened his arousal to the point of torture. Sweet torture, but torture nonetheless. "Don't move. I can't—"

Her hips rocked, answering his control with power of her own. Pulsing heat surrounded him. He moved, trying and failing to keep the rhythm slow. The pleasure was so intense—he'd come in an instant if he didn't pull back. So he exerted his last shred of control, withdrew, and kissed her. Only then did he give himself the exquisite pleasure of sheathing himself in her velvet heat. He lost it. He drove again and again, past the point of no return.

She clung to him—and he came in a flood of hot seed and sweet relief. They stayed that way for a few minutes. Skin on skin. Limb over limb. Tenderness overwhelmed him. His world view had shifted. She had taken him someplace new.

He eased back, not wanting to crush her, and in one quick twist, flipped her so she lay full length over him. He held her close and whispered, "What if we could make love like this every day and every night?"

She stopped nuzzling his neck and rolled away. The cool air was an insult on his heated skin, an unpleasant reminder of the world outside this room.

He ran his hand up her slim, strong back. "What's wrong?"

"Don't worry about my expectations," she said. "I believe in mutual pleasure and loving satisfaction. That's all."

"That's all?"

"You know what I mean," she said. "We can leave all the complications out of this."

She was every man's dream. Exquisitely responsive. Passionate. But her attitude mystified him. Why were her expectations so low? What if *he* wanted more? He smoothed her hair away from her beautiful face, now gone curiously still.

"We should get up," she said. "Your family is probably wondering about you and I need to deal with the locks."

"Let's get you some breakfast before we call that locksmith."

"You mean, before I call that locksmith."

"Whatever. We've got pancakes waiting for you at home and I'll be a lot happier after you eat. And then we can come back here and take up where we left off. If you're interested."

"I am," she said. "Why will you be happier after I eat? How does that work?"

"I don't know. But that's how it is. Come on."

They dressed with lazy, unhurried pleasure, watching each other, stopping to kiss and touch and discover how quickly they could turn each other on, just like that.

Walking home, he hooked his hand in the back of her jeans and tugged. "We still need to talk," he said. "You know that wasn't a random break-in."

"No."

One of the nice things about Meri—he rarely had to explain things. Unlike most people he'd known, she was right there with him.

"No, it doesn't add up," she agreed. "Why would they harass me now? Joe's attorneys finally came up with a big fat settlement on Friday."

"You didn't tell me that," he said in a goading tone.

"The process got delayed because of that blog post. Carolyn kept negotiating, pointing out that I hadn't actually given an interview to that reporter. Anyway. Why have someone break into my house when they're offering me a settlement? If they were trying to intimidate me, I don't see the logic. And no, I don't know what they would expect to find here."

Rob rubbed his forehead. "Too much smoke, Meri. There has to be a fire. If it is his people that keep breaking in—and who else would it be—there's something they want from you."

"I can't imagine what, except for my silence. And no one's tried to off me yet." The joke fell flat. Neither of them laughed. She stopped short. "Except—oh, duh. I said something to Chamberlain about a lab notebook that contained some of my notes, notes about the data that went missing from the database."

Rob looked at her, appalled. "What else haven't you told me?"

"You're taking this personally," she said.

"Damn straight," he said. "So where is this notebook?"

"I've looked, but I never did find it. It could be with all my furniture and the other stuff I put in storage."

"Did you look before they broke in the first time, or after?"

"Before."

They'd been standing outside his door. His mother waved from the kitchen window. "Later," he said. "We'll revisit this later."

After breakfast, Meri went home to meet the locksmith. Once the locks were changed and the house cleaned up to her satisfaction, she waited for Rob. As the afternoon inched on and he didn't come, she felt increasingly disappointed and then annoyed. With herself, mostly. Everything had changed and she didn't know if getting involved with him was smart. It probably wasn't. But she wanted him. She really wanted him. And she had a feeling she'd only scratched the surface of that need. Now that she'd had a taste of him, there was no going back. All he had to do was look at her and smile, like he had over breakfast, and she got all twitchy again.

Late in the afternoon, she walked down to the shoreline, determined to enjoy the day. She doodled in the sand with her toes, reluctant to go inside even as the light faded. The evening marine layer had started to drift in when she picked out a runner far to the south. She knew his long stride and watched him run toward her.

Rob eased into a slow walk about thirty feet away, breathing hard and wiping the sweat from his neck with the hem of his shirt. She stared at his lightly muscled stomach and chest. For the first time, she understood just how bloodless and lacking in passion her previous lovers had been. Or maybe she had been the one lacking. Because not once had she felt like this about a man, like she couldn't wait to have him again. Nor had she ever, ever wanted to jump any man hot and sweaty from a workout, his t-shirt clinging to his chest.

She had it bad.

His eyes skimmed her bare legs. "Aren't you cold in those shorts?"

"Not anymore."

"What was that professor's name again?" he asked.

"Dennis Chamberlain."

"That's what I thought."

"And?"

"I've been doing some research," he said. "A few years ago, the university slapped Chamberlain on the wrist. Conflict of interest. They found out he owned stock in a company he was doing a supposedly independent study for. Stock that performed very well. Guess who was one of the directors of that company? Joe Barranca. Those two have associated for fifteen years on various projects and companies."

"Surprise, surprise," she said grimly.

He dropped onto the sand beside her and propped his arms over his knees. His shorts slid up his thighs. She swallowed and looked away.

"I want to take you out to dinner," he said. "A nice dinner."

"Just me?"

"Yes, just you. My mom doesn't mind babysitting. She's tickled to death. Her words. So where do you want to go?"

"There's this place, kind of a hole in the wall, but really good food. We can take the ferry."

Meri leaned over the railing as the tiny barge hummed across the narrow channel to Balboa Island, a tiny speck of land between the peninsula where they lived and the mainland. "My brother and I spent a lot of time in this harbor," she said. "We learned to sail out of the marina here. Never past the jetties though. Our little sailboat wasn't designed for the open sea."

Rob nudged her sideways to shelter her from the wind's icy bite. "I had never been on a sailboat in my life until Bill took us out on his 30-footer."

Us. Well of course his wife had been with him.

"I grew up in a landlocked state," he said. "A few lakes and reservoirs but not much sailing. Anyone rich enough to own a boat had a motor boat."

She put her arm through his. "I want you to see this view—it's the best part of the ferry ride. Ready? Wait for it…wait for it… And—now!"

The channel suddenly opened wide and Newport Harbor sprawled before them, a bustling panorama. Tourists zipped past in an electric boat with a fringed awning. A yacht loaded with a corporate party cruised out to the ocean.

"That's my favorite part," she said. "Since I was little. You're going along the channel and then bam—the harbor just opens up."

A minute later, the ferry slip loomed. Rob squeezed her shoulder and they returned to the car. They bumped down the ramp and she directed him to the restaurant. She could smell the fresh bread before they even got out of the car.

While Rob scanned the menu, Meri eyed the rosemary rolls and chunks of steaming white country bread nestled alongside a dish of soft butter. By the time the waiter took their order, she'd eaten half the bread. "I'm sorry. Please take some before I eat your share, too."

He slid the basket back to her. "No. There's more where that came from. Eat."

She pushed the basket away on principle, and sipped from the glass of Sangiovese he'd ordered while her mouth was full.

"You mentioned a settlement offer," he said.

"I stuffed the papers in my purse so I could show you."

"Have you showed it to your attorney?"

"Of course she's got a copy." Meri dug around for the packet. "I only skimmed the first page or so, but I still can't believe they'd offer me this much."

"Let me see that."

She scooted around to read the contract with him. He scanned it quickly, pausing only to grunt a few times.

He looked up. "It's pretty much what I expected."

"$300,000. Crazy, right? I only expected a few months' salary."

"Meri," he said, "If they can get you to promise you'll keep your mouth shut, $300,000 is *nothing* to them. Nothing compared to the tens of millions Barranca personally stands to make in the next year. He'll stay majority shareholder. Anyway, if he's got people breaking into your house to find that—what did you say it was—"

"Lab notebook."

"They're obviously worried about what you know or any evidence you might have. I'm not convinced that attorneys can even resolve this."

"Who will?" she said. He didn't answer because there wasn't a clear answer. "I'm calling Joe on Monday to tell him I won't sign."

"Don't. You're better off having your attorney negotiate different terms. A delay isn't a bad idea. Let things cool down."

Meri listened with only half her attention. "I've already delayed so long, but the dollar amount is the least of my worries."

"Eventually, you'll accept some kind of settlement."

"I guess that depends."

"You'd be crazy not to," he said.

They stared each other down across the table. She blinked first, as she knew she would, but kept staring anyway. The waiter delivered their salads and brandished a pepper grinder until Rob waved him off.

"Eat," he said.

Rob dug into his salad. Even if she was too stubborn to eat, he certainly wasn't. He sighed and looked at her. On the ferry ride, her eyes had been soft and shining. Now those green eyes were hard as sea glass.

"Hey," he said. "I'm sorry I was rude. Eat your salad. Our food will be here soon."

Meri sat back and shook her head. Then she surprised him by laughing that sexy deep laugh and picking up her salad fork. "Do women always follow your orders?"

"I don't know what you're talking about. I don't give orders."

She made an incredulous face. "Right."

The waiter brought their pasta. Rob liked watching Meri eat. Her eyes closed when she tasted something she liked. A sensuous nature hid beneath that self-contained exterior.

He shifted in his chair. Even the way she moaned while she ate tortellini turned him on.

He wondered again about her background. Not that it really mattered, but her appearance did present interesting contrasts. Her green eyes were wide-set with thick dark lashes and her skin was beautiful, an interesting mix of light and dark tones. "What's your heritage?"

"A mix, like everyone else. Mainly, a combination of German and Mexican. Grandma's maiden name was Lopez. Her ancestors were native Californians, from old California that is, before the U.S. grabbed it from Mexico."

"You really do come from old money. Anyway, the combination is beautiful on you."

She smiled uncertainly. "You ought to see my mother."

"What are you talking about? You're a classic beauty."

"Nice line," she said. "I mean, thank you."

He lifted an eyebrow. "You don't believe me?"

"You have to understand—I grew up surrounded by beautiful girls. You couldn't walk for tripping over them. And if a girl isn't stunning to begin with, she's stunning by 16, courtesy of cosmetic surgeons on Newport Circle. No weak chins or big noses allowed. No chubby tummies, either. I didn't have those issues, but I was always the ugly duckling in the family."

"As I recall," he said, "the ugly duckling triumphed in the end."

"Not in Orange County. This place is lousy with swans."

They were on the way home when Meri said, "Are you coming over?"

"I wish I could, but I'm leaving for Taiwan—the trip has been planned for months. My flight leaves at 1 am from LAX."

"What—tonight?"

"My ride picks me up at ten."

"But you never even mentioned this. That's in less than two hours."

"I'm mostly packed," he said, not sure why she'd make this an issue. They had plenty of time and he hadn't rushed her through dinner. "I do have a favor to ask. While I'm away, would you consider staying at my house? That way I won't worry about you."

"That's sweet, but no thanks. I'll be fine."

He shook his head. Why wasn't he surprised she'd be stubborn? "Well, could you at least have dinner with my mother and Luke sometimes? She could use some help. Luke goes to bed at 7:30. I mean, in theory. And that's the time of day I'm worried about."

"I'll be happy to. I love your family and you've all been such good friends to me."

Friends. He pulled up in front of her house.

"Have a safe trip," she said.

He kissed her goodbye, hard enough to make her blink and stare. If she thought this was a friendship, she had another think coming.

9

Meri called her former boss at 7:30 on Monday morning. She knew Joe's habits. He would be at his desk by six, with no gatekeepers.

She hadn't asked Rob or Carolyn's opinion about calling; she already knew what they'd say. However, anything less than an honest conversation amounted to weakness in her view. She had no intention of weaseling out of a confrontation. It was past time to talk to her former boss directly.

Joe greeted her as if he'd fully expected her call.

Point blank, she said, "I'm not signing the contract, Joe. All I want is a fair settlement."

"You don't think what we offered is fair?"

"No. It's—bizarre."

"You'd be unique in that opinion, my dear," Joe said. "A confidentiality agreement is quite common. You've made up your mind then. You're certain?"

"Of course."

"Fine," he said, nothing if not calm and pleasant. "That's fine."

Meri paused, thrown. She was tempted to ask him why he'd risk everything. Sure he had a lot to gain. He also had a hell of a lot to lose by breaking the law and compromising consumer safety. He had accomplished so much in his career and made several fortunes. Why risk it all? But all she said was, "I won't whitewash the truth for you or anyone else."

"That makes two of us."

"I don't understand."

"No matter. In a way, we're on the same page, you and me. From here on, let the attorneys hash out the details. Good luck to you, my dear."

She disconnected, vaguely uneasy. He'd surprised her, once again. She'd expected him to be angry, or at least argue the issue. They obviously wanted her silence. Yet he'd taken her refusal of hush money without a ripple of protest.

For years she had believed in this man's integrity, looked up to his vast experience and knowledge. He had been a mentor, but only as long as she played her assigned role. He wasn't the man she'd thought and probably never had been.

The question nagging at her gut was whether she'd been willfully blind to his true colors. Maybe she had, in fact, sold her soul. If so, it was high time to reclaim it.

She started to make plans to attend the annual biotechnology conference in mid-March. She had attended for the last four years, twice as a speaker. Carolyn thought she was crazy.

"Why wouldn't I go?" Meri said when Carolyn questioned her. "I can kill two birds. Three if you count networking. When people see me there, going about my business, attending seminars and so forth, they'll see I'm not a nutcase. One of these days, someone will hire me."

"I still say you're courting trouble. They'll tear you down and humiliate you. Anyway, what other birds do you plan to eliminate on this trip?"

Meri grinned at her wording. "The guy from the National Institutes of Health, the one I've been corresponding with about investigating Barranca—he'll be there and we decided it was a logical place to meet. He might pull in a few other people to talk to me, too. Everyone will be in San Francisco that week so it's a good chance to meet people who can help me resolve this mess."

"That's two birds," Carolyn said. "What's the third?"

"I can keep doing what I always do. Learning the latest and staying current. No matter what happens, Barranca can't take that away from me. I won't allow it."

"And who's footing the bill for all this? You're not on an expense account anymore and San Francisco ain't cheap."

Meri blew a breath out. "This is why credit cards exist." She looked up then and smiled. "It's all going to work out."

During the week that Rob was away, Meri frequently joined his family for dinner. Though the hectic atmosphere took some getting used to, she soon found the noise and clutter as comforting as Betty Jo's southern cooking.

With them, she felt safe. Safe, healthy, and useful. She often helped Betty Jo with Luke, getting him bathed and in bed. The little boy continued to enchant her, charming her with new words and skills. In his own way, he was as relentless as his father. A force of nature.

She missed Rob. She didn't want to miss him. So she was ruthless with herself, knocking down every hope, every fantasy built on shifting sands. His departing kiss had left her yearning and mooning around like a fourteen-year-old. Which was unacceptable. She didn't do this. She wasn't someone whose life revolved around her latest lover and when he might pay attention to her again.

On the night before Rob was due back from Taiwan, Meri trudged downstairs, worn-out from putting Luke to bed. She heard voices. A thirty-something couple chatted with Betty Jo at the kitchen table. They were attractive, well-dressed, and clearly on a mission.

"Oh, Meri," Betty Jo said nervously. "I'm glad you're still here. This is Lisa and Dave. They live next door. Could you look at this?"

The couple produced paperwork, which Meri quickly scanned. It was a contract to bulldoze the beach in front of six properties, including Rob's. All six owners had agreed to share the cost of leveling scrubby sand dunes between their homes and the ocean.

"This isn't just cleaning up seaweed, is it?" she asked. "It says the contractor is going to clear away the dunes. Why?"

The husband, Dave, looked at her speculatively. "Rob already knows why. Have him sign his copy and drop it off by Friday. Everyone else has signed off. We need to proceed." His tone made it clear he expected her obedience.

She glanced from the papers to the couple. "Residents can't plow the dunes. People have trucked sand *in* to add to the dunes. But even that can cause problems. You have approval for this?"

"We're entitled to improve our view," Lisa put in. "Those dunes reduce the value of our home and deprive us of what we deserve. I know your father owns that house three doors down and has owned it forever. *You* don't have a sand dune blocking *your* view. Why shouldn't we see the ocean from our deck? Unlike you, my husband and I paid a great deal of money—our own money—for oceanfront property."

Lisa's defensive response convinced Meri they hadn't checked with the coastal commission or the city. She tried to explain. "Dunes are considered a vital ecosystem down here. You can't—"

Dave cut her off. "Look, are you on the title to this property?"

Meri shook her head.

"I didn't think so."

Lisa smiled at Meri mockingly and they got up to leave. Meri reread the contract while Betty Jo saw the couple out. She would have to warn Rob. These people were asking for trouble.

The next evening she was getting Luke into his pajamas when Rob came home from his overseas trip. He walked in, loaded down with luggage and briefcase, and Luke ran to him. With his son tangled in his legs and Betty Jo hugging him, Rob looked for Meri and gave her a slow smile. He scanned her, as if assessing any changes in her appearance. She felt awkward standing there, literally outside the family circle. After a few minutes, when she moved to leave, he said, "Stay awhile."

While he showered, Meri put Luke to bed. Betty Jo declared herself exhausted and went upstairs.

As soon as Meri walked into the kitchen, he pulled her into his arms. He held her face in his hands and kissed her, hard and hot. Hungry hands roamed, sliding up and down her body. He lifted his head, smiled into her eyes and said, "I missed you."

Another kiss, slower and sweeter. He was very warm and very male, demanding and giving at the same time. She explored under his shirt, where smooth warm skin and hard muscles waited, just for her. He did the same, sliding his fingers beneath the lacy cups of her bra.

"Meri." They jumped and moved apart when his mother called down the stairwell. "Don't forget to tell Rob about that paperwork you were so worried about. I'm going to watch a movie up here."

"Okay, goodnight," Meri called back.

"I think that was Betty Jo-speak for "Don't worry, I'm not coming back downstairs," Rob said.

They smiled at each other. He pulled two Coronas from the refrigerator, grabbed her hand and pulled her into the living room, keeping her close. They talked about his trip for a few minutes. He kept one hand on her at all times, whether it was stroking her hair or sliding up the inside of her leg. She'd missed him so.

Despite what she'd said, Betty Jo could be heard still moving around upstairs.

"Can you come back to my house?" Meri whispered.

"I just got home. I'd rather you stay over here."

"I'm not real comfortable with that," she said. "Your mom in the next room?"

"We'll work it out." His tone was confident; she could see he planned to talk her into staying. He propped his feet on the coffee table and swigged his beer. "What was that about paperwork I should know about?"

"Your neighbors have some kind of plan to bulldoze the dunes out front? They said you knew about it already."

"Yeah, so?"

"You can't just go move sand dunes. Not without permission and a very good reason."

"I have a very good reason. Improving the market value of my property. As for permission, no one will notice. We're only talking about dinky piles of sand. These dunes aren't huge. They can't be more than three feet tall."

She set her drink on a side table. He obviously didn't get it. "You're about to disturb a protected ecosystem. And the California Coastal Commission is infamously protective. They'll make you sorry."

He laughed. "What are they—the Mafia?"

"No, but you don't want to cross them. I've heard stories."

Rob drained his beer. Meri was your classic tree-hugger. She didn't grasp the big picture. And like anyone born into money, she didn't understand why others might want what she had taken for granted her whole life.

"Reminds me of an old joke," he said. "'What's the difference between a developer and an environmentalist?'"

She lifted her hands.

"'A developer is someone who wants to build a house in the woods. An environmentalist is someone who already *has* a house in the woods.'"

She half-smiled. "This isn't about a house in the woods, but I understand what you're saying."

"The joke definitely applies. I'll bet half the folks on that coastal commission already have a house with a terrific view. Canyon, ocean, whatever. Once they have theirs, they become real big on preserving nature—the part of the pie they didn't already slice out for themselves. Anyway, what do you think the commission will object to? Whose habitat would we disturb? The Newport sand flea?"

"If those dunes are leveled, the coastal commission will almost certainly object. It could cost you plenty in fines. Not to mention the aggravation."

Aggravation. Rob looked around for the TV remote and clicked on the Lakers' game. The construction loan on his new house had already ballooned past his pain threshold. The time had come to tell her. He hadn't meant to be secretive, not exactly. He'd held off this long because he'd guessed she wouldn't be enthusiastic.

"You may as well know," he said. "I'm listing this house for sale pretty soon. I've already signed the contract on a brand-new house."

"So you're moving away," she said quietly, so quietly he almost didn't hear her.

"It's up on the hill in Newport Coast. It'll be beautiful when it's finished. Problem is, as soon as I close, I'll have double mortgage payments. That's why I need to get as much as I possibly can for this place. An ocean view commands a premium. *That's* why I'm down with bulldozing the dunes."

"Rob, you can't control what your neighbors do, but don't go along. You have enough stress in your life without looking for more."

No doubt Meri was brilliant in her occupation, or had been. Witness the stacks of scientific journals piled in her living room. But he was far and away better suited for managing business decisions. What did she know about property values and real estate? Resentment emerged, resentment he hadn't even been aware of until now. "You've never had to swing a mortgage, have you, much less double payments. Daddy takes care of all that."

Her face dimmed. "It's true I've never owned a house. Until I got sick and moved over here, I paid my own rent, if that's what you're getting at. But my situation is irrelevant. What matters is that you understand the potential consequences here."

"So give me a number," he said. "Exactly what are these consequences?"

"I don't know, but I can check into it."

He fiddled with the remote. "You know one of my wife's better qualities? She knew when to back off. She never challenged me about things that were none of her business."

Out of the corner of his eye, he watched for the flinch. It never came. Meri sat ramrod-straight and composed. *Good.* He'd given her something to think about. She needed to watch that self-righteous attitude. He punched up the game's volume.

A minute or two later, she got up and let herself out. And he just let her go.

He turned off the TV soon after that. The Lakers had won. He was past caring. Bone-numbing exhaustion set in, no surprise after a demanding week and a 14-hour flight. He had liked coming home to her. Correction. He'd *loved* coming home to her. She'd been a welcome surprise. Sitting together in the late-night hush had been comfortable. Nice. The truth was, he enjoyed talking to her, liked how he couldn't predict what she'd say or where the conversation might go. That kind of connection didn't happen very often, not for him. Certainly not with his wife.

He'd admired Meri's cheerful spirit the first time they'd met, the first real time, on the beach. Tonight, with one thoughtless remark, he'd crushed that spirit. It wasn't fair to compare her to Julie. They were so dissimilar. Any comparison was absurd.

With some shock, he realized he hadn't thought about his wife in weeks. The grief had faded. When he did think about her, it was with faint regret. By now he'd learned how to cope with the guilt, to submerge it to a place in the deep.

And that's where it would stay.

Meri continued to help Betty Jo on occasion, but only after making sure Rob wouldn't be home. Several nights later, she knelt by the bathtub watching Luke imitate a duck. His vigorous flapping had soaked her from the waist up, but since she was already resigned to mopping the floor and changing her shirt, it hardly mattered. The duck suggestion had gotten him into the tub without a struggle.

Rob poked his head in the door. "Hey."

"Daddy!"

She closed her eyes in frustration. Betty Jo had said Rob wouldn't be home till after eight. Rob's eyes wandered to her chest. She looked down. The draft he'd let in to the warm bathroom made her look like a contestant in a wet t-shirt contest.

"When you're done, I want to talk to you," he said brusquely. When he closed the door, another gust blew across her chest.

Fifteen minutes later, she handed Luke over to his grandmother and sought out Rob. He'd changed into jeans and a t-shirt and was sprawled in front of the TV, watching another basketball game with his arms propped behind his head. The Lakers were losing to Phoenix tonight.

His rumpled sexiness grated on her nerves. Unsporting of him to show off. Why did he have to wear such low-slung jeans? She forced her eyes away from the gap between his shirt and waistband. The spot where his jeans dipped. The sight triggered a longing she didn't want to have. She didn't trust herself to be alone with him.

She lifted her chin. "I'm going home."

"You should change into dry clothes. I'll walk you back on the beach." His eyes lingered on her clinging top. "Put something over that."

"Yes, sir," she said mockingly. "I intend to. As soon as I get home. And if we walk the front way, I can be home in a minute."

"I need more time with you than that," he said. He pulled a windbreaker out of the closet and helped her into it. "I seem to do this a lot."

She had no answer. He grabbed her arm, led her out the back door and didn't let go until they were down the steps. The beach was cold tonight. She would never admit being glad for his windbreaker.

"I want to apologize," he said. "You shouldn't have meddled—but I didn't handle it well, either. I'm sorry."

Not much of an apology, was it? "Okay," she said anyway and curled her fingers inside her sleeves. He reached for her hand and slipped it into his pocket, which made her uneasy. Quickly, she added, "I found some cases on the Internet. Cases that'll give you some idea of the fines the Coastal Commission has imposed. I printed a few pages for you." And that's as far as she planned to stick her neck out. If he refused, she would drop the matter entirely. She took her hand back as they climbed her steps.

"Fine," he said. "I'll take a look at those."

She unlocked the door and he tried to follow. She held her hand up. "Wait here." When she came back with the papers, she said, "I know it's none of my business—"

"We've established that."

His attitude shut down any shred of attraction she'd been fighting. He'd made it easy for her. She said a curt 'good night' and shut the door in his face.

Rob stared, disbelieving, even as her new deadbolt clicked. He had fully intended to kiss her goodnight, at minimum. Now, out of nowhere, he had a caveman urge to pound on the door and drag her back into his arms. Where she belonged.

He walked down the beach for half an hour, brooding over what had to be sexual frustration, pure and simple. He had missed her. She was irritating, intelligent, and seductive in her own, almost innocent way. Tonight, when she'd looked up after he'd opened the bathroom door, her mouth had curved in unconscious welcome. And for a moment, he'd completely forgotten any barriers between them. The delicate outlines revealed by her transparent blouse turned him on so much he'd nearly scooped her into his arms right there in the bathroom.

And then she'd shied away.

For him, attraction, lust and lovemaking nearly always flowed along with a lazy inevitability. Never any urgency. Just a laid-back recognition of where things were heading. Even with his wife, even as a newlywed, he'd been content to let intimacy develop in its own good time. It always did, so why get worked up about it?

This need for Meri was far more urgent. And disturbing. A different business altogether. He wanted her, and not just her delectable body. He wanted the incandescent smile she reserved for Luke and he resented that he hadn't gotten one from her since the night he'd returned.

Rob stopped when he reached the boulders marking the harbor entrance. He'd lost track of how far he'd come. He looked at the damp, crumpled papers she'd gone to the trouble of finding and printing out for him. Now he would go home and read the damn things.

Meri watched Luke barrel toward a flock of shorebirds. The tiny birds power-walked ahead of him, their toothpick legs a blur. When he growled, the birds flew off. He brushed his hands in satisfaction.

She remembered a childhood chant for days like this, when hot offshore winds roared out of the desert. "Homeowner's fright, surfers' delight." A play on the old "red sky at night" expression. But fire danger was low this morning, with no red flag warnings. The Santa Anas were usually fairly benign in winter, delivering pristine skies and optimum surfing conditions. Today was no exception.

She looked at her watch and got up reluctantly. Time to chase him down for lunch and a bath. The oversized plastic bucket Betty Jo set out was already filled and cooling on their deck. Poor Betty Jo was flopped in her beach chair, depleted. The nanny hadn't been here for several days; her children were sick.

Meri wrangled Luke into the tub while Betty Jo brought out sandwiches and iced tea. They sat under the umbrella and let Luke eat his peanut butter and jelly in the tub. He lost interest after a few bites and began dunking his sandwich in the bath water. Then he was empty-handed, peering into the murky water. "Spongeblob go down."

Meri and Betty Jo exchanged shrugs. It was too hot to fuss and far too late to rescue the sandwich.

Betty Jo gestured at Meri's bikini top and swim skirt. "That's such a cute outfit. I think I saw one just like it at the S & M store in the mall."

Meri folded her lips to hide the smile. "I think you must have been at H & M."

"That's the one," Betty Jo said. "I noticed because it reminded me of a skirt Rob gave me one time—must have been twenty years ago. He'd earned his first real money that year, bagging groceries. On my birthday, I opened a box to find this darling white skirt with blue piping. I couldn't understand why the heck a mini-skirt would have built-in underpants." Betty Jo put her head back and laughed heartily. "I'd never seen a tennis skirt. Had no idea what it was."

"So why did he give you one?"

"That grocery store where he worked was in a high-class suburb. The kind of place where ladies shopped in their tennis skirts, or so I learned. So anyway. I put that skirt in my bottom drawer and that's where it's been ever since. Every time Rob asked me about it, I told him I was saving it for vacation."

Just then, Luke hurtled out of his tub. He had his eye on a brown pelican that had landed on a neighboring porch. Meri held Luke up to see. His little body shuddered with cold but he watched the immense bird with concentration until she put him back in his bath.

"So you never got to wear the skirt?" Meri said.

Betty Jo stared at the sea with a faraway look. "We didn't take vacations. When we had the money, we didn't have the time. When we had the time, we didn't have the money."

"I guess Rob wanted you to have what those suburban ladies had."

Betty Jo was struck by that idea. "I could never be like those ladies in a million years. Poor baby. He always wanted better. And who could blame him? We didn't have much." She sighed. "He's done so well for himself. He told you about that new house he's building—did he show you the pictures?"

Luke had his leg over the tub, poised to make a break. Meri grabbed a towel. "No, I haven't seen pictures."

"It's like a palace. Julie would have lov—" Betty Jo stopped herself. "She had a knack for decorating and fixing things up. She always wanted a showcase."

So the house had been something Rob had planned with his wife. The house was for Julie.

Later, after carrying Luke in for his nap, Meri went home. Restless and unsettled, she decided to take a long bike ride and work off her excess energy and uncertainty.

She set out on her bike and passed the raw section of the beach, bulldozed flat in the dead of night, two days ago. Yesterday she had seen a group of neighbors—a cluster of people in business suits—milling around, trying not to get sand in their shoes and looking awkwardly overdressed. One man had poured champagne into paper cups. They were toasting each other. Meri had never laid eyes on most of them. These people weren't usually outside—most of them worked such long hours they had no time to enjoy the lifestyle they worked their asses off to pay for.

She rode past her usual turnaround point and pushed an extra five miles up to Huntington Beach. The afternoon breeze kicked up, chilling the pooled sweat between her breasts. She had overdone it; wheezing had set in.

Several hours after setting out, she turned off the coastal path for home. What had been a slight discomfort had become a tight hard braid, constricting her chest. She hopped off near her back door and fished the extra garage door remote from her pocket.

Something moved at the edge of her vision, a fleeting movement near the side of the house. Her breath hitched and her heart rate accelerated. But it was broad daylight. The neighbors were out on their deck, within shouting distance. She calmed down, steeled herself to check the house, the alley, and then walked the perimeter. Nothing out of the ordinary. Except, as luck would have it, Rob driving in from work.

He pulled alongside her. "Are you all right?"

She nodded, so glad to see him and equally afraid to show it.

"I heard you helped Mom out again today. Thank you."

"My pleasure." She spoke in a flat tone, the only way to push the words out without sounding winded.

"Can you join us for dinner?"

"Sorry, I can't," she said. "Thanks anyway."

He gave her a penetrating look. "Stop being so polite and tell me what's wrong. Why won't you come over?"

She shook her head. "Plans." Talking took too much effort. All she wanted was to get rid of him so she could stop pretending she didn't feel ghastly.

His mouth formed a straight line and he nodded curtly. "Better offer, eh?"

She went inside and stood in the shower for a long time, letting the water hit her back. The steam helped somewhat. She dried off and threw on a lightweight beach dress over her panties. The house had absorbed the day's heat. It was too early in the season to be this hot. She went to find the inhaler she hadn't needed in many weeks, stopping to crack the back door open.

10

After dinner, Luke trotted out to inspect an intriguing pile of bulbous kelp and Rob followed him. He couldn't wait till they had a back yard. In the new house, he wouldn't have to watch his son every waking moment, constantly worrying about Luke wandering too close to the ocean.

Rob glanced at Meri's deck. A curtain flapped, catching his eye. Her back door was open. Had she actually said she was going out? She'd been vague.

He picked up his son and delivered him home to Betty Jo with a quick explanation. He sprinted back and approached Meri's door, listening intently for an intruder.

The loose curtain whipped against the doorframe. When he nudged it aside, he discovered her asleep on the sofa, curled in a ball with her back to him. Despite his annoyance, he grinned at the windfall view. Her short dress had hitched up to the top of her tanned thighs, exposing her curvy little backside.

He rapped on the glass as he walked in, hoping to scare some sense into her.

She flailed upright.

"What the hell were you thinking?" he said. "Laying here with the door wide open and your ass exposed."

Meri sank back against the cushions, pale and silent. Her eyes were too big for her face and her skin color wasn't right, somewhere between white and blue.

"What's wrong with you?"

"Asthma…flare-up." She panted between words. "This inhaler…might be defective…or something."

"Why didn't you tell me earlier? You have another one? Where?"

"My purse."

He found her purse in the bedroom, fumbled through it, cursing under his breath. "I don't see it."

A memory bubbled up from his subconscious, one he'd repressed. Julie convulsing. Holding her swollen body as steady as he could with one arm. They'd been stuck at a red light, in gridlocked traffic. He'd cursed himself for driving her to the hospital when he should have called an ambulance. But he hadn't known she was in critical condition until she started convulsing. He'd never felt so helpless in his life. Until now.

He went back to Meri, pushed damp tendrils off her face. "I can't find it, love."

"Try…medicine cabinet."

Two truths pierced him to the core. He cared about her deeply. And he sure as hell wasn't going to fail this time. Nothing would happen to Meri. Not on his watch.

He riffled through the medicine cabinet. And saw nothing that looked like an inhaler. "I can't find the damn thing," he yelled. "That's it. We're going to the hospital."

She couldn't understand what he said as he tore out the door. She floated and waited. The house cooled and dimmed. Maybe he wasn't coming back. And she couldn't breathe. She fought rising panic. *If a rip current takes you, don't fight it.* Tread water. Keep treading. Swim parallel to shore. Except none of those lifesaving tips applied when facing a huge wave. The wave was about to break.

She had a choice. Get pounded by its terrible energy or dive under. As always, she chose to dive but the wave proved too strong. Her head got pulled backward. She went under and tumbled in the impact zone.

She surfaced when he touched her face. "Let's go. Come on now, sugar." He wanted her to sit upright. That "sugar" was kind of cute. It would have sounded silly coming from any other man. From him—just right.

When she woke, an overhead light hurt her eyes and a machine beeped behind her head. She was in a bed, with a dim memory of Rob driving her here. He'd driven very fast.

A nurse appeared next to her. "You're a lucky girl. That gorgeous fellow in the waiting room has been bugging us every five minutes. If he weren't so cute, I'd think he was a pest. I'll go out now and let him know you're all right."

They wheeled her away for various tests then and the admitting doctor said they'd keep her overnight. She waited for the next few hours, thinking Rob might come back, but he didn't. Then again, he'd already given up his entire evening for her. She was glad he'd gone home.

When he walked into the room early the next morning, Meri sat up and smiled, determined to have her say before he had a chance to give her a hard time about—well, anything. "You saved my life. My airways were closing up. If you hadn't come along, I would have been in real trouble. Thank you."

"And now?" Rob said. "How are you now?"

"Hanging in. They're getting the discharge paperwork ready."

"So what did the doctor say? Surely that wasn't just an asthma attack?"

"Maybe. The doctor thought there might be more to it. I'll see a pulmonologist on Monday. I'll find out then."

He scraped his chair closer to the bed. "When is your family coming?"

"They're not." She got busy with the knots on her hospital gown.

He looked startled. "Hold on, after we got here last night, I grabbed your cell and left messages for the three Darrow's in your contact list. Your dad. Your brother. Someone else—a woman."

"That would be my sister-in-law Nina—Bella and Kelsey's mom. Thanks for doing that, for letting them all know."

"Did you hear back from them?"

"My brother and my dad texted back. And last night I called my mom in Oregon, so she's aware."

"But no one is coming for you?"

"Dad only just got back from Aspen yesterday. Jordan's in San Diego. It's no big deal."

"Yes it is."

Ordinarily she took her family's self-absorption in stride. Seeing them through Rob's eyes forced a comparison she didn't want to make. She felt fragile, ready to shatter at a moment's notice. She took a shallow breath and blew it out. "How's everyone at your house?"

"They're fine, Meri," Rob said, watching her this whole time and missing nothing. He stayed until she was discharged. Neither of them brought up her family again.

He put her into the front seat of his car. "You're going to my house until you're better. And don't even think of arguing because I'm not doing that. I'm not arguing with you about this."

She studied the planes of his face as he drove. His jaw was set, like he'd made up his mind about something. He kept his hand on hers most of the way home.

When they arrived, Betty Jo and Luke made a fuss, making Meri a nest on the couch, delivering blankets and snacks. Luke stuck his teddy bear beside her. Rob shooed them away and Betty Jo took Luke outside. While Rob worked, she slept. When she woke next, the sun had already set. Rob sat reading at the other end of the couch with her feet in his lap.

"How're you feeling?"

"Okay, I think." She inhaled cautiously. "Much better."

"Your color's still not right."

"I'll be good to go in the morning."

"We'll see," he said, with a pinched expression she wasn't used to seeing.

Remorse caught at her heart. She probably felt better than he did. Sudden illness was bound to upset him.

"Truly, I'm fine," she reassured him.

His mother talked her into eating fried chicken with them. "I'm turning in early," Betty Jo announced as she cleaned up the kitchen and then bundled Luke into bed early.

Rob insisted Meri change into the nightgown and robe he'd retrieved from her house.

"Your back door was open," he said, when she came out of the bathroom. "Which is weird because yesterday when I—" He looked pinched again, even nauseated.

Meri went over and touched his wrist. She doubted this had anything to do with an unlocked door. He stood at his door and stared out at nothing. There was only the dark beach and the black void of ocean beyond that. This is how he'd been that night at the emergency room with Luke. Not really here.

Operating on instinct, Meri wrapped her arms around his torso and turned her face against his chest. She didn't say anything. Whatever demons he battled, he hadn't ever shared, except for the time he told her about his father. Even that day, horrified as he'd been with himself for yelling at his little boy, Rob hadn't looked like this—sick or sick at heart, more like.

He returned to her then, with a start, as if surprised to find her in his arms. She held on, listening to his heartbeat. He tucked her head between his neck and his shoulder and held her in place without attempting to kiss or converse. They stood silently like that for a long while, together but separate. His mother moved around upstairs and then, with a definite click, closed her bedroom door. Meri smiled into his shoulder. Betty Jo wanted them to know she was in for the night.

Finally, she said, "So did you lock my back door?"

"Yesterday? Yeah that's what I meant. I locked up before I took you to the hospital. Remember, I put you in the car and then ran back in to get your purse?"

"I wasn't entirely with it," she said. "Honestly, no idea what happened. But are you saying that tonight, just now, my back door was open when you got there?"

He nodded uneasily.

"Open-open or just unlocked?"

"The sliding door was unlocked. I checked around and nothing else had been touched, broken, or otherwise messed-with, at least nothing obvious. I'm positive I locked it last night."

Meri didn't like any of the possibilities. Her father would have told her if he'd come by. Jordan was in San Diego. That's why he couldn't make it to the hospital. Whatever was happening, it had spiraled out of control. What did these people want from her? What did they expect to find? Or were they simply trying to terrorize her? She sighed shakily.

Rob kissed her, soft and tender this time, more for comfort, she guessed. "I'm not letting you stay there," he said. "I don't care if you think I'm some kind of chauvinistic tyrant—it's just not going to happen, Meri. Not while I have a pulse. So don't start with me."

He looked so unhappy and tense; she couldn't bear that. "Okay." She rested her cheek on his chest again, because she loved doing this and who knows how many chances she'd have?

She didn't know what would happen after tonight. Sooner or later she'd either go home or move over to Jordan's place until she figured out her next step. Rob would be making his own plans to move on. As would she. Her father usually started the rental season at Easter—only five or six weeks away now. Maybe she'd go stay with Carolyn, who hadn't, in point of fact, actually offered. No matter what, everything would change.

Later, he kept his arm around her while they watched a movie on TV, a political thriller. Preoccupied by his near-constant touch, she couldn't follow the movie's convoluted plot. When he wasn't smoothing her hair, he trailed his hand up and down her leg or rubbed her back in light circles.

As the credits rolled, he captured her ankles and tugged. She yelped and landed in a reclining position with her legs draped over his lap. Her robe and nightgown had hiked up. She tried to smooth the gown but the fabric was caught beneath her bottom.

His eyes flared and he tickled her from the soles of her feet to the inside of her knees, making her jump. Before she knew it, he'd trailed up her leg and stroked the tender skin on her inner thigh.

She shuddered and panted in her effort to sit up. "Too much."

He stilled his hand. "Can you breathe?" When she nodded, he said, "So what is it then?"

She gave him a small smile. "I feel very strange right now. Turned on, excited, and scared out of my mind."

"Scared? Scared of what?"

"Falling in love with you." She swallowed hard and sat up straighter. "I didn't plan on saying that." When he said nothing in response, she gave him a sidelong look. "Sorry. I think everything that's happened has—well, I'm missing a filter between my brain and my mouth today."

"Don't be sorry. Would falling in love be so bad?"

The cards were on the table. "Maybe. Probably. Shit. Yes."

"I told you already, we're not arguing," he said calmly. "I won't even debate. Not tonight. Give me your feet back."

She'd curled her feet behind her. "Why?"

"A foot rub, that's all. Lord girl, what did you think? Hasn't anyone given you a foot rub before?"

"Other than your mom, no."

He held out his hands. "Poor deprived bunny. Come on, I don't have all night."

She lifted her bottom, adjusted her nightgown, and put her feet back in his lap. When he started on the toes of her left foot, she moaned.

He grinned. "Like it?"

"Oh my God. I had no idea." Her eyes widened when he circled the ball of her foot with his thumb. The sensations bolted directly to a pleasure center in her brain, back down to her lower spine and finally curled right between her legs. Tense and relaxed. Hot and liquid. All things, all at once. If there was a heaven…

"I need to tell you something," he said.

She opened one eye.

"In a minute," he said distractedly, playing "this little piggy" with her toes. Then he looked up. "So, you were right."

"About what?"

"I couldn't talk them out of it. Their minds were made up. They didn't have you to tell them what's what."

"Who and what are we talking about?" she complained. He dug his thumb into the arch of her foot. "Ouch!"

"You ought to be patient," he said. "The coastal commission came down on them like Thor's hammer."

She sat up, forgetting about the foot rub. "Already? Someone must have complained."

"Turns out a city planning guy lives a ways down the beach. He noticed and got a member of the coastal commission to come down here. My neighbor Lisa said he knocked on her door, pretty irate."

"Wait a second. You said the commission came down on 'them'. You didn't say 'us'."

"That's right. Not me. Them. Every property owner who signed that contract has been threatened with big fines, maybe even a lawsuit. Not only that, they're going to have to restore that stupid patch of sand with native plants. This thing could cost hundreds of thousands of dollars to put right. A real mess. And I'd be right in the middle of the mess if you hadn't saved me. I owe you one."

"That's good. I mean, it's not good for your neighbors, but I'm relieved you're not part of it. What made you change your mind?"

"You did. You went to all the trouble of researching and highlighting and circling. Made those little notes in the margins for me. As though I hadn't behaved like a jerk. I'm sorry I didn't listen to you."

"That's all right," she said. "I know I stuck my nose in."

"It belonged. I want your nose there."

She watched him uncertainly.

"You were smart and stubborn enough to stand up to me," he added. "It was a new experience. I'm not used to having someone challenge my decisions—not outside of work, anyway. I'm grateful."

"Does that mean you'll rub my feet some more?"

"Only if you agree to go upstairs and get into bed first."

She raised her eyebrows.

"I'm going to tuck you in, that's all," he said in an aggravated tone.

Once upstairs, she sat on his wife's frilly bed and observed him sleepily. This was her first time in his bedroom with him. Last time she'd slept alone. The room was messier tonight, with Rob's sweatshirts and jeans hanging off the chairs and his books and mail piled on the dresser. Now the room looked more like him.

He pulled back the covers. "Come on."

She scrambled in and turned on her side to face him. "Are you sure about this? What will your mother think?"

"That I'm watching over you. That's what she'll think."

Her eyes closed of their own volition.

"Should I sleep on the couch again?" He didn't sound enthusiastic.

She laughed under her breath. "Sugar, just get in bed."

"You called me 'sugar'."

She was too tired to think about the startled pleasure she heard in his voice and fell asleep even before the mattress dipped.

Meri woke up freezing. She huddled into the bed's warm center, encountered his body and then drew back in alarm. She'd forgotten where she was.

"You all right?" he said.

"Fine."

He pulled her back under the duvet. "You're cold."

She tried to relax but her thoughts raced. Gradually, his warmth spread and her eyes adjusted to the dark. She lay there for a long time, watching him sleep. He was very sweet, really. When he wasn't ordering her around.

A long time later, he opened his eyes and caught her staring. He reached out to stroke her hip and drifted back to sleep, her nightgown bunched in one fist. All night long, whenever she stirred, he tightened his hold, anchoring her. She didn't mind.

Sometime before dawn, Rob turned on the bedside lamp. He'd heard her say something—he was certain. "What?"

"You came back," she whispered. "I thought you left."

He cupped her cheek. She wasn't really awake. "Go back to sleep." As tempting as she was with her sleepy eyes and soft mouth, he knew she needed more rest. He stroked her hair. She had crept into his heart, with her unique blend of naiveté and intelligence. Lately he'd been fantasizing about making love to her in his new master bedroom. She'd like the fireplace. And the privacy they'd have. He'd let her shop for the bed. Women liked that sort of thing.

He had planned to take things gradually. Was it just two days ago he'd thought that? But now he needed to keep her safe. He wanted the right to touch her when he felt like it. He wanted to argue with her in the afternoons and love her every night. He rolled over. Worry could be an exhausting business.

Sunday morning was foggy and cold. Rob bullied her into dressing warmly before they went down for breakfast. Meri felt strange when she walked into the kitchen but Betty Jo welcomed her warmly, without blinking an eye.

Rob lifted Luke into his high chair for a second breakfast and they all tucked into scrambled eggs, grits, sausage, and hot biscuits dripping with butter and honey.

"I sure am going to miss your cooking," Meri said to Betty Jo with a replete sigh, and then jumped when a glob of food whizzed past her ear.

Rob looked up from his plate, ignoring his son flinging grits at the wall. "Are you going somewhere?"

"I can't stay here forever. In fact, I'm driving to San Francisco within the week. There's a meeting set up for next Monday—investigators plus scientists on a regulatory committee. They need information from me about the clinical trial and what I know. Most of them have to be there for the biotech conference anyway so it's a good chance to get everyone together. And this way I can *do* something, instead of waiting around for more bad things to happen."

"Bad things," Betty Jo said. "What bad things? Your health?"

"No, I'm fine now. Just problems with my work situation." While she spoke, Meri dangled a sausage above Luke's high chair tray. When he dropped his spoon to reach for the meat, she deftly whisked away his bowl of grits. He claimed the sausage with a triumphant grab.

"Now where have I seen that trick before?" Betty Jo mused.

"Shamu Stadium at Sea World," Rob said. "The day after Christmas. Mom, do you mind if Meri and I take a walk after we clean up here?"

"Go right ahead," his mother said, beaming. "You two have lots to talk about."

Meri glanced at Rob. What was this? Maybe he was going to tell her about his plans to move. She'd wanted to ask him about that new house last night more than once, but chickened out every time. He said nothing further and continued to wipe grits off his son with a washcloth.

"I'd like to run down and check my house," she said. "Plus I need some clothes."

"As long as I'm there too—fine with me."

Fine with him? Recalling his troubled expression last night, she refrained from making a sassy comment and went to check her phone. There were two missed calls from a number she didn't recognize and a voice mail.

Half an hour later, she and Rob stepped into a wall of fog so dense they couldn't see the ocean. "I just talked to Carolyn's dad," Meri said. "She didn't show up for dim sum this morning. She was supposed to meet them at the restaurant. It's Lunar New Year, so it's an especially big deal that she wasn't there. And she's not answering her phone."

"It's Sunday, maybe she's sleeping in. Or went home with someone last night."

"Could be, but her dad was upset. He said she always calls. I'll try to reach her again this afternoon."

"Let's go around to the front," Rob said, "and go in that way. I want to go in first. Give me your key." He did a walk-through and then beckoned her in. She packed clothes and cosmetics into a tote bag while he waited in the living room.

"I can't find my phone charger," she called. "It might be in the car." She walked into the garage and flicked the switch.

She noticed it right away—the same smell as that other time. And then, out of the blue, an olfactory memory came back to her. Bryan Haskell had worn that cologne. He'd been wearing it when he'd fired her. That's where she had smelled it. Not on the lab assistant as she'd thought.

Now she knew Haskell had been in her house. Twice. At least. And in this garage within the last 36 hours. Her car looked as it always did. A boring sedan with nothing unusual about it. Windows closed. Door locked. She scanned the garage but saw nothing else different.

Rob stuck his head in the garage. "Mom just called. The Harbor Patrol and a police boat are anchored at the Wedge."

11

"A surfing accident?"

"I don't know."

Together they went out to the deck and squinted south at the cluster of boats anchored near the jetty.

"Do we know what happened?"

"Mom said a neighbor knocked on the door to warn her to keep Luke off the beach and away from the area."

"Wait a second." She went inside and found binoculars. After adjusting and peering for a minute, she handed them to Rob. "I can't tell what's going on."

He took a look. "Me neither."

"Did you smell cologne in the garage?"

"Cologne?" he said, as if she were off her rocker.

"Yeah, that's what I said."

"What does cologne have to do with anything?"

She explained about Haskell and her suspicions.

"So you're saying this man may have broken into your house—"

"At least twice," she said.

"—and did who-knows-what, for reasons we don't understand. You think he may even be the inept burglar. And that he came back yesterday? Again, for reasons unknown."

She lifted her shoulders. "I know, right? But, in fact, I haven't been home since Friday night. So sometime since then. You said the back door wasn't locked when you were here yesterday—early evening, wasn't it?"

"And this Haskell is the same guy your company claims is the real culprit in setting you up. The guy they fired."

"That's what they said."

"Who did?"

"Well, Carolyn did. That's what Barranca's lawyers told her."

"This is…this is getting strange."

"Welcome to my world, sugar."

He wore a half-dubious, half-amused expression. "You're really calling me that now?"

"Looks that way." She moved closer. If there were a way to fit herself into his side without giving away how much she needed him, she'd do it in a heartbeat.

He looked through the binoculars again, lowered them and shook his head, as if to clear it. Then he paused. Looked sideways at her. And smiled. He caught her hand and held it against his heart.

She melted inside. What a guy. Even now, in the midst of this, he thought to reassure her. That's when she knew.

She loved him. His touch. *Him.* A hard and cynical pessimism—a conviction she'd had as long as she could remember—dissolved away. So this is what love felt like. She couldn't know his feelings but how nice to know love *was* possible for her. He hadn't said anything last night when she mentioned falling in love. She tried to be objective, to evaluate what sort of future they might have, assuming he wanted one. How would she fit into his life?

Short answer? She wouldn't. Their fundamental differences were, well, fundamental. Neither did she see how she could ever give him up. She decided not to think about the inevitable end. After all, she'd never truly been in love before. In like and in lust, yes. Not in love. Why not enjoy this while it lasted? Wasting precious time over-thinking it would not change the outcome.

More people had gathered on the beach. One of the police boats roared off. "Let's go down there and see what's going on," she said.

"*I'll* go. You head home and stay warm."

"You've got to be kidding me."

"Meri," he said, with a warning note.

"Rob," she mimicked.

"You were just in the hospital."

"What if I go in and find a coat?"

"And a hat," he said, fingering her cold ears. "You don't have much protection up here."

She loved it when he touched her with those long, strong fingers. She loved it a little too much. "You mean I don't have much hair. Fine, I'll get a hat."

"But not the scarf," he said. "Please."

"Whatever you say, sugar."

"Now you're just laying it on too thick."

Despite the icy fog, a small crowd had gathered near the Wedge. Another Harbor Patrol boat roared in as she and Rob made their way there. People were holding up their phones, taking pictures of an object stuck in the huge pilings. When Meri and Rob approached, one of the bystanders broke away to stare at his phone.

"Are they rescuing someone?" Rob said. "Is that a surfboard?"

"No, it's not a rescue operation," the man said. "Recovery. They found a body. Says it right here on the local news site."

Rob drew her away from the crowd. "You don't want to see this, do you?"

She craned her neck. "I doubt it's a surfer."

The man with the phone chimed in. "Probably a drunk who just washed up here. That's what happened to a lady at the marina last year. She was walking home from a bar and took a wrong turn off a dock. They didn't find her for days."

Rob steered her away from the group. "Let's go."

About an hour later, when Luke was down for his nap, they were sitting in the kitchen with Betty Jo when Meri's phone rang. "It's Carolyn's Dad again," she said, and answered.

Rob heard a choked-up voice say to Meri, "They found our girl at the beach. Drowned."

Betty Jo heard too. She clamped her hand over her mouth and stared out the window, horrified.

Rob had only met Carolyn once. He watched Meri, who seemed unnaturally calm as she spoke on the phone. After an initial stunned silence, she asked a few questions in a steady voice and listened. "I'll meet you there," she said and ended the call.

Expressionless, she turned to him. "I have to go. They need me."

"Where?" Rob said.

"The coroner's office," she said. "Mr. Ling shouldn't do this alone. His wife is beside herself. I could hear her wailing in the background. He doesn't want her to see Carolyn. I was her oldest friend and the one they know the best. They've known me since middle school. They were always very kind to me. I'll get ready." She walked upstairs, moving like a robot.

Rob insisted on driving her. Meri didn't try to argue. Other than thanking him twice, she said very little on the drive to the coroner's office. He found her extreme composure worrisome. He reached for her hand and held onto it. She didn't react or squeeze his hand in return; she only stared straight ahead.

Finally, while they were parking, she said, "I still can't quite accept that was Carolyn we saw in the rocks this morning. I feel like I should have known. I don't know why. They put a blanket over her, I guess. If you hadn't suggested we leave, I would have stayed and gossiped, waiting to hear more detail. I even wanted a better look. Now I'll get my wish."

Rob wondered if self-disgust—the only emotion she'd shown since hearing the news—was preferable to shock. He wasn't so sure.

The process of identifying the body didn't take long. Rob waited in the lobby with Mrs. Ling, a tiny lady who collapsed when she saw her husband's face as he and Meri emerged. No one said a word. They didn't have to.

Rob helped Mr. and Mrs. Ling out to their car. Meri drove them home while he followed. She only stayed a minute once she got them inside. "I can't help," she said, rejoining Rob. "What do you say to someone who's just lost their only child? I don't know what to say. But I have a lot of questions. I need to speak to someone who can explain what happened."

Her color had improved but he didn't like that eerie calm she maintained. "I'll make sure we find out who that is," he said. "The authorities may not know much just yet."

He made her go lie down when they got home and kept everyone away. While she slept, he made phone calls. A Detective Shyu had been assigned the case and said he'd come interview them the following night.

She didn't sleep long. When he went to check on her, she was wide awake and shivering, staring at the ceiling. He kept her beside him for the rest of the day. Luke played on the floor nearby and his presence seemed to help. She didn't eat much and remained silent and sad, finally falling asleep in his arms in front of the TV.

He checked on Meri at 8:00 on Monday morning. Still out cold. If sleep was a cure for shock, she was healing. He'd watched over her all last night, too aware of her soft, sweet curves cuddled up against him. And devastated as she was, he couldn't do much more than hold her.

He made a fresh pot of coffee and took advantage of the rare quiet time to get some work done.

She drifted into the kitchen at 9:00. With the morning sun at her back, her cotton nightgown was nearly transparent. Her long legs were outlined in all their delicate beauty. He re-settled himself in his chair.

"No work?" she said.

He gestured to his open laptop. "I have been working, but no, I'm not going in today. More important things to do. Get dressed and I'll make you some toast."

"Where is everybody?"

"At the park. The nanny is here too, so Mom has plenty of help. You don't have to worry about them."

Though her voice and manner were stiff, he was relieved to hear her chatting about inconsequential things. She'd need to talk about her friend sometime; however, as far as he was concerned, that talk could wait.

Cool air streamed through the open kitchen door. While Meri stood there checking out the clearing sky, he was treated to a side view through her thin nightie. She eventually noticed where his eyes lingered and hustled off into the shower.

He carried coffee and toast outside and waited for her. He put his head back and closed his eyes, listening to the distant lap of waves and the gulls calling to each other. Sunlight warmed his skin and sank into his bones. He rarely had a chance to kick back and sit for more than three minutes, much less relax, on a weekday morning.

She came out a few minutes later in a sweater and jeans, bringing the smell of citrus shampoo with her. "I miss my coffee mug."

"What's wrong with this one?"

"I have a thing for big mugs."

"That must be why you like me."

"Right, that must be why. No really, I just like drinking coffee out of big mugs. I used to have this giant stainless steel one at my office—everyone laughed at it. They called it my sippy cup. But I always knew which mug was mine. I even remembered to grab it when they walked me out of there. I lost track of it since. That's the problem with moving."

"What time is your appointment?" he asked.

"Is *that* the reason you didn't go to work? It's not necessary. I've been taking care of myself for quite some time, dear." She darted a quick look at him, checking to see if he'd noticed the endearment.

He reached out and easily pulled her onto his lap. Her soft bottom molded against his thighs. She shifted her weight. "Relax," he said. "I can't vouch for my control if you keep wiggling."

She sat very still. "The appointment is at 11."

Meri didn't know she could compartmentalize tragedy. But since that phone call, she had done that very thing, over and over. It only worked for short stretches, until the impact hit anew. Forgetting horror was either an amazing skill or just plain cold-blooded. Sitting here in the sun with Rob, she'd forgotten about Carolyn for a full minute. A peaceful minute. And now, back to reality. Yesterday had been real. Carolyn was dead. And she still could not understand how that could be true.

She relaxed into Rob's chest. "Do you know what Mr. Ling said to me in the car after we identified her body? He said he was glad I'd repaired the friendship. I didn't know what he meant. He said Carolyn used to talk about me all the time when we were kids—that she had always compared herself to me. The way he spoke, it was as if she and I had had a huge falling-out when we were teenagers. But we hadn't. I would have remembered that."

"You did the right thing, meeting them at the coroner's office," he said. "That took courage."

"I don't know," Meri said. "I feel vaguely guilty. Was she over here on Saturday looking for me? Her car wasn't parked here—her Dad told me her car was found a few blocks over yesterday. She didn't call me or anything. The last time we talked—Friday night when I was at the hospital—she said she had something important going on the next day. I remember she asked me if I'd be home on Saturday and I said probably not." She glanced at Rob as if embarrassed. "I kind of hoped I'd be here with you."

"I'm glad you hoped that," Rob said. "You had it right."

"I don't think her parents have a clue what happened. And they weren't in any shape to answer my questions or ask any of their own."

"They will, once they get over the shock. And get the full autopsy results."

"Carolyn liked to party, but she never partied alone. Men loved Carolyn and she loved them. Someone must have been with her Saturday night before she drowned. How could she have fallen in? Why was she out there on those rocks?"

"She may have washed up at the Wedge, but we don't know if that's where she started out. Or how long she was in the water."

Meri went on. "And then there's the question of the unlocked back door at my house. She definitely had a key. But I didn't see any sign of her yesterday morning. And what about the fact that I think Haskell was there also? Why would those two have been there together?"

"We don't know that they were. There's a lot we don't know. The cops will be asking questions. And if they don't, I'll take you down to the station myself. But first we need to get you to this doctor's appointment."

Rob won over the office staff with his charm, naturally. After the exam was over, he breezed in to join her for the consultation. Not that Meri minded. She was secretly grateful she didn't have to ask for him.

The pulmonologist pulled up various reports on his computer and perched nearby, turning the screen so they could see the results he'd compiled. Meri's doctor had sent over electronic files, plus various lab reports had been collected from different sources. For the first time, all her charts and results were assembled in one place.

"Once I heard you'd been admitted over the weekend," the doctor said, "I pulled some strings and got some of your tests re-done. Also I got some of the earlier samples and had them run a few more esoteric and unusual tox screens and analyses." He flipped his glasses up on top of his head and looked at Meri with a half-smile. "You're one for the books, Ms. Meri. One of the more interesting cases I've seen."

Rob cleared his throat. "We're glad you find her case interesting, doc, but maybe you could elaborate."

"First, and most serious, the samples."

Meri leaned forward, shaking off the apathy that had dogged her since yesterday. "What samples?"

"When you first became ill." He scrolled to find the dates. "Last October. Your doctor took all kinds of samples and tests. Those screens he ordered then were standard ones. He had no reason to suspect anything unusual so he didn't look for anything unusual. Here's where we got lucky. Some of the samples he collected back then were frozen. You may recall he collects samples for his own, unrelated research. Anyway, I was able to order more specific tox screens. These are not screens we ordinarily request. After all, none of your doctors is a forensic pathologist. The results just came in. Now we have our first break-through piece of information."

"Indicating what?" Meri said.

"Poison," he said. "Well, that may be putting it a bit dramatically, but in essence, you were exposed to something toxic."

She felt dizzy. "When?"

"The samples from—let's see, it's March now—four months ago—indicate the presence of heavy metals. These are not substances one would ordinarily ingest accidentally."

He went on. "And this exposure would have taken some time and I'm guessing—with my limited expertise—repeated exposure over an extended period. I'll be referring you to someone better suited to this sort of analysis. But at least you have an idea of where to start. This isn't going to be easy to come to terms with," he said, nodding at her and then Rob, in turn.

"What specifically poisoned her?" Rob said. "How? Something she ate? Something she breathed in? Accidental or deliberate?"

"I don't know any of that. I will say, however, that the exposure appears to have been systematic, over a period of weeks. It would explain why your hair fell out."

"*That's* why I lost my hair?"

"I believe so. You'll learn more, of course, as you go on. As to how this occurred, I can't say. Here's the good news. Your prognosis is good. The recent samples are normal. Whatever happened, you're recovering."

"So that's why I was so sick all those weeks last autumn? It wasn't from a virus or stress at all."

"That virus-like illness you suffered through—most likely from the same toxin."

"But it didn't kill me. What about in future? Residual effects?"

"No," the doctor said. "Not enough to kill you. Whatever it was, it was low, slow and steady exposure. You'll need to be followed, but my guess is, you're going to be all right. Now this next thing—"

"There's more?" Rob said. His features were chipped in stone.

"Plenty," the doctor said. "I ordered a more specific tox screen that revealed fentanyl in your system. Do you have a prescription for a pain killer that you forgot to tell us about?" His tone made it clear he knew she didn't have anything of the kind. Now he looked at her with part-suspicion, part-sympathy.

"Of course not," Meri said. "Why would I have that? It's a pretty strong opiate. Used for cancer patients, right?"

"That's correct. The tox screen I requested shows a very high level present the last time you went to the doctor."

"When was that?" Rob said.

"That would be...the day I was supposed to talk to the journalist, but I couldn't. That was when they caught me in my pajama top?"

The doctor's eyes went wide. "You do have an exciting life."

"I thought it was a relapse," Meri said. "But clearly something else must have happened. Something more sinister." The memory of that day made her dizzy and ill. "What about my respiratory problems? That's what sent me to the hospital a few days ago."

"Right," the doctor said, putting his glasses back on his nose. "Here we have yet another puzzle. Your asthma, as far as I can see from your records, hasn't been a serious problem until the past couple of months.

"So the breathing problems stem from the same exposure?"

"I don't think so. I believe your lung issues are probably unrelated."

"That's a relief," Meri said.

"Actually, it isn't," the doctor said. "I'm seeing evidence of insidious cumulative damage that can only be caused by inhaling ultrafine particles. I understand you're a scientist.

You know the surface area of adult lungs is big as a tennis court?"

"Okay," Meri said apprehensively.

"And the alveoli are more vulnerable than the airways. There's only a thin separation between blood and air. So damage is more likely to occur there than in your airways. What have you been exposed to, environmentally?"

"Did you breathe in manufacturing or lab fumes at work?" Rob said. "In the lab?"

She shook her head even as the doctor kept talking. "If that's the case—if you've been exposed to ultrafine particulates, those can travel deep into the lungs. And they clear from the lungs more slowly than larger particles. Whatever caused this, it's from something you inhaled—somewhere, somehow."

Rob and Meri exchanged glances and spoke at the same time. "The inhalers."

12

When they got home, Meri went right upstairs. Alone. She changed into comfy yoga pants and flopped onto Rob's bed. No. Rob and Julie's bed.

Questions bounced around her head in an endless game of pinball.

For months now, she'd thought Barranca wanted her sidelined, but not permanently silenced. Yes, he was willing to hang her out to dry in the process—making sure the world thought her greedy, stupid, or just one hot mess. He'd trashed her career, her credibility and character—making her look like a drug-addled idiot. As bad as all that was, she hadn't ever believed herself to be in serious danger. She thought she understood the game. She hadn't.

This—this was a killing game. And Carolyn's death couldn't be a coincidence.

If there was ever someone who could poison another person and get away with that, it would be Joe. He was a world-class expert in toxins. Some substances were approved by the federal drug administration, some were not. Bacterial toxins, in all their terrible beauty and ancient uses, were a particular specialty of his. If anyone knew about the intersection where beauty met death, it was Joe.

Rob came upstairs. "Let's get out of here. We've got a lot to talk about and I don't want to have these conversations near the family. We need privacy."

"What have you told Betty Jo?"

"Nothing. She only knows that you've been through a lot today."

She put her hands on her growling stomach. "I'm starving."

"I got that covered."

Her sensible self knew she ought to be focusing her energy on figuring out her next move. And yet right now, she didn't have the will to do anything except go along with his suggestions. For the moment, she'd allow herself to be swept along by his energy. His certainty that everything would turn out okay.

Rob tossed a basket in the back seat and opened the door for her.

"I smell fried chicken," she said.

"What else? It is a picnic. And I am from the south."

They drove down Coast Highway. By mutual agreement, they were taking a break from the insanity of the last few days and all the question marks that remained. They'd have to talk to the cops, probably tonight, but for now, he wanted to give her a break. She needed it and so did he.

Strip malls gave way to undeveloped foothills on the left. On the right, the ocean flashed in and out. As impossible to ignore as Meri was. The events of the last couple of days had left him reeling. She, on the other hand, projected that spooky calm again. Almost serene.

He took a left and proceeded through a stone entry into a new development.

"When did this road get built?" she said. "This canyon has been back country my whole life. You could only access it by hiking in through El Moro Canyon." She tipped her head to look at the rows of huge palm trees that stood like sentinels, newly installed with their fronds still bundled straight up. "Those palm trees are absurd here."

"Why absurd?"

"They're not native trees. Stuck in the middle of so much natural beauty—they remind me of giant can-can dancers with skirts up around their heads. A symbol of the development insanity. This was the last natural stretch of coastline in the county. I hate to see it disappear."

"It won't all disappear," he said. "See that canyon up there? That's designated as permanent open space. The developer announced it will never be built up. It'll stay that way."

"You're referring to all those steep and unstable hillsides?" she said, pointing. "Those are the designated open space?"

"Yes."

"So these developers blow their own horns and hire publicists to blather on about how environmentally sensitive they are—when all they're doing is taking credit for preserving land they can't build on anyway."

He shrugged. "You might try to see the positive aspects. If I didn't know you better, I might think you were a negative old crank instead of a young woman. Although— what are you—thirty? Maybe you are an old crank."

She didn't laugh.

They made a few turns and passed tracts of unfinished Mediterranean-style homes with busy construction crews and a platoon of earthmoving tractors. The farther they climbed, the larger the homes became, with three- and four-car garages and bigger lots. They kept driving up a single paved road that curved to the summit.

The homes trickled off. Here the land was virtually untouched, dotted with scrub sage and a few rusty boulders. California poppies flamed orange against the olive-brown hillside.

He pulled to the curb in a new cul de sac with a single Tuscan villa under construction. They got out and looked around. No one was here. No construction noise or workmen's shouts disturbed the hilltop. Only the rustle of wind in the sagebrush.

"Those people will have a great view, won't they?" Meri said. "With the ocean out the back and the canyon in front. And it smells so good up here. See, I can be positive. It's not that hard in such a beautiful setting. Are we looking for a trailhead?"

"No." He went back to the car and retrieved the basket and blanket. "Come on, I want to show you something."

She followed him, picking her way through the scrub bordering the dusty sidewalk. "You're not going to make me walk a mile before you feed me, are you?"

"Just a minute. I want to show you something," he repeated. He walked up a stone path that curved into the villa's courtyard.

"Should we be trespassing like this?"

"It's okay. No one's here. What do you think of this home?"

"It's not a home. It's a mansion. Do you know the owners?"

"The deed gets recorded tomorrow. And then the clock starts ticking. Until I get rid of the other house, I'll have two mortgages—and this one is a mother of a payment."

She froze. "Wait. *This* is your new house?"

"Close your mouth. You'll catch flies."

"I didn't know. You should have said."

He caught her hand in his. "I know it looks a little barren now. But the landscapers haven't finished yet. Once they landscape, it'll be a lot nicer. Much greener. Italian cypress will go there and there. The reflecting pool will get filled up, of course. Take a look at this wing. The architect was going for the Tuscan style. But then Julie told him she wanted the breezeways to have a Mission look. So I said fine, whatever the lady wants."

He realized his mistake right away. Meri's mouth had flattened. He gave a mental shrug. Nothing he could do about that now. She'd get over it. He went on. "So then our architect modified the plans and we ended up with a blend of styles."

She tried to smile and did a bad job of it. "Very nice. Shall we sit out here?"

Rob unlocked the front door. "You don't want a tour first?"

"Ah, sure. Let's do it."

Their footsteps echoed on the marble in the foyer. He took her straight through to the back wing. The kitchen would impress her with its giant windows and gourmet appliances. Every woman who'd been here loved this kitchen.

He showed her all the features. She didn't say a word about the center island that was bigger than a bedroom. She only nodded, her face a polite mask.

And now, even to him, the space looked more like a cold cavern than a kitchen. Marble countertops cast a blue-gray gloom on the unfinished space. An oversized chandelier dangled over the vacant spot meant for a kitchen table.

He showed her the wide window that overlooked the terraced hillside. You could see for miles up and down the coast. Surely she couldn't deny this view was a jaw-dropper. He really wanted her to love it. Everyone else considered the house spectacular.

She murmured polite noises without really saying anything.

He should have known better. Meri wasn't everyone.

Meri tried to say all the appropriate things. The effort gave her a headache, but she would keep up the pretense for as long as necessary. Rob was so proud. To him, this was the ultimate achievement. Who was she to rain on his parade?

In the formal front room, shrink-wrapped taupe sectionals waited to be assembled. Since the scale of the rooms was ginormous, the furniture had to be equally ginormous, she supposed. That sofa would comfortably seat six ogres.

"Custom-designed," he confirmed, nodding at the sofa and an intimidating table in the dining room. "Cost me two arms and two legs."

She laughed uneasily.

Half the house would never be used for anything other than parties. Perhaps that's why he wanted this showplace. Although—what kind of neighborhood would this be for Luke? His grandmother or the nanny would have to drive him everywhere. She forced another smile. "Well, it's interesting. When will it be finished?"

"A couple of weeks."

She told herself to be happy for him. This was what he wanted. According to his mom, his lifelong dream. Rob's life. Rob's dream.

Not hers. Her parents had split up smack in the middle of building a lavish home they had called their 'dream house'. An already shaky union had collapsed under the weight of the expensive project. The family never moved in and they'd sustained a heavy loss. Her father still spoke bitterly about that big house. Her mother never discussed it. She'd moved into a grand home with her next husband and chose to forget.

When Meri declined a tour of the bedrooms, he took her elbow. "Let's have that picnic."

They spread the blanket on a clean corner of the back terrace and sat near the ledge that overlooked his steep backyard. While Rob told her about plans for an infinity pool, she unpacked the picnic. Betty Jo's fried chicken, a sliced baguette, fruit, and chocolate chip cookies. She noticed champagne in its own cooler. Neither of them made a move to open it. They ate in silence.

Leave it to her to fall in love with a man who wanted the lifestyle she'd rejected long ago. If anyone had told her she'd find herself in this position, she wouldn't have believed them.

Rob said, "What's funny?"

"Nothing."

She wrapped up the leftovers and packed them away, standing up to shake the crumbs off. She needed to go back to her own life, the life interrupted months ago. Only problem being, now she was a different person. Now she would know what she'd been missing. Before meeting him and his family, she hadn't thought of love in a homey, everyday sort of way. What it felt like when you had someone looking out for you, making sure you ate right and taking care of you.

She hadn't known how it felt to have her presence truly matter. To anyone. And then there was the sexual tension—the promise of that kind of loving every night? If it were anything nearly as good as that one time, she'd be missing out on the best.

Rob stepped into the backyard strewn with construction debris and cigarette stubs. "I have to talk to the contractor about cleaning this garbage up. See that big rock there in the corner?"

"That's not a rock. It's a boulder."

"Want to see?"

"Hell, yes." For the first time since she'd gotten out of the car, she felt genuinely glad for him and for Luke. Glad father and son would have this new adventure. They had each other and they would be fine once they were settled in their new home.

He reached for her hand and together, they scrambled to the top of the boulder.

"How cool is this?" she said. "Luke will love it when he's older."

"Or now. I wouldn't put it past him to get up here on his own."

"Me neither," she said. "Nice that you didn't move this when they graded the property."

"Nice had nothing to do with it. It weighs a ton. We left this bad boy right where we found it." He took a deep breath. "So, here's what I wanted to talk about. I think you should move up here with us."

She turned her head slowly. "You're not serious."

"Yes, I'm serious. When I sell the beach house, we can all move up here. You'll have time to look for a better job. Or not. Whatever you want. My mom wants to go back to Tennessee soon, but we can keep Letty on. I'll give her a raise to make up for the longer drive." He paused. "Why are you looking at me like that?"

His hopeful expression tore at her. She thought her heart ached a few minutes ago, but that had been a superficial wound. As tempting as it was to leap off this rock and walk away, she owed him an answer. "It's way too soon."

"Too soon? You've known us for months." He looked closer. "What?"

"I'm sorry. I didn't expect this. You surprised me." She walled her pain behind a resolute face.

He waited a beat. "Are you going to elaborate?"

"This is not me," she said, jabbing her thumb at the stucco monstrosity behind her. "I don't want this life. It's your dream. And Julie's. Not mine. I'm not her. I will never be like her."

"Who's asking you to be? So it's the house you object to," he said, lifting a strand of hair stuck to her cheek.

"No. Your house is lovely. For you. We want different things. And if you're honest, you'll admit we're not exactly well suited." She held up her hand. "Let me finish. I know you weren't proposing, but someday you'll need a wife. Someone to organize parties and run a big home like this.

Someone who's into being a rich man's wife. Knows how to socialize and how to support you in your goals. You're not going to find her if I'm in the picture." She looked down the hillside, her gaze unfocused. "I take that back. You will find her. And I don't want to be here to see that happen. That will really suck, watching you fall in love with someone right in front of me."

"What are you talking about?"

"I think you're on the rebound."

"It's been two years," he said.

"Yeah, and how many relationships have you had since your wife died? How many people have you slept with?"

"Two. Since you're asking."

"Oh," she said, taken aback, wishing she didn't feel hurt. "So there was someone else before me. My mistake."

"I didn't care about her. I would have hooked up with anyone that particular night. It was the day after Luke's first birthday. I got a babysitter and went out drinking at the Balboa Bay Club with some friends, so desperate and horny I went home with the first woman I met that night—friend of a friend. She was hot. We had sex. That's it."

"But you didn't see her again? Even though she was hot?"

"I said she was hot. I didn't say I liked her."

"So that *is* a requirement." She closed her eyes, disgusted with herself. "Sorry."

The rising afternoon wind filled the silence. One part of her wanted to put aside misgivings. Misgivings as big as this boulder. He'd have the same doubts, once he thought about it. Once he had some perspective.

"Anyway," he said. "Point taken. I agree it might appear I'm on the rebound. Except—I'm not."

"You've heard about widowers and remarrying too soon, haven't you?"

"I can see you're burning to tell me."

"A lot of men who've lost their wives take up with someone else very quickly. Too quickly. And eventually, when the lust wears off, they find themselves tied to a woman they might not have chosen under normal circumstances. I'm surprised no one's warned you about this."

He rolled over her objection like it was an old can in the road. "If you need extra time to be convinced, you can have it. And I didn't mention marriage because I didn't want to scare you off. So here's plan b. I'll consider a long engagement. We'll get married whenever you want. I remember how complicated wedding plans can be. We could have the ceremony here. I'll bet we could fit 200 people back here."

Meri shuddered. She wasn't poor Julie. He might as well get that through his head. "You're not listening."

"I'm trying to," he said, sliding from the rock and reaching for her hands to help her down. "You keep changing your story. First, it's the house. Then it's not the house. It's our values—even though we like being together. Then you come up with a new excuse. Now you say I'm on the rebound. You're one confused lady, Meri."

"Maybe I'm sensible."

"Maybe pigs fly." He left her, climbing the slope back to the house. "I'm going to lock up. Do you want to come in? Use the bathroom before we go?"

"No." She walked around the yard while she waited for him, kicking cardboard coffee cups into a pile. This was the right thing to do. Going along with his plans would lead to even bigger heartbreak later. His ambitions and choices would mean leading a life she couldn't tolerate. Even if she learned to shoehorn herself into the role of a manicured wife, how long could they last? Only as long as she denied her real self.

She followed a red-tailed hawk's gliding circles above the adjacent canyon. If she ignored the patchwork of green suburbs edging up the scrubby hills, she could almost forget where she was. And forget about time passing. The afternoon was almost over. Down deep, she had never believed she was wife and mother material anyway. She knew exactly who she was. The fun auntie. The last thing she could ever be was the kind of woman he needed.

Rob came out of the house, seemingly cheerful and relaxed. He offered up the smile she had come to consider her very own, the one he reserved for her. She had rejected him a few minutes ago and he was barely fazed. As if she hadn't said anything at all.

He gently spun her around to face the canyon. Then he lifted her hair and kissed the back of her neck. "If you need more convincing," he said, sliding his hands up her back, kneading her shoulders, "I can remind you of how great we are together."

"Oh, I'll remember," she said, laughing a little, dying inside. Her bottom pressed into his thighs.

"Maybe I won't take no for an answer," he whispered, tickling her ear. Her eyes fluttered closed and she forgot everything except his soft heated lips on her skin. He kissed his way down to the hollows above her tailbone, punctuating his kisses with endearments. "You'll say 'yes'…yes I need you…yes we need each other…you can't deny this. You know it's true, Meri, so why pretend otherwise?" He held her hips and with relentless skill, kissed his way back up her spine.

His cock pressed into her rear, insistent. Demanding she acknowledge his need. She pushed back with desire just as hot and stubborn. She stood on her tip toes, letting his erection tease her sensitive cleft. One last time.

She even laughed. As did he. His hand came down her belly and then lower, searching. He touched her with a pulsing rhythm. To pay her back. She understood; she was past laughing now.

He stayed behind her. One of his hands roamed her breasts. The other started a fire. He slipped his hand inside her waistband and slid down her belly, then farther, moving his long fingers between her legs. She moaned low in her throat. He taunted with the heel of his palm pressed hard above her clitoris. He moved his lips to her neck while his thumb made hard circles verging, but never on, the center of her need. She pushed against him, matching the tempo he set.

"Please," she begged. He continued to taunt her, first low, then high. Finally he muttered something about not being able to wait anymore. She was so lost in need she didn't notice at first that he had put her hands on the rail as if to brace her. He kneeled, slipped her jeans down and moved her panties aside. Then his quick tongue was there, promising fulfillment, taking her way past arousal. He licked just off-center until she could have screamed in frustration.

"Here it is now, love," he whispered. His breath tickled her there. Even that was erotic. Her whole body trembled. "I've got you. Hold still and I'll give you what you need." She squeezed her eyes shut, overwhelmed. Then quivered when he held her inner thighs to hold her steady. "Relax. Let me take care of you."

She shook when his tongue, pointed and hard darted into her. A few hard flicks had her bearing down on a piercing need. She convulsed and cried out. She would have collapsed on the ground if he hadn't caught her. Then he was on his feet, turning her in his arms.

"You now," she said. She unzipped him, stepped out of her pants and braced her back on the wall, heedless of the scratchy stone. "Oh damn it. I don't have a condom." She could have cried. She almost did cry.

He kissed her so sweetly then. "It's okay, we can wait. I can wait."

"I can't," she said. "It's a safe time. And it's my last…"
She had almost said her last chance to make love to him.
She grabbed the base of his cock and claimed him.

"Are you sure," he said, groaning the words and then
entered with a long possessive stroke. He took his pleasure
fast. She welcomed the strong thrusts. She wouldn't have
been satisfied with anything less. She wanted to give him
what he had given her, complete and profound relief. He
groaned deeply and she thought he was going to come.
Instead he withdrew and turned her to face the canyon
again, back where they started. He bent her forward, held
her shoulders and entered her from behind.

"Too deep?" he asked hoarsely. She shook her head and
tilted so he could penetrate deeper. That drove him over
the edge and he pounded for the last few strokes. He came
with a moan that almost became a shout when she
squeezed the last drop out of him.

"Now tell me we don't belong together," he said, still
grasping her shoulders as he kissed his way up her neck.
"You know we do, sugar. I love you."

Flushed in afterglow, she shivered as her body cooled.
How crazy, she thought, that her first whole-body
orgasm—the intense kind she'd heard about but never
experienced—happened now, quite possibly the last time
she'd be with him. And how crazy that he'd just told her
he loved her. Now—right when she couldn't let herself
believe any of this. The sense of intimacy, so vivid a minute
before, faded. The gulf between them was palpable, though
he was still right here.

Until she shivered in his arms, he didn't notice the
advancing fog. The sun would disappear any minute. He
wrapped the picnic blanket around her and sat her down
on the back steps.

He started out strong, like he'd planned. "I love you."
He paused. Her thunderstruck expression wasn't the

ecstatic one he'd hoped for but he barreled on. His mind was made up and he was determined to have his say. "I want you to be happy. I don't want you to dumb down or polish up or whatever crazy notion you have. I know you're not Julie. I loved her too, but not in the same way. This is stronger—I know it already. You have passion, intelligence. You're great with Luke. He needs a mother and he already loves you and you love him."

"It's not fair to use your son."

"Why not? If it gets me what I want. End justifies the means. Plus, I need a strong partner. I get that now. I didn't know what I was missing."

He watched her carefully. She chewed her lip and though she wouldn't meet his eyes, he suspected she was on the fence. She needed a little push. He'd only thought of the next idea on the drive here, but hey, whatever it took.

"Listen up. Plan c," he said. "When you do move in with us or we get engaged—your choice—I guarantee you'll have a shot at your dream research. That vitamin lotion stuff you talked about? Let me handle the business side. I can make it happen."

Her eyes were hard chips of bottle-green glass. "Why are you talking like this, like you're negotiating a business deal?"

"Come on. You're not usually so touchy. I see opportunities. It's my instinct. And it's carried me right here. To the back steps of my big new home. With a beautiful woman. I've been working for this moment my whole life. So—what do you say?"

She glanced around like a cornered animal. "This is all too much. My friend died yesterday. This morning I learned I was poisoned. Now I'm getting a marriage proposal? It's too much to take in. I can't believe you'd expect me to try."

"Relax, will you?"

"I don't know how to make you understand."

"Just go along with me. Let me take charge."

He expected her to argue with him again, but she didn't. She only watched him with a hopeless, strained expression, like she'd given up on him.

Ten minutes later, they were driving down the hill too fast. After Rob squealed through a second turn, she asked him to slow down. His choice of words had been revealing, she thought, when he'd told her how much he cared. Every other word had been "I". He probably did care, but all these plans were more about *him* than anything else. That speech and his conditions for marrying convinced her she'd been right to turn him down. He had known her weak points and didn't hesitate to exploit them. He'd known what to use as leverage. His son. Her work. Their lovemaking. Spectacular sex wasn't enough to build on. Although it might have been fun trying.

Her instincts for self-preservation were finally kicking in. She'd fallen for a man who had no hesitation about manipulating people to get his way. And he'd almost succeeded. She had seen his caring side and believed that's who he really was. When in fact, he'd coldly calculated every move.

He was silent all the way home. That jaw, set so firmly and stubbornly, pretty much said it all. He was a steamroller. And he'd run over her one time too many.

13

Betty Jo met them at the door. "There's a Detective Shyu from the Newport Beach Police Department waiting to see you Meri. He's in the kitchen."

A rather young-looking detective sat with a cup of coffee, watching Luke play with blocks. He stood to shake her hand. "Need to ask you a few questions," he said, "about Carolyn Ling and the night she died."

"I've been expecting you," Meri said. "We have a lot to talk about." Betty Jo hovered in the kitchen looking scared, and Rob braced his arms on the back of a chair, about as fed up as she'd ever seen him. She'd spare them from having to witness this conversation. They'd had enough stress. "I'd like to move the conversation to my house, detective. A few doors down from here."

"No problem."

"I'll just run and get my things," Meri said, reassuring Betty Jo with a smile. To Rob, she said, "Can I have a word?" He nodded and followed her upstairs.

When they were alone, she said, "I'll go over to Jordan's tonight, after I'm done talking with the detective. Then you can relax and stop worrying about me. One less thing on your plate, right?" She crammed items into her tote bag and grabbed her toothbrush from the bathroom. "Okay?"

"I agree," he said stiffly, looking at the floor. "You should move on. Better for all of us."

His words were a kick in the teeth. But he spoke the

truth. This was the right choice.

"And then," she said, "I'll be driving north in a few days."

"I thought the conference was next week."

"I have friends up there. Job possibilities."

He met her in the middle of the room and threaded his hands through her hair. The heels of his palms were warm and strong behind her ears. He finally met her eyes. She saw mingled fear and animosity in his. Yet even now, his hands steadied and soothed her. She blinked. No matter when or where, his touch always made her feel good. Better than good. She almost raised her hands to his face, and then stopped herself in time.

He let go. "You *will* follow up with that new doctor they want you to see? You need to figure out how you were poisoned and the ramifications. Which reminds me, where are those inhalers—the ones we think are corrupted? They're evidence."

"I'll find them."

"The cops need to be briefed. That guy downstairs better listen to you. If he doesn't, you let me know. This needs to end. If the police don't deal with him soon, I'll go after Barranca myself."

"You wouldn't do that," she said, resigned to the lecture. She didn't mind his bossiness now that they were about to say goodbye. He was simply being himself—strong and stubborn. Like her.

"Sitting on my hands isn't an option so you better keep me informed. After what he's done to you, I'd love to go after him."

"Don't even think it. You have a family to consider. Luke needs you." Another reason to get herself out of here. The most important reason of all—to draw the circling sharks away. If anyone got hurt, she'd never forgive herself.

She looked around one last time. "I guess that's it." She had been safe here. And cared for. Rob and his family—

they'd given her so much. She was departing a much healthier woman. Not happier, but that was a different matter. Her happiness was her own issue, her own responsibility, not his.

"I want you to know I'll always be grateful for everything you've done for me." She tried to kiss him goodbye, but he turned at the last second so that her lips brushed his jaw.

Once downstairs, she hugged Betty Jo and Luke and then joined the detective, getting away before they saw her weep.

Detective Shyu scratched his jaw. "So you're alleging this Dr. Barranca was involved with your friend's death. If you'd told me this last night, you would have gotten a different reaction. However, a lot of people want a piece of this Barranca guy. After I spoke to your friend—"

"What friend?" she interrupted.

"Robert McLain," the detective said, searching her face. "Isn't that the guy I just met?"

"Yes," she said. "Of course. I didn't know you two had already talked."

"Yesterday and then again this afternoon. Which was the first I heard of these allegations that you'd been poisoned."

Meri sat back, at a loss. He'd talked to this detective *twice* without even mentioning it to her. Were these misguided attempts to protect her or high-handed controlling tactics? Did it matter anymore?

"This case is a mushroom cloud," Detective Shyu added. "It just keeps spreading. Already today I talked with regional federal investigators from multiple agencies. Both the FBI and the Securities and Exchange Commission have opened investigations."

"I didn't know that."

"At least one of the securities investigators interviewed

your friend some weeks ago. About another matter."

"Who—Carolyn?" she asked.

"No," he said patiently. "McLain." He watched her. She could see he wondered if her reasoning ability was impaired. Maybe it was. SEC people had questioned Rob? Why wouldn't he mention that?

"Do you know why?" she asked.

"I'm not at liberty to say. But let's return to you—this afternoon he told me you have reason to believe you were poisoned by this Barranca guy, or by someone who worked for him?"

She looked at the ceiling in frustration. Events had swirled out of control. Not that she'd had much control over this drama to begin with. "I do, yes, but I want to talk about Carolyn first. Can you tell me anything about—about how she actually died? The cause of death?"

"We'll have preliminary autopsy results tomorrow morning. Final results will take a lot longer. Toxicology—easily six to twelve weeks."

"That long?"

"It's a process," he said.

"Joe is extremely knowledgeable about all kinds of toxic substances. He would also know which would be difficult to trace."

"Duly noted. Even after the cause of death is established, it'll take time to build a case."

Anger kindled in her gut. Barranca wouldn't get away with these crimes, no matter how powerful he was. She'd do whatever she had to do. After that...after that she'd figure out how to get through the rest of her life.

Detective Shyu pushed his card across the table. "Meanwhile, one of the federal investigators from back East said he's already got plans to meet you in San Francisco."

"The conference next week," Meri said.

"It's good you're already in touch with the experts," he

said. "Definitely not my area."

"It's not a problem if I leave town?"

"I'll get back to you." He tapped his pen against his knee. "This case is getting more convoluted by the minute. Quite a leap from white collar crime to murder and back again."

"How long will it take to bring charges?"

"Hard to say. If even half these allegations are true, something will stick. In the meantime, keep a low profile."

They talked for over an hour. The young detective hadn't been gone for more than five minutes when the doorbell rang again. He must have thought of another question.

She swung the door open. "What did I—"

It her took a full second to identify the man in front of her. Not a stranger. Bryan Haskell. In that one slow-motion moment, she registered his changed appearance. A soul patch goatee grew on his chin, and he'd become a dirty blond.

She didn't have a chance to speak, much less scream. He shoved a cloth into her face. She lashed out at him. Hard fingers dug into her cheekbones and acrid fumes burned through her nasal cavities. Then darkness.

Rob had just tossed the garbage into the cart when a white van moved through the dark alley. Vans weren't common in this neighborhood. Maybe that's why he looked twice. No markings, other than a rental company name on the license plate frame. None of his neighbors drove a white van.

With an involuntary glance at Meri's house, he headed back inside to finish his catch-up reading for work. Not that he'd actually comprehended any of it. He couldn't stop remembering her face after he'd rebuffed her kiss. That ripple of hurt she'd quickly masked with a parting smile. He'd wanted to inflict pain and he had. The petty satisfaction hadn't lasted more than a split second.

Rob had almost reached his doorstep when he heard a screech. The van, now out of sight, had taken the turn too fast. Once on the street, the van peeled out. He thought for maybe two seconds. Then he ran.

He reached her front door and burst in. "Meri!"

He called her name again and checked all the rooms. The lights were on and a glass of water sat on her kitchen table, along with her phone. He sprinted home to grab his keys. "Meri's in trouble," he yelled up to his mom. "I'll call you." And then he jumped in his car and took off. There was no time to call anyone.

The van had a significant head start; however, only one major boulevard linked this peninsula to the mainland. To reach Coast Highway or the freeway, the driver had to take the boulevard. Multiple traffic lights and congestion all but guaranteed stop and go traffic all the way to the bridge spanning the inner harbor. After that, the van would either get on Coast Highway or keep going inland, straight on to the freeway. He'd never find it after that. He had to locate that van before it crossed the bridge.

Meri surfaced and knew right away she was moving. But confined. The floor vibrated beneath her. A car, then. Something else, something dark hemmed her in. A canvas bag? She struggled to make sense of this and on an intake of breath, got a dizzying lungful of whatever it was he'd used to knock her out. A foul-smelling cloth cut into the corners of her mouth. She couldn't reach for the gag or spit it out. Her hands were tied. And her feet. She kicked and bucked and got nowhere. An attempt to scream produced only a muffled grunt.

Impossible not to hyperventilate. A weight held her down. Too strong. Just like when she was a kid and a wave's churning pressure kept her down. She wasn't underwater now. But she couldn't get out of this bag. And she couldn't breathe. The acrid smell overpowered her. When the darkness came again, she was almost grateful.

After an interminable ten minutes creeping along Newport Boulevard, Rob glimpsed a white van in the right lane about fifteen cars ahead. When the light changed, Rob weaved through traffic, prompting a few angry honks. He'd narrowed the gap to about seven cars as they approached the bridge.

Once over the channel, the van took the ramp for Coast Highway. Rob followed and joined the traffic flowing south on a commercial stretch. The van drove fast but he kept pace, still seven or eight cars behind. At Jamboree, the van's driver floored it through a yellow light. Rob got stuck there, fuming and struggling to maintain visual contact. The van sped south and Rob kept his eyes on the white blur until it disappeared over a rise. He used the button on his steering wheel to call the police. When the light changed, he accidentally hung up on the dispatcher.

He accelerated and tore ahead. A bit of luck gave him a clear stretch after the intersection. He drove as fast as he could, straining to catch another glimpse. Yacht brokers and restaurants lining Coast Highway gave way to office buildings and strip malls.

Far ahead, a white vehicle turned right. When Rob reached that turn, he took it. The dead-end street wound around the back of the harbor, with private entrances to yacht clubs and marine businesses. There were numerous parking lots and driveways but no sign of the van. He called the police again while he drove in and out of four or five lots, constantly swiveling his head. That van had to be here somewhere. At the end of the street, he noticed a small sign for a public launch site. Close to ten minutes ticked by while he searched through rows of parked cars.

Finally, he spotted a white van nearly hidden behind a charter rental shack. Rob pulled in next to it. He checked the van, which appeared empty, and then sprinted to the marina. It was fairly quiet at this time of night and the docks were empty. A large yacht slowly navigated a narrow side channel. In the distance, a sailboat rounded a corner, about to merge into the main channel. He ran back to the rental shack.

A leathery man looked up from the desk. "We're closed."

"Did the person driving that white van charter a boat from you in the last few minutes?"

The man shook his head. "No."

Rob looked out at the harbor in desperation, casting about for another possibility.

The man said, "No, I mean he chartered it this afternoon. A Catalina 30. He said he was coming back with his gear later. Which he did. Then he took off a little while ago. Twenty-four hour rental."

"We have an emergency," Rob said. "Call Harbor Patrol."

While he waited, Rob checked the locked van. It told him nothing.

A Harbor Patrol vehicle pulled up and a Newport Beach police cruiser arrived almost at the same time. Rob told the officers what he knew about Haskell, which wasn't much. He couldn't even remember the man's first name. The charter guy verified that he'd rented a boat to a thirtyish white guy and witnessed him lugging a very large gear bag onboard.

The Harbor Patrol deputy began a squawking exchange with his dispatcher. Their back and forth dialogue proceeded at a maddeningly slow pace, with none of the urgency Rob wanted—that Meri needed—*right now*. The police officer, meanwhile, left on another call, explaining that his department would coordinate with Harbor Patrol.

Rob stood on the windy dock with his only hope—a deputy who, while friendly, did not seem unduly concerned or inclined to react quickly.

"The Harbormaster is on his way," the deputy said.

Rob examined the Harbor Patrol insignia on the deputy's uniform. These officers were competent professionals—he could see that. But he wanted more than competence and Meri needed every possible advantage.

"So you're actually with the County Sheriff's Department?" Rob asked. The deputy nodded.

"Here's a coincidence," Rob said. "I manage a big chunk of your pension fund." It was true. He did. "We outperformed the market last year. I'm expecting pretty decent returns this year for you officers." He'd never say such a thing—practically promise results—under ordinary circumstances. But the deputy had no way of knowing that.

The officer immediately perked up. He asked Rob a few questions about his pension. Rob patiently answered, though it was the last thing he wanted to talk about.

The Harbormaster, a man who introduced himself as Lieutenant Jack, arrived on the scene. Rob didn't have to repeat himself. The deputy briskly explained the situation and even reported Rob's connection to their pension fund.

"Do you know this man's destination?" Lieutenant Jack asked.

Rob shook his head, more than ready for action of some sort. "Maybe I should just rent a boat and go after her myself."

"Sir, that's not advisable. There's a small craft advisory in place."

And indeed, high winds buffeted the marina, noticeably gustier than usual, blowing from the east in wild gusts.

"Nights like this, the wind roars down the canyons," Lieutenant Jack said. "It comes through those hills and blasts out to sea. This is not a night for a landlubber."

Nausea woke her. Then a rocking motion. A raw wind cut through the opaque bag she'd been stuffed into. *Was this a body bag?*

Her breathing and heart rate sped up as panic took over. She fought for control. Forcing herself to calm down, she breathed in and out, conscious of every short, precious breath. If she got sick now, she would choke on it and probably suffocate before he had a chance to kill her. She didn't want to die like this, trapped in a bag. If she had to die, let it be under the sky, the stars, or the water. Not here.

The movement beneath her had changed. Not humming like an engine and not rocking as much as skimming, rising, then falling. She heard hollow, muffled slaps of water. Sailing. She was sailing. In a fairly quiet zone. Maybe not quite out of the harbor? She listened carefully to the snap of the sail, the rattle of rigging, and a man talking to himself. Haskell. The crazy bastard.

He'd gotten her after all. And it didn't look good. Why would he drag her out here if *not* to feed her to the fishes? Once he tossed her overboard, that would be that. Tied up and crammed in this bag, she didn't have a chance. Even if by some miracle she freed herself and swam for it, hypothermia would kill her in a matter of minutes.

The air turned colder as they headed into the wind. At least she thought that's what that were doing. She huddled into the fetal position. Exposure might kill her before Haskell did. She was wearing the same yoga pants and light jacket she'd worn up on the hill with Rob earlier. Today? Yesterday? A lifetime ago. She had no idea how long she'd been unconscious.

His muttering had increased. He bitched about the motor, the obstacles, and the fickle wind. The mainsail waffled. He didn't know what he was doing.

"Haskell," she called through the bag. The word came out garbled.

"Huh. You're not dead after all." He wasn't far away so she must be in the cockpit.

She tried again. "Where are we?"

"I can't understand you. You're gagged, fool. Plus you're in a bag. What are you doing in there? You should get out." He laughed, short and ugly.

She didn't give up. "Where are we?"

"Just shut up, would you? I have no idea what you're saying. Be quiet. We're not going far."

She didn't like the sound of that. But he hadn't tossed her overboard yet. That gave her a shred of hope.

She worked at the gag for a while with her jaw, tongue and even her teeth. Though still nauseating, the fumes had subsided. Soon the gag had loosened. "Where are we going?" she called, only slightly garbled now.

"A marina."

"Which one?"

"I'm going to San Pedro. *You* won't be going that far."

She felt sick again. He would need a very good reason not to toss her overboard. She raised her voice. "Why?" He didn't say anything. She tried again. "Why are you going there?"

He laughed. "You sound retarded. I'm having a conversation with a retarded gear bag. The adventure begins. I guess it doesn't matter now. You're already dead."

She heard him move. *Oh, God, was this it?*

The zipper ripped open and the wind whipped her face. Haskell hovered above her, a vague outline. She blinked. Even the night sky seemed too bright. He yanked the gag down below her chin. Then he zipped the bag up again.

"That special needs voice was annoying me," he said, moving away. "Joe's yacht is moored up there. He's waiting for me—or he will be, once he gets away from that spoiled brat he lives with. We're casting off for Mexico in the morning."

She'd had no idea that Bryan Haskell and their boss were romantically involved. Joe had often referred to Derek—his domestic partner and eventual husband—as the love of his life. Everyone thought they were happily married.

"San Pedro is a long sail," she called. "It's not easy at night, especially if you haven't done it before. You'll need help. I'm an experienced sailor." She wasn't, but from the sound of things, she knew more than he did. "What kind of boat is this?"

"It's a 30-footer."

"It's not easy to sail a 30-footer alone."

He snorted. "You always did underestimate me. I saw it on your face every time we met. You thought you were hot shit and people like me only existed to serve you or get in your way. Didn't you."

Her throat hurt. She needed water. "What are you planning to do with me?"

"You'll find out soon enough," he said. He made a noise of frustration. Was he talking to himself again? She strained her ears and in a moment of calm, heard him mutter, "Why won't he answer?"

The sails filled with a loud crack, a sudden gust. Next she heard a thud when the boom made contact with something. Haskell cried out.

Hope soared and then was dashed when he cursed and jostled the boat with a series of bumbling movements. He must not have seen the boom coming. He had no idea what the hell he was doing out here. Other than disposing of her.

But this gave her an advantage. Her only advantage.

Her bag tumbled to one side when the boat listed. He cursed again as he tried to maintain control. Even the boat felt confused as he vacillated, trying one maneuver after another. He was getting more frustrated by the second so she bided her time, waiting till his anger settled into anxiety. A few minutes passed.

From all the rattling and flapping, she guessed he hadn't turned far enough into what must be a very brisk wind. He didn't understand how to harness its energy. Which meant they were sailing far slower than necessary. Desperate to get out of the bag, she gathered her breath and yelled, "So you know about all the shoals, right?"

Silence.

She tried again. "There's hazards all along the coast."

"So?"

"There's one infamous shoal by the Queen Mary. It's tricky. A lot of people get in trouble there." A friend had run aground there once. That tidbit was the extent of her hazard knowledge. "I can show you where it is."

"You won't show me anything." He cursed again. "Shit, it's cold out here. No one told me it would get this cold."

"If you'll let me crew, I can cut your sailing time in half. Don't you want to arrive in half the time? Get out of this wind sooner?"

The boat shifted and rebalanced. He was moving again. With no one at the tiller, the mainsail flapped, echoing the so-called captain's confusion. She heard the squeak of his sneakers as he came closer.

He'd had enough. He was going to throw her overboard.

14

Joseph Barranca had been surprised and grateful to fall in love at age sixty-two. Even now, ten years in, their mutual devotion was the envy of all their friends. He knew how lucky he was. He also understood the need for compromise and tough choices that other people, including his husband, could simply not comprehend or accept gracefully.

Tonight, for instance, he had told a little white lie about indigestion. He'd been soaking in their huge marble tub for an hour now, to avoid Derek's hurt stare. Sidestepping amorous overtures was the most practical solution. For them both.

There was no way he could fully satisfy his much-younger husband this evening, not without resorting to a pill and he simply never did that. He prided himself on his natural potency. He didn't do pills, not any sort, except aspirin or the like. Even that was a rare weakness. Admirers often commented on the irony of a pharmaceutical wizard who hated taking pills. He'd long ago accepted this eccentricity in himself. And so had Derek, once they'd committed to each other.

He nabbed his phone from the side of the tub and read five long messages from Bryan Haskell, the love-struck moron. He'd gone rogue with these plans and assumptions about their future together. Had Bryan *seen* Derek? Why would Joe give up a trophy like Derek? As if rolling around the captain's quarters of his new yacht constituted a relationship. Talk about wishful thinking.

Derek hated the drive up to San Pedro so it was the one place Joe had all to himself, ideal for extracurricular activity. But that's all it was. If Bryan had been stupid enough to believe sweet nothings whispered in his ear, tough luck.

Pragmatism always held sway. From the start, Joe had intended to send him away after he'd played his part. And if Bryan hadn't misbehaved, he would indeed have received a tidy sum to sail off into the sunset. Possibly to Mexico where no questions would be asked and he wouldn't have had to work another day in his life. Pretty good for someone like Bryan, a man of middling intelligence and looks.

Regrettably, a different solution would now be required. Bryan's most recent text said he had decided to deliver the package to San Pedro. He'd be dealt with. Joe really preferred to hire someone for this sort of thing and always hired through an intermediary to protect himself. He'd been meticulous thus far, but time was critical and Haskell a loose cannon. He'd eliminate Bryan himself tomorrow morning.

Outside the bathroom window, a Queen palm rattled in the wind. A fierce offshore wind tonight. Not good news for the drought-ravaged canyons.

Joe's fingers hesitated and stilled as he planned his next move. This turn of events meant certain variables and possibilities were still in play. What he really ought to do was ensure a complete clusterfuck for Meri Darrow and that annoying fund manager—just in case. He quickly texted new instructions to his man on call.

Haskell unzipped the bag and yanked the gag around her chin to pull her upright. "If you want to crew," he said,

"then crew. Make yourself useful instead of a dead weight."
He moved back to the stern. "Ha. *Dead* weight."

Her hands and feet were still tied. She extricated herself from the bag in a series of butt hops and rolls. At one point, she fell into the hold, landing hard on her ribs. Haskell snickered. Crawling out took a few minutes and involved folding and unfolding her body, banging her elbows, knees, and shoulders repeatedly to get traction up and over the ladder. Once she'd heaved herself up on the bench, she paused to rest and get her bearings. As soon as she stopped moving, her teeth began to chatter.

Her eyes had adjusted. The jetty lights were well behind them. No hotels or commercial buildings sat on the adjacent shore. Just homes. Far to the north, the high-rise apartment buildings of Long Beach flickered. Light clusters that must be Seal Beach and Huntington Beach curved along the coastline in between. They were maybe half a mile offshore.

They'd already passed the Balboa Peninsula. Somewhere back there, Rob and his family were snug in their little house. Safe in bed by now.

Haskell didn't warn her when he decided to jibe and she nearly got hit by the boom. Her reflexes were deteriorating. If she didn't preserve what body heat she had left, hypothermia would set in. It probably already had. Her fingers were going numb. At this rate, she'd be dead from exposure before he had the chance to kill her. She spotted an old life preserver. Even that would help cut the wind.

"Can you hand me that life jacket?"

Haskell enjoyed another laugh at her expense. "Why would I do that?"

"It'll help me retain body heat. If I'm frozen, I can't help. And you need my help sailing this thing."

He ignored her. Now that she could actually see his tension and the frequent disappointed glances at his phone, she had a better sense of the real situation. He still didn't know Joe Barranca was playing him. Using him as he used everyone.

The dynamics of this love triangle were pretty much the same as a straight couple. Haskell was the classic 'other woman'. If he thought Joe would leave his husband, he harbored some grand delusions.

Meri hugged her core, the best she could do with bound wrists. "So you're sailing up to Joe's yacht," she said. "Why would you need two boats to go to Mexico?"

"First of all, as soon as I'm ready, I'm going to throw you off this boat. That's practically a done deal so you can start kissing your ass goodbye. Second, Joe isn't sure which boat we'll sail to Mexico. Of course we'd both prefer his yacht. It's a palace compared to this tub but Joe says it's too conspicuous in some ports south of the border. We don't want to attract the wrong sort of attention. The criminal element."

Meri would have laughed if she felt even a fraction more secure. Joe's reasons likely had more to do with the convenience of a deadly accident at sea. And not just hers. As soon as Haskell got rid of her, he'd have outlived his usefulness to Joe.

"It's going to take all night to get up there at this pace," she said. "If you want to arrive in half the time, untie my hands and feet."

"Nice try," Haskell said. "Not happening. I'll take my chances."

"I won't be able to help you. How about just my feet?"

"Hows about you shut the fuck up."

Anger burned beneath her ribs. This evil little prick had caused her enough grief for one lifetime. "We're sailing into one of the busiest ports in the world. You need to be ready to take evasive action because the freighters cannot see us. You know that, right? If you wander into a shipping lane, we could be pulverized. Look north. There's one freighter going out. And there's another coming in. We're heading into the Port of Los Angeles."

"No, we're going to San Pedro."

"That *is* the Port of Los Angeles. Last year some people in a yacht got killed by a freighter in the middle of the night. The freighter ran right over them and kept on going because no one on board had the slightest idea. They said they didn't even feel a bump. The bodies were never found."

Haskell's body language told her she'd gotten to him.

The sail waffled. He looked up nervously. "Is the wind changing?" he said to himself. "Something's different." He swiveled to scan the black expanse of water heaving around them.

Without warning, a violent gust punched the sails and the boat heeled. Haskell slid into the corner of the cockpit. After another nervous glance at the uncontrolled mainsail, he came over and sliced the cord binding her ankles. "You're still gonna' die, you know."

Pins and needles pricked her feet. She flexed her ankles. Why hadn't she ever taken kick boxing? She scooted over to trim the sails. He sat and watched her work.

"Did you kill Carolyn?" she asked, after she got the boat stabilized.

Haskell scoffed. "Someone else botched that detail."

"Detail?" Meri failed to keep the outrage from her voice.

"Joe hired the lowest bid. Never a good thing. The hit man, thug, whatever you want to call him, came on the wrong fucking night. He was not the brightest button in the box. Right address, wrong female. He must not have paid attention to the physical description."

"So you weren't at my house the night she died?"

"Oh, I was there," Haskell said. "Earlier that evening. She was a bit of a pistol, wasn't she—your little China Girl.

She fucking hated you. She probably enjoyed shoving those pain killer lollipops in your mouth."

"That's what she used to knock me out? Prescription lozenges?"

"Bingo. A fistful of those sponges on a stick. It wouldn't have taken more than a few minutes. Not her idea though. Joe has quite a supply from that father who refuses to die. Do you know that old man is *still* not dead? He's like 95 and he just won't die."

Rob couldn't sit in that waiting room and drink coffee out of a Styrofoam cup, not at a time like this. He paced back and forth in front of the Harbor Patrol station, scanning the harbor entrance, though he knew he wouldn't see anything. She was out there somewhere in that choppy dangerous sea. Was she alive?

If he hadn't been such an asshole, she'd be safe and warm. Maybe even in his bed. He could have convinced her to stay if he hadn't been such a jerk up at the new house. If he hadn't allowed his temper to take over. He could have talked her into staying if he'd put his mind to it, if he hadn't let his hurt pride rule.

Lieutenant Jack came outside and stood with him for a few minutes. Rob asked for the third time, "How long will it take to find them?"

"No guarantees, of course, but I've got two patrol boats out now. One searching north, one searching south. The Coast Guard will deploy a helicopter shortly. If they're out there, someone will spot them within a couple of hours."

His phone buzzed. His mother again. "Rob," she said. "It's your new house."

"What about it?"

"The fire department just called. It's on fire."

"A fire?" he said incredulously. "Are you fucking kidding me?"

"Language!" his mother said.

"Let it burn. I have insurance."

"They want you to go."

"I can't do that. We're still looking for Meri." The phone beeped mid-sentence. "I've got another call."

"It's probably the fire captain," she said. "I gave him your number."

The fire captain was adamant. "Sir, you're the homeowner, correct? You need to get up here. Now."

"How bad is it?" Rob said.

"Bad enough that I've got six firefighters risking their lives to save your home. It's not good. Now we've got a wind event starting. Your home is at the top of the canyon sir and this situation is volatile. We believe the fire started in your garage. We need to know what your contractor stored in there. I'll be expecting you."

When Rob disconnected, he was shaking. She needed him too; he knew this like he knew his own name. How was it possible—that he'd have to make this choice? The house or Meri. There was no contest. What if they brought her back hurt? He couldn't leave.

Nor could he stay while those firefighters were working to save the house, possibly even the whole canyon.

Lieutenant Jack clapped him on the shoulder. "You better do as the man says. Look, there's nothing you can do here. You already did the most important thing by alerting us. I'll be in touch by phone. We've got this."

Rob looked at the whitecaps beyond the breakwater. It tore him apart to leave without her. Was she alive? "Call me the minute you know."

Haskell began relying on her to decide when to come about and when to trim the sails. Soon all he did was grip the tiller. He kept an anxious eye on the freighters in the distance as they drew closer. He had stopped looking at his phone.

"Which way now?" he asked at one point.

She would have smiled if her face wasn't frozen. He had no clue their roles had reversed. Whether this was due to the dropping temperature or an inkling that his lover wasn't so eager for a rendezvous after all, he wasn't the same overconfident stooge who'd heaved her onto this sailboat.

She'd considered Rob overconfident when they first met. Strange to think of her perceptions of him then, versus now. She'd thought him arrogant. He did have that tendency when he thought he was right. And he nearly always thought he was right. One thing about Rob though—he had never once asked her to be someone else. He accepted her: Meri the nerd. The ugly duckling turned swan turned ugly duckling.

She huddled into a ball and dipped her chin to gain some warmth. If she didn't rescue herself soon, she'd have all of eternity to discuss inner beauty with her grandmother in heaven. The key would be dislodging Haskell from the cockpit. He had at least fifty pounds on her. With her hands tied, she didn't see how she'd shift his bulk anywhere, much less on deck and overboard.

"I'm getting up," she said. Creeping and shuffling, snatching for balance at whatever she could with stiff hands tied together, she edged to the cubby where she'd spotted the life jacket. In a half-crouch, she hooked her foot around it and pulled it out. It took several attempts before she succeeded in flopping it over her head.

The jacket wasn't tied and it wasn't fastened, but it covered her chest and core. It definitely helped shield her from the wind. The small success gave her a mental boost, as well as physical one.

"Haskell," she said. "My inhalers were corrupted with something. What was in them?"

"No idea. Came from one of those knock-off companies overseas that make shit medicine. A lot of crooks out there, you know. And our boss knows them all. He knows everyone."

"He wanted to kill me with my own asthma medicine?"

"No, just mess you up good and proper. The idea was to keep you sick all these months, and out of our way. And the strategy worked. Until it didn't. Joe was strangely fond of you. God knows why. He didn't want you dead, not at first. He thought it preferable to sideline you and avoid unnecessary scrutiny. I planted those inhalers when I broke into your house. Genius, right? You thought stuff was stolen? It was *delivered*."

"But you broke in to both my apartment and my house. Several times."

He shrugged. "Wasn't always me and it wasn't always about the inhalers."

"What were you—or they—after?"

"I'd overlooked something last fall."

"Do you mean my lab notebook?"

He sneered. "Like anybody cares about your high school notebook. No. I'd missed a small detail that day I had the sublime pleasure of seeing your ass kicked out the front door."

"On the day you got me fired."

"I got so much shit from Joe over that one little oversight. I hate disappointing him. That's why I kept searching. He thought there was a chance there'd be trace evidence. He's funny that way. Such a perfectionist. But that's what makes him a great man."

"What 'oversight' are you referring to?"

"You still don't know? Your coffee mug, you idiot. You made it so easy for us. Joe and I, we laughed about that. How easy it was. Getting you to swill that coffee, day in and day out."

Wrapped in a thick robe, Joe peeked in on Derek, who slept deep and well, as always. Lucky boy. He took the phone into his dressing room to check the latest messages. The last one demonstrated a shocking lack of mental acuity. Why in the world would Bryan think delivering Meri Darrow to him on a platter was a bright idea? Joe didn't care about killing her himself. Why would he?

Bryan reminded him of a feral cat depositing a dead bird on a doorstep. A ritualistic offering to prove devotion. Joe didn't need a goddamn dead bird. Just drown the fucking bird and be done with it. What a pain in the ass.

Joe finally responded to the barrage of absurdities. He texted, *"Finish the job NOW."*

No point in rushing up to San Pedro tonight. Bryan wouldn't get there for hours yet. However, Joe did prefer to be locked and loaded for the morning, so to speak. Except that metaphor didn't fit. He despised firearms. They were barbaric. He knew much cleaner ways to deal with unfortunate situations like this one. His solutions were better. Elegant. No fuss. No muss. Well, of course there was always muss. That was someone else's problem—the mopping up. He operated on a higher plane and he knew, without false modesty, genius lived by its own rules.

This new development had its advantages. The narrative had now changed. Bryan would become the mastermind, the obsessed and unstable young man who'd murdered two young women. The man who'd altered the clinical trial data and committed multiple crimes. Joe himself would remain untouched, heartbroken by an incomprehensible turn of events. Bryan's disappearance could actually improve the various spin scenarios and outcomes. Joe would emerge unscathed.

He opened his personal safe and pulled out the vials he kept for emergencies. One dose for Meri Darrow just in case Bryan didn't follow orders, one dose for Bryan, and one back-up. He thought for a moment, went out to the bedroom coffee bar for a bottle of Derek's favorite overpriced water, carefully added the back-up dose, and then screwed the cap on. Keep it simple. If all else failed, all he had to do was hand Bryan a bottle of water after engaging in some hot and sweaty activity, then toss him overboard before the body stunk up the yacht's new interior.

Joe packed his elegant arsenal into his small Gucci carry-on and zipped it up. There. All set for the morning.

The city lights of Long Beach gave her hope. As did the sight of a returning cruise ship heading for the port. It gave her an idea.

"Haskell. Heads up! We're on a collision course."

He startled and looked around with his mouth open.

"See that cruise ship? It's going in on a direct tangent. At the speed we're going, we'll collide."

"What do you mean 'at the speed we're going'? We're sailing. They're steaming. It's not even close."

"Yes, but look where that cruise ship is. It'll take a while to get in. We'll be in that same place at the exact same time. And once we are, we'll be in trouble. Serious trouble."

"How do *you* know?"

"I've been on one of those cruise ships—weekend to Mexico thing. I know the approach. I know the course they take. It's like this." She held up her hands, forgetting they were tied. "Well, I could show you the angle if you cut these cords."

"Forget it," he said. "I'm not falling for that trick."

She didn't have to fake her exasperation. "Trick? I'm trying to save your ass. And we're going much faster now, haven't you noticed? The wind is with us. It won't take long to sail right into that ship's lane. They may or may not see us in time."

She had no idea if he would take the bait. His posture changed. He leaned forward and cast anxious looks towards the cruise ship as their paths converged. He was buying it. The closer they got, the more intimidating the ship became, now maybe 200 yards port side.

"There's a way to slow our speed," she said. "We tack starboard."

"We attack starboard? Attack who?"

"No. Tack. We shift direction." More or less. "We'll have to jibe and you'll need me to be ready to cleat the lines. I can do it if you free up my hands."

"I'm not untying your hands, you stupid cunt."

She was glad he'd used that word. It would make everything easier.

"We should head in towards shore," he said, "and then go back out when they've passed. We'll just get out of the way."

"There are shoals. All along this part of the coast. It's dangerous, especially at night."

"I don't believe you."

She thought a moment. "There's an old saying. 'There are three types of sailors: those who have run aground, those about to run aground, and liars.'"

"Then what do we do?"

She turned away and half-smiled to herself. "I'll do the best I can with my hands tied. I think the only way this can work is if we're methodical. Work together like a machine. I'll tell you each step as we go. Right?"

They tried it for a while and as she guessed, he couldn't follow her directions. She used words he didn't know and contradictory moves, changing course constantly. He got nervous, trying and failing to keep up. The combination of high winds and choppy conditions added to the chaos. She milked his fear for all it was worth.

The cruise ship came closer. Though she didn't think they'd be mowed down, her instructions were, in fact, keeping the sailboat in the shipping lane. It wasn't hard to act panicky at the sight of the gigantic ship bearing down on them. They could see its churning wake and the way it dwarfed other vessels.

Meri got ready. "I hear the engines," she called over the wind. "It's too close."

Haskell stood in a half-crouch. Even in the dark, she saw how pale and shaky he'd become.

"Come about," she yelled. "Hard-a-lee."

He froze. "What? What?"

"Sharp turn! No, the other way!"

He looked around wildly as he moved the tiller and the moment's distraction cost him. As they came about, the boom swung fast. Meri ducked with time to spare and heard an audible thwack. His reflexes had slowed from the long hours of exposure. He stumbled and fell sideways. His head hit the fiberglass edge. But not hard enough. *Shit.*

On his feet now, with his arms out, Haskell flailed for balance. The boat rocked violently. The uncontrolled boom swung back and hit him again, across the torso. He fell against the tiller and then flopped forward, landing on his hands and knees.

"Help me stabilize this thing," he cried, crawling aft and getting tossed around like a rag doll. Meanwhile, the sailboat had moved in a wide arc, still in the path of the approaching ship. Now she actually did hear the thrumming of the ship's engines, closing in fast. The chaos gave her a decent chance to dislodge him from that cockpit.

"We're out of time," she said, popping up. "That ship's gonna' hit us. We should jump for it." She made a break for the forward deck, praying he'd chase her.

"Get back here you stupid fucking cunt."

She scrambled up and over the deck, heading for the bow. The pulpit and its triangular railing was her best hope—as secure a place as any to face him down. One last time.

Behind her, he cursed again. "That's it. You're done."

She edged forward. The closer she got, the scarier it became. Wide open gaps on either side of the bow revealed the ocean as it rushed up—and plunged down—again and again. She dropped into a crouch and fit her back against the pulpit railing, riding the bow as it rose and fell. There wasn't any good way to hold on, not with bound hands. So she braced her running shoes on the deck. Her legs were strong enough to kick him overboard. Survival seemed less and less likely but at least she could take him with her.

Haskell came for her, even as the cruise ship loomed. Beyond reason now, he had the knife out. He didn't care about the tiller. He didn't care that they were still too close to the ship. He wanted her dead.

She stared at his contorted features, wishing his wasn't the last face she'd see. He was almost here. He'd finish this. But not before she gave him one hell of a kick.

And then he moved faster than she expected, diving with his arm outstretched. Fire and pain exploded in her calf. She screamed. He twisted the blade in her flesh and it hurt too much to scream.

The cruise ship roared past, with room to spare. Haskell craned his neck and watched it go by. He turned back with a grim smile.

With the knife still stuck, Meri drew her knees in. If he wanted to stab her with this knife again, he would have to come and get it. That would be her moment of power. If necessary, they'd go down together.

Through a blur of pain, she saw a wall of water, moving toward them, gathering power. The ship's wake had fused with a wave. The swell knocked into them and the boat heeled at a crazy angle.

He fell with shocking ease. She caught a glimpse of his face, disbelieving and white against the dark abyss. A wave enveloped him. His head didn't even bob up. His fight ended in a blink.

She fell too, of course. She clawed at a loose mooring line as she slid. And for a second, miraculously, she held on. But her fingers were too numb and she wasn't strong enough. The line slipped between her fingers.

And then she was gasping in water so icy her muscles seized up, paralyzing her. She had no control. Her elbows remained tight at her side, keeping the life jacket on, even as the waves tried to rip it off. She'd never been so cold. This wouldn't end in a blink for her. These minutes would become an eternity, until she passed out for good.

So this is how it ends. She thought about Rob and the way his smile dazzled her. About Luke's sweet face. About the children she would never have. And she screamed at the heartless sky.

It might have been a minute. It might have been ten minutes. She could not feel her body anymore. A blessing. She'd never known you could see shadows on the sea. But shadows they were, directly below the clouds, playing over the ocean and playing tricks with her eyes. She saw other boats. Or vague shapes that might be whales. The shadows morphed and merged, from ocean into mirage and back into ocean.

This would not go on much longer. Interestingly, she felt as if Rob were with her. In spirit. What a lovely hallucination. If this was death, she was all for it. She saw the light. A circle, in fact. She'd always wondered about the beautiful light so often mentioned in reports of near death experiences.

There it was—a circle of light moving over the water, illuminating the foaming whitecaps. A whirring noise. She tilted her head. Imagine that. A helicopter. She closed her eyes against the glare. She couldn't lift her arms to wave.

A litter appeared, dangling above her. A rescue. This would be a rescue. But if they expected her to reach for that basket or hop into it, they were sadly mistaken. She couldn't do anything except float like a jellyfish. For a little while longer. Maybe she'd make it after all.

15

Someone held her hand and she opened her eyes to see Rob's face above her, creased with concern. She smiled. "Don't look so worried. I was just taking a nap."

He watched her as if she might disappear.

"Don't you look nice," she said. "Prettier than me."

He kissed her. His lips were softer than she'd expected and he tasted like coffee, warm and sweet. Coffee ice cream.

"How are you feeling?" he said.

"Not bad, actually. Your hair is wet. Did you just get out of the shower?"

"A while ago." A funny look crossed his face. "I'm sorry I couldn't get here sooner."

"They've been keeping me pretty busy. I understand you were the one who alerted the Coast Guard. Well done."

"Are you sure you're okay? The nurse said you weren't doing well at all when you first came in. She said they were more concerned about hypothermia than the wound. Your body temperature dropped to something like 34 degrees."

"It's good now. I don't need warming blankets anymore."

He examined her scraped up arms. "Where did he stab you?"

"Right calf. Hurt like hell. The salt spray didn't help. The wound is kind of deep, they said. But the doctors weren't particularly alarmed. The trauma team sees a lot of knife and bullet wounds. One stab wound is child's play compared to what they see here on a typical Saturday night."

He went around the side of the bed, lifted the sheet and skimmed his fingers around the bandage. Right away she noticed a pleasant warmth. When the nurse's assistant checked the dressing earlier, Meri had flinched. Now she relaxed. As always, she felt better the moment he touched her. But it went much deeper. Seeing him made her happy. His touch was the icing on the cake.

"When can I take you home?"

She couldn't stop smiling. What a sweetheart. "Tomorrow. But Jordan will come get me. I already told him he didn't have a choice. He'll pick up clothes from the beach house."

"I'd rather—"

"It's fine, Rob. Really. But there is one thing. I don't have my phone with me so—"

"I brought it for you."

"Good thinking."

He looked sheepish. "Betty Jo's idea. Also brought your wallet, in case you need medical cards or identification."

"How'd you get all this?"

"Your front door wasn't locked."

"No, I guess it wouldn't be." Meri gave Rob an edited version of the story, skipping over the worst parts.

"I chased the van," he said. "But I couldn't catch up in time." He wore that look, the sickened gray expression she hated. "So, is it over? That crazy fucker is dead."

"Yeah he's gone. He drowned. I don't know if he washed up yet, but he's definitely finished. But I'm afraid it's not over. Joe Barranca is still out there, no doubt going about his business. As far as I know, he's still the keynote speaker at that biotech conference in San Francisco. I suppose I'll see for myself next week."

"You're still going?" he said incredulously. "That, I can't allow."

"You can't allow? You're seriously saying that to me?"

"Yes, I am. And proud of it."

She stroked his stubborn, sweet jaw. He turned his mouth to kiss her palm and then her fingers. "I have to do this," she said. "For me, for Carolyn, for all those people in the clinical trial that suffered side effects without follow-up. Anyway, whatever happens, it won't happen quickly. They can't pin anything on him directly, not yet. This will take time."

"I don't give a shit how they go after that asshole," he said, holding her hand against his heart. "So long as you're not in danger."

"You're over-protective."

"I've got my reasons." His expression was an odd mixture of possessiveness, longing and ferocity.

Stunned to see his eyes glisten, she opened her arms. "Come here."

He moved in and with a long sigh, laid his head on her breast. They stayed that way a minute.

"Tell me," she said.

Rob tucked a lock of hair behind her ear and sat on the bed. "I wasn't protective of my wife. Not at all. If I had paid attention, she might have had a fighting chance. I was careless with her. I had no idea she'd skipped a bunch of appointments with her obstetrician."

"Why would she do that?"

"Julie hated office visits because they weighed her every time. She'd gained a lot of weight, more than she expected to. I know now, from talking to the ladies at work, some women gain more weight than others. No one likes it but it's not the end of the world, right? Julie was obsessed with the scale. Anyway, I didn't take her concern seriously. She was upset about how 'fat' she was getting. I got impatient, more than once, and told her to stop whining. But I knew she'd been having headaches. And—I forgot about this until just now—in one of our last phone calls she told me her ankles were swollen. I was travelling a lot back then, on long trips out of the country two out of those last three weeks before—before she died. I should have asked more questions. Hell, I could have done two minutes research online and learned the danger signs. But I didn't."

This was the most he'd ever said about Julie's death. After all this time, the words had poured out of him.

"So what exactly did she die of?"

"Eclampsia," he said.

"I've heard of pre-eclampsia."

"I hadn't," he said. "The doctor told me she probably had pre-eclampsia for some time. But I wasn't around much and when I was, I wasn't paying attention. Later, I learned her doctor could have caught the blood pressure problem and addressed it quickly. Since she'd skipped the last couple of appointments, no one had checked her blood pressure. If I'd cared more, if I'd bothered to learn what those symptoms meant, she wouldn't have died. I failed and now my son will never know his mother."

"Have you been torturing yourself about this?"

"Mostly trying not to think about it. And mostly succeeding. But then I met you. And it didn't take long to realize how much I liked you. And wanted you. God, how I wanted you. And it's only getting worse."

"Worse?"

He took her hand again. "I'm screwing this up. No, I mean it's better. I only want you more, not less. And I thought there must be something wrong with me because you were so obviously unwell at first. You looked so ill that day we met on the beach and then every time I thought you were getting healthy, you had a relapse. At least that's how it appeared. I know how selfish I must sound. Falling in love with you has been…painful."

After a mental wince, Meri nodded. Strange that she'd never understood this before. How love and pain were braided together.

"It's been great, too," he quickly added. "But only fools refuse to learn from tragedy. And I'm not a fool. Your safety takes priority over everything. You were in serious trouble last night."

"Rob, you aren't responsible for me."

"You're wrong," he said simply, without rancor. "I should have looked out for you instead of sulking like a teenager. Like it or not, Meri, we're connected. We are all too far gone in this to pretend anymore."

"We?"

"It's a package deal. You've got me and Luke and mom, too. No matter what you tell yourself, no matter what you said about me not being your kind of people—you have us and we have you. There's no going back."

Tears filled her eyes. How had she gotten so lucky?

He kept talking, on a roll now. "If I can take action to prevent harm to someone I love, I'm damn well going to take action. And you have to let me. You can't expect me to sit back and wait for something bad to happen. I can't do that. Not with you." His voice cracked on the last word.

"I wouldn't expect you to," she said, starting to cry. Because now that she understood him better, she also understood what this meant, going forward. This bond was awesome. And it wasn't always a good-awesome. Strong feelings like these—their feelings for each other were a huge responsibility.

"Don't do that," he said. "Don't cry. I don't want to make you sad."

"I'm not sad. Just overwhelmed."

He reached for her and their kiss was slow. His lips and tongue soothed and explored, both tender and sweet. The sweetness deepened into something else until they broke apart, short of breath.

He released her. "Are you warm enough now?"

"Oh, I'm warm."

He ran a finger along the side of her neck stroking the delicate skin there as if he loved its texture. She turned her head so she could feel his fingers on her cheek, against her lips.

Meri's phone vibrated with an incoming message. She glanced at it. "I don't recognize that number." She read a few words but didn't keep reading because the message didn't make sense. "Spammers."

A nurse came in to check her vital signs and Rob stepped out of the way.

"I'll go out now and give them your insurance cards," Rob said. "Be right back."

The phone buzzed again. After the nurse left, Meri checked it. Someone had sent a photo of Luke and Betty Jo on the beach in matching sun hats. Cute but taken from far away. Who had sent this? It wasn't Betty Jo's phone number. A friend? The nanny? She went back and read the first text message more carefully. It said: "You'll go second."

The new threat hit her hard. Luke and Betty Jo were in danger. And probably Rob, too. If she hadn't had these last sweet minutes of happiness with him, the shockwave may not have been so bad. Those minutes hadn't been reality; they had been pure delusion. She'd been stupid to think they could go back to normal. Nothing would be normal again.

As she checked the beach photo once more, it dissolved. Whoever sent it had used one of those apps that erased the message. There was probably a way to retrieve it if one had the luxury of time.

Another photo arrived. Taken closer up, this one also showed Luke and Betty Jo, this time with the nanny at a restaurant. Meri recognized the local sushi place. She'd been there with them and remembered Betty Jo marveling at Luke's capacity for and love of sushi. They went to that restaurant often.

Meri looked anxiously at the hallway, hoping Rob would return in time. He didn't. She gritted her teeth and seethed as the photo disappeared from her screen.

A ping. This time an incoming e-mail. Meri opened the e-mail to find a medical journal article. A case study about a neurotoxin derived from the pufferfish. Tetrodotoxin. A toxin well known to sushi chefs adept at removing the poisonous parts of the fish. The case study detailed several instances of poisoning, both accidental and deliberate. The poison caused paralysis and eventually respiratory failure. Death.

When Rob finally returned, she demanded, "What was your mom doing with Luke today?"

"They were going out for lunch."

"You have to go home. Now." She told him about the photos and the article.

Distraught didn't begin to describe Rob's face. He took a deep breath. "He's probably bluffing to scare you into backing off on that meeting next week, right?"

"Probably. And it's working."

He called his mom immediately, spoke to her, and disconnected. "She says everything's fine. They just got back from the restaurant. How long does it take—if they— if they ingested poison?"

"I don't know," she said. "I'll see what I can learn from here. Call me."

He kissed her hard on the lips and then rushed out the door.

She stared at the empty doorway. Even if this proved to be a bluff, the risks were simply too great, the consequences too scary.

The trauma of the last 24 hours cut deep, a fresh, gushing wound far worse than the knife wound. And now this. Rob and his family weren't safe. And with her in the picture, the odds were worse.

No one got sick, not even a tummy ache from the sushi. So it had been a bluff. Rob had checked them all into a hotel. Once out of the hospital and moved in with her brother, she'd called Rob to say she couldn't visit, using her recovery as an excuse. He wasn't fooled; she knew that. He hadn't pressured her about anything since then. He hadn't even asked her to quit cooperating with investigators. She wondered if she would be as brave if her child had been threatened. She didn't think so.

For the next several days, both in the hospital and out, Meri met with numerous law enforcement officers, gave statements, answered questions, and weathered questions about Haskell's death. Harbor Patrol said he'd been seen struggling to transfer a large gear bag into his rented sailboat. The combined evidence and statements seemed to convince the cops.

The federal investigators were another story. They expressed doubt about collecting sufficient evidence to prove that Joe himself was behind the clinical trial's doctored results. Meri had already made her decision. Her doctors and Detective Shyu had cleared her for travel. She didn't want to go to San Francisco, but she'd come too far to back down now.

On the day before she left town, Bill Bard, Rob's boss called her. "We need to talk." They agreed to meet for a drink at the Montage in Laguna Beach. She could guess what was in store, but she owed it to Rob to be courteous.

Later that day, Meri limped into the hotel lobby in a long fuchsia dress she'd chosen because it hid her leg. And because her pride demanded that she look good. She didn't know why looking good made a difference, but it did.

She recognized the tall man in the bar from their meeting last fall. After settling into club chairs and ordering drinks, Bill cleared his throat. "I want to be straight with you. Rob's in trouble. You seem to care about him."

She nodded.

"You heard about the fire?"

On a sharp intake of breath, she said, "No."

He looked at her curiously. "The fire at his new house?"

"Is Rob okay? Did anyone get hurt?"

"He's fine. No one was hurt. But arson is suspected."

"When did this happen?"

"Two nights ago. Monday night. Well, technically, early morning hours on Tuesday."

Appalled, she kept quiet. Early Tuesday. Right around the time she'd been rescued. He'd come to the hospital on Tuesday, late morning. After the fire. And he hadn't said a word. Another significant thing he hadn't shared.

"I've even got video." He pulled out a tablet. "It was still burning at sunrise. Made the morning news. You can see it better on this."

He pulled up a news clip of flames shooting out of the villa's windows. A blood-red glow lit up the dawn sky. "Dramatic, right? The news stations love a fire, especially during a drought. Luckily, the fire didn't spread too far and no one was hurt. I understand there were some recent threats against him and the family." He shook his head, as if unconvinced, and made a face. She wasn't sure if he doubted the threats or the identity of the real target.

"So now we have yet another shitstorm," he added. "I don't know his insurance situation—the fallout remains to be seen, especially if arson is involved. It's bound to be messy to sort out since the title only just transferred. The house is salvageable but it won't be cheap. Rob is under tremendous financial pressure. He had no business buying that place but the wheels were put in motion some time ago."

He went on. "Rob McLain was—is—one of the brightest guys I've ever hired. And that's saying something. He's got it all, smarts, work ethic, people skills. You already know this."

She nodded again.

"I'll give you the benefit of the doubt here. What you apparently don't realize—his career is in a tailspin. He's lost his edge, his spark, and his drive. He's not putting in the hours. Most people in his position are in the office at five a.m. and they're not out of there until seven at night. Recently he's had to take—how many days off?—because of you and your, uh, situation. Situations. You understand he was already at a disadvantage because of his wife's passing. We were all sympathetic. Up to a point. And we passed that point some miles back.

"I like the guy. I consider him a friend. But he can't continue like this. I've put him on notice. He's on a performance improvement plan and believe me, I don't often waste my time with that bullshit. If and when someone's not performing, I don't care who they are, they're out. No second and third chances. We don't do that. No one's immune, all the way up the chain. It's brutal, but it's honest."

"So what are you saying?"

"I'm saying, if you love him—hell, if you like him—do the right thing. Let him go. You're aware of the rumors about you?"

"I'm aware of some rumors." She didn't care about the public shaming anymore. People would forget.

He now regarded her with pity. "I can see you haven't heard the worst. Word got around you were providing insider information to Rob. He had to contend with some unpleasant interviews with the regional Securities Exchange Commission office a while back. Luckily, that came to nothing. But the investigation didn't do his career any good, I can guarantee you that. You really didn't know this?"

"No. How would I provide inside information? I've been out of the company for almost five months."

"But you were in a position to know significant facts about the company's products," Bill said. "We're all under tremendous scrutiny and since the market is especially volatile right now, no one likes a gray area. And that's what you are. He is under massive stress. He more or less admitted you've got him all tied up in emotional knots. And that you've dragged him down."

An unpleasant sense of Deja vu crept over her. Rob had used that phrase when he lost his temper with Luke.

"Since you entered the picture, his home, his career, and even his kid's safety have all been compromised."

Meri looked at her untouched drink. How did one argue with the truth?

"From what I can see," Bill said, "your problems aren't getting any better, they're getting worse. You've made a hash of things. And all this drama with that drowning in Long Beach the other night and your attorney friend found dead in the Harbor? I don't see how you can recover your career. But that's not why I asked you here. Rob's a good man. Better than most. If I'm honest, a better human being than me. I'm a son-of-a-bitch and I know it. Which is why it's unusual for me to step in. But that's the effect Rob has on people."

He shook the ice down in his drink and shrugged. "Look, the kindest thing you can do for him now is go away. And stay away. In any case, I've told Rob he needs to distance himself from you publicly. He agreed."

She met his eyes. "I understand." Nothing could surprise her anymore. All she wanted was to get away with her dignity intact. She fumbled for cash.

"I'll take care of it," Bill said. "For what it's worth, I'm sorry things played out like this."

She got up and walked into the cool March evening. The last traces of buttery light washed over Laguna Beach and a thin band of red dawdled in the western sky.

Why hadn't Rob told her? Didn't he realize she had a right to know? Or perhaps that over-protective tendency of his had kicked in. The point was moot. He hadn't turned away when she needed help. And he'd paid a price. But he'd never complained or flung recriminations about the consequences. Now it was her turn to do the right thing.

16

Meri stepped inside the dim ballroom. And exhaled. She hadn't realized she'd been holding her breath. Things weren't so rosy for Joe Barranca, after all. A sparse crowd waited for the keynote speaker, less than 50 people in a room designed to hold 500. These people had shown up for the same reason she had. Morbid curiosity.

The podium light switched on. At 11:01, he clicked his laser pointer at the title slide. Here he was, ready to hold court, come hell, high water, or disgrace.

She wondered at his audacity. By the third slide, half the audience had left the room. A few sycophants stayed. True believers in their charismatic visionary.

Joe kept talking, his well-oiled delivery the same as if a standing-room only crowd hung on every word. She noticed his husband, ever the supportive spouse, sitting in the back. She'd always liked him. He deserved better.

She joined the exodus. She'd heard this speech already. Far more interesting material awaited her elsewhere.

An hour later, she strolled past the ballroom. The doors were open. Joe was packing up his computer, wrapping and stowing cords methodically. She took a deep breath for courage and walked up the center aisle. There were hotel workers in the back of the room. Joe wouldn't hurt her in public, not physically. Not his style.

She stopped a few feet away. "You didn't cancel."

"There you are. I've been expecting you. I don't cancel speeches."

"You know this is all over, don't you?"

"My dear," he said in a flat voice, "it doesn't end here. I've started over more times than you've had orgasms without batteries."

He waited for her horrified gasp. He wouldn't get it. The raw cruelty under his well-groomed mask shouldn't surprise her. It had been there the whole time.

"Do you really want to go to the wall on this?" he asked, almost philosophically. "People will suffer because of your actions today. People you love."

"Threats? Still?"

"Regarding those federal investigators you're meeting this afternoon—" He paused while a smile played around his mouth. "Did you think I didn't know? Dear girl, I've been so forbearing. Giving you plenty of rope. And you've used it so efficiently." He ticked off items with his fingers. "First, we have your record of opiate use—illegal use of someone else's prescriptions—"

"If I can't prove it, how will you? I'd really like to know."

"You'd be surprised what's possible in this world," he said calmly. "Then there's your instability, ethical breaches, and your friend's mysterious death." Joe wagged his finger. "Not to mention poor Bryan Haskell's demise. Which leads us to your paranoia and delusions. Your credibility is at an all-time low. But go ahead. Knock yourself out with those investigators. Do what you think is best. What's the worst that could happen?"

He snapped his fingers at a worker. "Bring us some coffee. A carafe and two cups."

Her attention clicked on his smooth, untroubled face. "I'm not staying for coffee."

"Water, then. The tap water here is awful. I've got bottled water." He unzipped the leather bag at his feet.

"Oops, not here. Never mind, we'll have the coffee. Don't you have questions? I felt sure you'd wonder about your attorney friend. No one has been very helpful, have they? I'll bet that young detective hasn't told you a thing. Face it my dear, I'm the one—the only one—with the answers to your questions. Haven't you wondered—did Carolyn Ling suffer? Did she truly understand how she had betrayed you? And if so, why would she do it? Why did she go to your house the night she died?"

The worker placed the coffee on a bar table nearby. Joe followed and then beckoned to her. This might be her chance to get the truth. Of course he could lie. However, his narcissism and giant ego might take precedence over caution.

He kept talking. "Don't you want to know what made you so ill? How we did it? It was quite clever."

He didn't realize Haskell had already told her most of it, except the actual toxin he'd used. She could try to record the conversation. She put her handbag on the next table, and with her back to him, pressed the audio 'record' button on her phone, leaving the purse open. It might work. She'd even practiced this in the hospital while fantasizing about ways to bring him down.

He'd already poured her coffee. He smiled to himself as he poured his own. He knew exactly what she'd been doing just now with her back to him. Just as she knew what he'd been doing.

She picked up her cup and watched his still-handsome face as his eyes followed her movements. "So what made my hair fall out?"

"In your case, thallium. Sometimes classic solutions are the best. As you know. The doses were mild. Not enough to kill you."

"My doctor said I was poisoned over a period of time, probably weeks before I even got fired. Why?"

"It had been apparent for some time that the trial results were going south. I managed to keep the lid on the data, but I knew I couldn't hide it from you forever. You were too close, too involved, and, as I had already figured out, incorruptible. Ridiculously so. I started planning months before the deed was done. And so I had Bryan spike your—your water."

She noticed the slip. The water hadn't been spiked. If it had, her whole department would have been sick. He just wanted to avoid the word 'coffee'.

"I didn't think it would be necessary to kill you," he said. I always had a soft spot for you. I was your mentor, after all."

"Tell me about Carolyn," she said quickly. He was too observant. He'd notice her lack of interest in the details.

"She was greedy, of course. To her credit, she recognized a fellow pragmatist in me. Her death was a mistake. I thought you were still wearing the wig at the time. I gave my hired help a description and he confused Ms. Ling for you. Details, details. They'll be the death of us all. You'll be interested to know, in the end, your friend had second thoughts. She definitely wanted to see you fail, but she didn't want to see you die. Then again, neither did I, not until you became so uncooperative. Ms. Ling insisted on removing those inhalers from your house after you landed in the hospital. Bryan was the one who'd put them there for me. By the way, thanks for saving me a trip to San Pedro last week. You did me a favor when you killed him. You're more like me than you know. Bryan stood between you and what you wanted—life. It's as simple as that sometimes. People don't know when to get out of the way, do they?"

An anxious-looking woman in a suit interrupted them. "Dr. Barranca, I'm the hotel manager. I need to speak with you privately, sir. It's urgent."

"I'm working," he said, irritated.

"It's regarding your—your husband."

He cocked his head indulgently. "Has Derek maxed out the credit card in the gift shop? Again?" He chuckled. "I don't have time for this, sweetheart. I'll straighten it out later, whatever it is."

"Sir, it's an emergency."

Joe raised his eyebrows in mock dismay. "We'll have to chat in the back of the room, then. I can't leave this room."

Because he needs to see this happen to me. He actually believed she'd drink that coffee. Meri watched him confer with the hotel manager who spoke to him now in low, urgent tones.

Suddenly Joe cried out. "No!"

Meri and everyone else in the room froze.

He doubled over, as if in terrible pain. The noises coming from him were harsh and agonized. Horrible, braying cries as he howled like an animal. But it wasn't physical pain. He cried, "I have to go to him." He tried to run to the door but the manager and a few workers held him back.

The manager said, "Sir, you don't want to see him like this."

Joe crumpled into a chair. His persona and power dissolved, right in front of Meri's eyes. A security team arrived. Soon they led him out, sobbing.

One good thing about a male-dominated conference— the ladies room was empty. Meri dumped the coffee in the sink and then realized she'd destroyed evidence. Shaking with reaction, she washed her hands and then sagged onto a dainty chair with her arms wrapped around her middle.

A sudden death. Derek seemed fine when she saw him earlier. Whether accident or suicide, she wouldn't be surprised if the death could be traced back to Joe— whatever the actual cause. Revulsion and anger coursed through her. She thought about the human wreckage Joe had created. A path of destruction. One that led right to his own door. He'd loved Derek and he'd destroyed him, too.

She sat up and looked at herself in the mirror. Her eyes were red and her mascara had run. But she looked like herself again. He had not destroyed her. She had not allowed it. And that's when she knew she was strong enough to see this through.

In fact, the meeting that afternoon wasn't too bad. She told the truth the best way she knew how, sticking to the facts and staying concise and unemotional. The investigators, two men and one woman, were polite, business-like and thorough. None of them knew what had happened to Derek. She didn't bring it up.

They asked the right questions. When she told them about the debacle of the data monitoring committee and Chamberlain's belief in his methods, they listened closely.

One of the number-crunchers spoke up then. "If I'm correct, the clinical results weren't deleted at all. They were hidden. Under millions of lines of code. He didn't have to purge anything to obscure the truth. He just buried it."

An hour later, she was done. They stared at her as she gathered her things, waiting for her to leave. She hesitated, wondering what would happen next. They weren't supposed to say anything yet about their conclusions.

One of the men took pity on her as he walked her to the elevator. "Don't worry," he said, "we're going to get him."

"And the patients in the clinical trial? The anti-aging cream?"

"We've got a team following up with every single one. No permanents effects are expected. And that drug application will be permanently shelved. It's over."

A text message from Rob awaited her. "Come home."

She didn't go home. She'd been hired for a temporary job—a research project at UC-San Francisco. They were willing to pay her decent money for six weeks of work. Not corporate scale of course, but decent. And even offered her a place to stay—housesitting in a loft on Potrero Hill for a university couple on sabbatical.

Around the corner from the loft, a shuttered coffee factory still retained the scent of roasted Columbian beans in its bricks. When she stepped outside, a ghostly trace of coffee followed her down the hill.

On her first night there, she stared out the window. If she craned her neck, she could see the bay—a smudge of blue. Not the same as home. Her longing for Rob was a fierce ache.

When she called to explain she wouldn't be returning soon, Rob surprised her by laughing abruptly. "You don't understand what's between us, do you? You're more scared of the happiness we could have had than any bad guy. Now you're walking away with no idea what you've just given up."

"Look," she said, "it's a job. I haven't earned any income in almost five months."

He hung up on her. After that, she returned maybe one out of five calls he made to her. He stopped trying after a week or so. More than anything, she wanted him to succeed and meet his goals. Recharge his career, move into his dream house, and most of all, live happily, the way he'd always planned. He was better off without her.

Detective Shyu called Meri two weeks later. "Barranca's in custody. The judge was convinced he's a flight risk, so he won't even get bail. There's more to come. I've got plenty of leg work remaining to gather evidence of multiple poisonings—you, possibly that husband of his, plus your friend Ms. Ling, depending on what the toxicology report says. The D.A.'s office believes they have enough evidence for a jury to convict him. That recording you made will help. Add on the pending federal charges and Barranca will have a tidal wave of trouble even his battalion of lawyers can't hold back. By the way, tell your friend Rob he doesn't have to hound me anymore."

She didn't tell Rob. Talking to him was painful and now that he'd stopped calling, it wouldn't be fair to stir things up again. So she stuck to her plan and left him alone. Her job was absorbing and her colleagues fantastic. They mentioned the possibility of future collaborations. They'd won a grant and needed more researchers. She was working six days a week. Even so, she was lonely. She found herself asking her colleagues about their families more than she would have in the past. Rob had pulled her off the sidelines of life and now she'd never be the same.

She refused to fall apart. She had a healthy, strong body to take care of—one thing she would never take for granted again. She climbed the city's steep sidewalks without huffing and puffing. Her figure filled out and her hair grew long and lustrous.

The irony didn't escape her. The two things she had lost last year—her health and her career—were now flourishing. As the weeks went on, she found, increasingly, those things were hollow without Rob. Every day she threw herself into work and every night she longed for him.

The longing wasn't eased by news Jordan gave her over the phone one night.

"Guess who I ran into last night at the Crystal Cove Trader Joe's? Your friend Rob. I didn't remember what he looked like. He remembered me though."

She sat up straight. "How did he look? Is he okay?"

"How the hell would I know?" Jordan said. "Guys don't ask stuff like that. But now that you mention it, he looked tired. Did you know he's moved?"

"To the new house?"

"That's what he said."

One day when her six-week stint was nearly complete, she was approached at work by a pretty woman of South Asian descent who seemed to know her.

"I wondered if I'd see you up here," she said, shaking Meri's hand. "I'm Priya Varanasi."

"Sorry, have we met?"

"Once. You wouldn't remember. You gave a presentation at my office last year. I asked a question about product safety?"

"I remember you now. What are you doing up here?"

"I'm visiting one of your colleagues—he's done some breakthrough work. Lots of commercial potential." Priya smiled shyly. "It's really a personal visit. Anyway, I don't work for Rob anymore. Actually, I have his old job."

Meri's heart fell. He had lost the job after all. That second chance his boss offered had run its course. She hurt for Rob. And for herself, if she were honest. He'd sustained this blow without telling her. And what about the financial strain of his two mortgages? That had to be intense.

"He was a wonderful mentor," Priya said. "He still is."

Meri smiled sadly. "I thought you said he left the company."

"He left the department. He made sort of a lateral move—a back office role that requires very little travel and hours that aren't so crazy. Every time I see him, he teases me about all the gray hair I'm going to have from this job."

Meri gazed at the young woman's perfect, glossy head. "Why would he tease—you mean he *chose* the transfer?"

"Oh, yes."

Rob had made the decision to walk away from the high-powered job. It hadn't been made for him. He hadn't been fired because of her.

Priya glanced away from Meri's stunned face, casting about for a new topic. Then she grinned. "Have you heard about his house? We all thought he'd lost his mind."

"It is a bit much."

Priya looked baffled. "I suppose. In a way."

Meri wrapped up her obligations. Arrangements and solutions fell into place—dominoes in the path of her resolve.

She flew back to Orange County on Friday. Afraid something might go wrong, she didn't call him until she landed. When he didn't answer, she sent a text and left a voice mail. At least now he knew. She was coming home.

Outside the airport, a soft marine breeze blew her hair—now shoulder-length—off her neck. The air was pleasantly mild, warmer than San Francisco by about twenty degrees. She was home.

She let herself into her brother's condo at 5:00 p.m. He'd agreed to let her crash for a few nights and borrow his car. He was in San Diego with his new girlfriend. Pizza boxes covered the kitchen counter. Ants marched across his stovetop. She wrinkled her nose and decided the mess wasn't her problem. Unless she ended up back here tonight. She showered, tugged on fresh jeans and a t-shirt, grabbing a cardigan and her bag on the run.

Thirty minutes later, she turned into Rob's gated community, passing through the giant palm trees she remembered. The neighborhood looked more settled already. Families were starting to move in. As she drove higher into the hills, the houses became stucco mansions, with fewer and fewer per block. She drove into the last cul de sac. Here too, landscapers had performed magic, transforming chaparral into garden. White iceberg roses spilled over dwarf boxwood hedges in Rob's front yard. And his house looked immaculate. The fire damage had been repaired.

She idled across the street. A new crossover SUV sat in the driveway with its trunk open. A tall blonde in a yellow sundress walked across the courtyard. She glanced over at

Meri before she unloaded grocery bags and went in. She was attractive, polished, and assured. She looked exactly right for Rob. And belonged here in a way Meri never would.

A too-familiar sense of isolation set in. Too late. A man like him would not wait around indefinitely. This woman would want the same things he did.

And yet…a small voice whispered in her head, how could this woman understand Rob the way Meri did? He needed someone to both ground him *and* challenge him. And then there was Luke. What if his new mom expected him to sit still all the time? Color inside the lines. Stay clean.

Meri's first instinct was to run and hide, to find a dark corner and lick her wounds. However, she had survived these past months and come through stronger. She would go in to say 'hello'. He would introduce them. They would be civilized. And it would kill her to stand there and smile at Rob and his new love.

She made a U-turn and now had a better view of the courtyard. Two boys played with remote control cars. Bikes and scooters leaned on the inner wall. The kids were surrounded by discarded toys and jackets. Their stuff. Lots of it. A baby sister cried somewhere inside the house.

The obvious, glaring truth lit up like a neon sign. He did not live here. Another family lived here. She had worked herself into despair over nothing. Which she would have known right away if she weren't so half-crazed with longing.

She got halfway down the hill before pulling over next to a playground. Tears streamed down her face. She needed to find them. Her own family.

Rob picked up on the fourth ring. "Where are you?"

She held the phone tightly. "I'm in Newport Coast, looking for you."

"I thought my mother must have told you where we are. She mentioned *you* often enough."

She scribbled his directions on the back of a receipt. He lived off Pacific Coast Highway much farther south, between Laguna Beach and San Clemente.

"We'll be waiting," he said.

She hung on to those words as she drove through the long spring dusk. The turn-off was a narrow road that dropped steeply to the ocean side of the highway. Tall hedges blocked views of the community. She came to a guard shack. She slowed, peered in. Nobody manning it. Since there was no gate, she proceeded, only to meet a T-intersection. A new developer's sign pointed left. An old redwood sign indicated "Sandy Cove" to the right. Rob evidently forgot to mention this turn.

She had a choice. Left would take her uphill to the newer part of the community. Those houses would have killer views. The homes on the right were close to the beach, likely much older. A car appeared in her rear view mirror and she turned right to get out of the way. The flat neighborhood would be easy to scope out first. She'd look around and then headed up the hill to find Rob's house. He'd have picked a newer place, for sure.

She passed a community park and several streets named for sea creatures. He'd said to turn right after Urchin. Maybe they lived down here, after all. She read the signs aloud as she passed. "Starfish, Sand Dollar, Anemone, Urchin." Urchin was a cute street name.

Here it was. *Barnacle.* Terrible street name. She'd actually thought he was joking at first. She pulled up to the curb.

This couldn't be correct. She double-checked the address. It was right. A rambling cottage slumped in front of her, its board and batten exterior painted fresh green. The freshness ended there. It looked like an old summer home, never intended to be used year-round. Aside from its location, which was fantastic, the property was remarkable only for its dilapidation.

17

She let herself in through an old gate halfway off its hinges. Overgrown junipers blocked the windows. No doorbell. She knocked on the screen door. They didn't hear. She propped the screen with her shoulder and knocked hard on the front door. Her heart pounded even harder.

Then she saw him through the door fanlights. His face was thinner, yet so familiar and so dear. He flung the door open, scooped her up and hugged her hard enough to knock the wind out of her. He held her head tight against his shoulder.

"Thank God," he said. "I thought I'd have to go to San Francisco and kidnap you."

She lifted her face. His sweetly careful kiss answered the most important question. He hadn't changed his mind.

She pulled back to examine him. He was different. His jeans hung off his hips; he needed a belt. Dark eyes focused—zeroed in on her with the same intensity—and yet doubt shadowed those eyes. Even now, in joyful reunion, he was more watchful than before. Less brash and sure of himself. He had his own questions, she saw, questions her kiss hadn't answered.

He ran his hands up and down her arms as if he didn't believe she was really there. "You found us."

Luke hung behind his father's legs. "Doo found us."

She gathered him in a hug. He had grown. He wiggled out of her arms too soon, then ran off, only to pound back within seconds to show her a fistful of polished river pebbles. "Big rocks," Luke said.

She looked at Rob, delighted. "He knows the word 'big'."

"Big rocks that won't go anywhere they shouldn't go," Rob said.

"Unless he throws them through the window," she said, in a whispered aside.

"Hadn't thought of that."

"Yet."

"I've got something to show you, too," Rob said, pulling her along to a screened side porch. Luke trailed them, telling her about his new house. She understood most of his words now.

Rob pushed the side door open. "Careful. These stairs are ancient."

He kept her close as they walked into the twilight. A sharp marine breeze had kicked up. Overgrown hedges blocked the view but she knew the ocean was out there, beyond the garden. She could smell it. A jumble of chairs sat in a semi-circle around a flagpole.

"This is lovely," she said.

"Watch this," Rob said. Luke danced next to him, begging to help. Rob picked him up. Together they raised a flag. It was a handmade flag—a green margarita glass stitched on white canvas. Both boys turned and looked at her expectantly. When she didn't say anything right away, Rob added, "It looks a lot better when the wind blows the other way."

Tears had filled her eyes. "It's absolutely wonderful. You remembered the margarita flag. I can't believe you remembered that. Have you used it yet?"

He leaned in to kiss her, as if he couldn't help himself. "Not officially. We only got it last week. And we haven't met too many neighbors yet. We were waiting for you. Come on. You're cold out here."

Luke ran ahead. Rob kept his arm around her and led her inside. Toys and unpacked boxes jammed the small house. She stood in the circle of his arms, watching Luke. They didn't talk for a while. Being together was enough.

Then he touched her nose. "You *are* here for good?"

"If you're ready for me."

He laughed and shook his head. Luke ran up with a magnetic dinosaur to show her. Once he'd gone back to his toys, Rob said, "I'm sorry about what I said to you on the phone—when I lost my temper—I think it was frustration. You know, *that* kind of frustration."

She put her arms around him and tucked her hands into his back pockets. "We can fix that later. Tell me, how did you end up down here?"

"After the fire, I got an offer from a couple who really wanted the house. They got a good deal and by then, I was more than ready to unload it. And relieved not to have the burden. Meanwhile, I had an agent on the lookout, waiting to pounce on whatever came on the market down here. We're renting now; we have the option to buy. I didn't want to decide without you."

"This is so far removed from your villa. You must really love me." She leaned back and scanned his face, not quite believing her luck.

"Why else would I be such a glutton for punishment? Six weeks, Meri."

"You didn't give up on me."

"I couldn't."

She shook her head. "I've never known anyone like you."

"Persistent?"

"Try stubborn. Relentless. Even though those qualities drive me crazy—and doubtless always will—I love your strong character. I love you."

He went very still. "That's the first time you've said it."

"No, surely not. I've told you."

"First time." He watched her solemnly. There was vulnerability underlying his strong personality. The part of him that belonged to her.

"What a coward I was. Not anymore. I'll tell you every day."

When Rob carried Luke off to bed, she looked around. The bathrooms and kitchen here were so old they were fashionable again. Assuming Rob even liked the retro style, he'd want new appliances and fixtures to make the house halfway comfortable. The house was one story, with three bedrooms, one and a half bathrooms, and a funky kitchen overlooking a small, fenced backyard. Perfect for Luke. But was it perfect for Rob? This was a far cry from the fabulous villa. No showcase here.

She was staring out the back window when he returned. He slid his arms around her waist and asked her reflection, "Like it?"

"The house? I love it. You knew I would. But do *you*?"

"Surprisingly enough, I do. It needs a lot of work, but I like a challenge."

"Mind if I go after that shrubbery?" she said. "I'm certain I can improve your view."

"Our view," he corrected her. "Is tomorrow too soon?"

"That can be arranged."

"When are you moving in?"

"Is now too soon?" she said. He stopped her laugh with a kiss that left her breathless. "What really made you decide to give up your new house? Was it the financial strain?"

"Every time I went up there, dealing with insurance adjusters and contractors, I felt uneasy and lonely. It's too big. Too isolated."

"What about the infinity pool you wanted?"

"Maybe. Someday. This place has its compensations. Most important, you'll be happy here. The beach is only three blocks away. Close enough to enjoy but far enough so I won't worry about Luke and the water. I understand everyone chips in for a lifeguard for the summer season. I couldn't arrange for the Shake Shack to relocate, but we do have a couple of entrepreneurs selling Hawaiian shaved ice on weekends. Your surfboard's already in the garage. You're not going without me, though."

"Do you want to learn to surf?"

"Hell no. I'll watch. You can teach Luke." He led her to the sea grass sofa she recognized and pulled her down on his lap.

"Did you raid my dad's garage for the board?"

"I called him and he met me over there."

A note in his voice alerted her. What had her father said? She shifted off his lap. "What's wrong?"

"I told him you'd be coming home to live with me, sooner or later. Hope you don't mind."

"Not at all. He probably wondered why you'd want someone like me. Not the warmest character, is he?"

"We'll get along fine. As soon as I asked him about his golf game, he was downright pleasant." Then he grunted in exasperation. "You're not the ugly duckling anymore, Meri. Remember that. You're a beautiful, intelligent, desirable woman. I want you because I'm in love and I don't want to go through life without you."

She held his hand to her heart. Mere words seemed inadequate. So she just watched him with her heart in her eyes.

"Give me your feet," he said, gesturing.

"Huh?"

He bent down, slipped her sandals off, and settled her feet in his lap. "Go on." He pressed the balls of her feet with his thumbs.

She lost her train of thought for a moment, nearly going under with pleasure. "Whoa. I might be having a teensy orgasm here."

"You were saying…"

She hesitated, unwilling to burst the bubble of happiness they'd created. Life wasn't a fairy tale. Though it sure felt like it at the moment. He continued to rub her feet and watched her patiently.

"There are things we need to talk about," she admitted. "Things you should know. I confronted Joe at the conference. I was so mad and sick of being a victim." She told him about Joe's attempt to poison her one last time, and the surprise of Derek's death. "It turned out to be an accident. As sad as it is, it was fitting punishment for Joe, because he really loved him. Derek accidentally drank from a water bottle Joe had doctored for someone else. Possibly me. I think they've added Derek's death to the list of charges."

"What about Carolyn's murder?" he said.

"Detective Shyu is still working on that. A couple of weeks ago, Carolyn's mom sent me an old diary of Carolyn's. I don't know if she actually read it first—I hope not, because it wasn't a sentimental journey. More of an explanation. Maybe that's why she sent it—because it was all there. If you can believe this, Carolyn kept a chart detailing all the ways I'd wronged her, all the perceived insults or offenses over the years, most of which I was completely unaware. The resentment went all the way back to middle school and a science fair I won. Later, she didn't get in to her first choice university, but I did. She thought I got in because of family connections. The animosity and bitterness staggered me. I'm still not over it."

"You could have called me," Rob said. "You should have told me about all this when it happened."

"And you should have told *me* what you were suffering through all along. Going forward—for this to work—you will have to share. No more secrets. Even if you mean well, it's not okay to make unilateral decisions. Julie might have been okay with it but I'm not."

"I know. I'm working on that."

"Which brings me back to the reasons I stayed away," she said. "I couldn't see how things would work out with you. With us. I learned you'd paid a price for helping me— and then I was warned off."

"By whom?

"Bill Bard."

Rob's face darkened. "He had no right to interfere. I'd already come to a decision. He just didn't know it yet. I was done with the brutal hours and sacrifices. It's not worth it. All I had to do was observe how Bill's choices have played out. His marriage isn't great. His kids don't like him. I ran into his son Miles one day playing beach volleyball. You should have heard the way Miles talked about his father. With real contempt. Bill's wife—his kids—all the family members operate independently, never together. No real connection or respect. I don't want to see contempt on my son's face." He interpreted her cautious smile. "Okay—not counting normal teenage eye-rolling. There is a difference."

"You've got a bond with Luke that's solid," she said. "You're already close and you're a great father. Kids don't come with guarantees, but what better way to start than this?" She pulled her feet back and kneeled to kiss him. "And you'll be a great partner too. After everything we've been through—you never once asked me to be someone else. And you never once blamed me for the fall-out you suffered."

"Like I said, my decision was all but made," Rob said. "Once I decided to move off that track, a huge weight rolled off me." He slipped his hand possessively up her back. "What about you? I don't want you to regret leaving your job in San Francisco."

"That one is over but there may be more work in future. I have some irons in the fire—some people to talk to. I'll figure it out. I may need to fly to the Bay Area from time to time."

"Of course."

"My work will always be important," she said. "But you—we—come first."

He pushed her back on the throw pillows, supporting his weight so he didn't crush her. He caressed her stomach where her shirt had ridden up. His lips were warm and sweet. Summer nectar.

He was in no hurry, but she was. "Is Luke asleep? Are your curtains closed?"

"Looks that way." He went back to kissing her, more urgently. "You're mine, you know."

"Yes, I do know." She had her hand inside his waistband. His skin was surprisingly satiny. More so as she slipped her fingers lower.

"I like this new confidence. You wear it well." With a sharp intake of breath, he stilled her wandering hand. "Since there is a chance Luke will pop up like a jack-in-the-box, what do you say we move to the master bedroom?"

"Works for me." She hopped off the couch.

He took her to the bedroom. "It's pretty small."

"Not as I recall," she said, peeling off her t-shirt.

His eyes shone in the dim light. "I was talking about the bedroom. Take off your jeans."

She curled her thumbs in the waistband and inched them down. He eased her onto the bed.

"Now you," she ordered, a small smile curving her mouth as she watched him undress to boxer briefs. The ribbed knit hugged his muscular thighs. "Very nice. Except you've got no butt anymore."

"You're one to talk, skinny-bones." He unhooked her bra and threw it over his shoulder. "Wait a second." He cupped her breasts and ran his hands over her hips. "Your figure. It's different."

"I know. I have one. How about that? What do you think?"

"I love it. You're gorgeous."

She looked at his erection, jutting through his boxers. "I'm happy to see you, too."

Playfulness was forgotten when they came together, greedy for each other. And she was ravenous. He lifted her hair to nip at her neck below her ear and taste his way down to her breasts. She tugged his hair none too gently and dragged him back up so she could kiss him while she wrapped her legs around his back. "Quick and hard," she said. "I can't wait."

He smoothed her legs apart, pausing only to stroke the soft skin of her inner thighs. He entered with a gritty thrust. She tensed in shock. She'd forgotten his size.

"I'm okay," she said breathlessly.

He leaned in and kissed her, waiting for her to adjust. His mouth was hot and tender. She wanted his mouth everywhere. So sloppy, so sweet, and so male. She had wanted him since the day she saw him sitting on the beach. And she always would.

She got so slick her body relaxed and let him in. As he stroked, she moved and tilted her hips so he could go deeper. He was hers now. To take. She could keep on taking him, again and again. She rocked with and against him, refusing to let go. He came in a hot flood that felt almost as good as a climax of her own. They were together.

He laughed shakily with his face buried in her hair. "Sorry about that."

"You gave me what I asked for."

"I missed you more than you'll ever know," he said, dead serious. "No more long separations." He flipped her to his side and pulled a sheet over her hip. "I bought these sheets for us last week. And washed them so they'd be soft for you."

"Pretty confident, weren't you?"

"Yes. And no. The truth is, I couldn't allow the possibility that you weren't coming back. So I had an active fantasy life. But real life is so much better." He'd launched an onslaught as he spoke, circling her breasts with his thumb, watching her nipples respond. "Are you going to let me be your fantasy?"

She was proud of her body, proud to surrender and give herself over to him and everything she needed from him. He roamed, touching her all over, using his mouth and fingers to tighten her need into a taut string only he knew how to pluck. He tormented her in an agony of pleasure, licking his way down her body.

He had her writhing on the sheets. "Please," she whispered.

"My woman says 'please'," he said wickedly. "I'm going to have fun teaching you to leave your manners at the door, sugar."

They were done with words then. Paradoxically, as her need climbed, she fell deeper. He took her into a dark chamber where energy gathered, waiting. She rose from that deep place on a rush of anticipation. He finally covered her with his mouth, teasing, taunting, and fluttering. His fingers moved, enhancing the climax. She contracted around him. Her whole body shook with its power. He forced the pleasure from her in waves, massaging, distracting her from nearly unbearable stimulation as the pressure built all over again. She called his name and came once more. He knew what she needed. And he gave it to her. The fulfillment mirrored her love for him. It grew and blossomed, only to blossom some more.

Much later, cradled in his arms, she said, "Do you want more kids?"

"Sure. Don't try to tell me you don't because I won't believe you."

"No, I do. I've been scared to hope, though."

"That you can have children?"

"The whole thing." She waited for him to say something. When he didn't, she poked him in the ribs to see if he had dozed off. "I prefer to be married first."

A laugh rumbled through his body. A little embarrassed, she squirmed to get some distance until he held her so firmly she couldn't move at all.

"Ah," he said. "You want to be asked again. Why didn't you say so? Will you marry me?"

"Yes. But Rob—"

"No buts," he said, exasperated. "I'm going to start foaming at the mouth if I hear any buts. You belong with me now. With us. Accept it."

"I do! You must know I'm flying blind here. I didn't grow up in a happy family. And as much as I love you and Luke, sometimes I'm scared to hope for 'happily ever after'."

His arms were heavy on her back. "What's it going to take to convince you?"

"Don't say it like that," she said, distressed for him. "I didn't mean to hurt you or spoil the moment, my darling. I'm convinced I want to marry you. This is who I am, though. I can't *not* wonder what will happen."

He sighed. "I know. And I want—fully expect—you to share your worries so go ahead." He reassured her with a lopsided smile.

"So here's my big but—"

"You have a little butt."

"That was too easy. I totally handed you that one. Seriously, family life is wonderful in fair weather. It's a fragile business, so dependent on everything going along smoothly. And whose life isn't rocky at times?"

"You're right," he said. "No one's life is trouble-free. But that's nothing new for either of us. I'll watch your back. You watch mine. We'll figure it out together. We're strong people, right? We've each had more than our share of character building. If we're determined to make it work, we will."

"You really think so?"

"I don't do anything badly. Except wait for you. Or suffer fools." He laughed. "So there are a few things." Then he spoke in the private voice he saved for her. "Loving you is something I'll always do. And I'll always do it well. I'm going to make you happy. We'll make beautiful babies and teach them to be sensible and kind. And we'll love them. And each other. Always." He patted her stomach for emphasis.

"You're not going to worry too much if, or when, I do get pregnant?"

"Can't promise complete sanity. One night last month I seriously considered driving straight up to San Francisco with Luke asleep in his car seat. I was all set to surprise you. Betty Jo talked me out of it over the phone. She said you'd come back. And she was right."

Meri played with the hair that curled on his neck. She'd always loved touching him here. Now she could touch it— and him—whenever she wanted. The power of that intoxicated her. He lifted her to rest on top of him and smoothed her back from shoulder to bottom. She rested her chin on his chest and felt his response tickling her belly.

"So we're going to take the leap."

He fanned her hair with both hands. "I'm not letting you go. I insist you marry me."

"Insist?" She exaggerated his bossy tone.

"I want and need you to be my lover, partner, and wife. Please."

She kissed his neck and then worked her way to his ear. "Much better."

"I don't think I've heard you giggle before. Tell me that answer again."

"Yes. I'll keep saying it all night. Yes."

He rolled and she let herself roll with him. She was strong enough to catch life's waves, to ride them out or duck-dive when necessary. He would be there.

If you enjoyed this book, please consider posting a review now on your favorite online bookstore. Whether short or long, reviews are much appreciated.

About the Author

Noelle Greene lives in Northern California with her husband. She grew up in Tennessee and Wisconsin, and has lived up and down the West Coast since. Her background includes working in Silicon Valley marketing communications, running a school library and raising two sons. She enjoys putting her own twist on popular romantic themes and really does believe in the power of love to change the world.

To receive a free copy of the next release, visit either site below and sign up for a (non-spam) mailing list.

http://www.noellegreene.com

http://www.facebook.com/NoelleGreeneRomance

Acknowledgments

Thanks to my fantastic beta readers Susan Shyu, Zoe Drazen, Rebecca Amthor and Sarah Amthor. Tom Pinkel helped with the sailing scenes, as did my dad, Donald Pinkel, who taught me that "hard-a-lee" means "duck" and that sailing isn't for sissies. Sara Pinkel helped with medical details. Nancy, Mary and Ruth Pinkel, Joji Ruhstorfer, Rose Simon, and Mary Kuckens were great sounding boards. Also, thanks to Jena O'Connor for her editing and romance savvy; Scarlett Rugers for her cover design; and to Victoria Curran for extensive notes way back when. The environmentalist joke in chapter nine is from Dennis Miller. Thanks Bruce, for all those long walks at Crystal Cove.

Also by Noelle Greene

Lover's Intuition

**A psychic must use her gift to save the skeptic
she loves.**

Camille Jorgensen is starting over in a small town after
a heartbreaking loss. On the night she meets reclusive
billionaire Will Holloway, her sixth sense suddenly goes
haywire. Although Camille's intuition whispers that evil
will strike, she doesn't know when, why, or where.

Sweet, sexy, and possibly delusional Camille is Will's
New Age nightmare. She's the only woman to detect deep
passion beneath his cool facade. But tenderness checked
out of his soul long ago, and logic—unlike the people he
loved—has never abandoned him.

Available in ebook or paperback